The Widdershin Widow

J M Samland

Dyingstar Press LLC

An Award-Winning Novel

The Widdershin Widow is an award-winning novel! It took gold in the "**Gothic**" and "**Women's Historical Fiction**" categories at the 2026 Spring BookFest awards!

This is the first time I submitted a novel for award consideration, and I'm absolutely tickled to win with one I'm so proud of. With Gothic works, the environment itself becomes another character, broody and deep. Historical fiction, as I describe at the end of the book, required a great deal of research into the location specific to the era the story is set. Succeeding in women's fiction, as a cis man, was a definite validation of my growth as an author.

Try as I might to be humble, I'm very proud of this win and elated to be sharing Violet's story with you.

For Katie

Yes, I know you're Kate to everyone else, but being the only person who still calls you Katie makes me feel like a very special little brother.

I've written novels at someone's suggestion, but have never written one *for* someone. This is the very truest sense of a dedication, and I can hardly think of someone more deserving.

You suck.

From the Author

As with all of my books, the end result of *The Widdershin Widow* looks nothing like what I first intended. What started as a deep exploration of depression came out as a statement about women's rights and independence, or lack thereof.

My parents have researched genealogy my entire life. My childhood was lunches in graveyards and long hours on the floor in courthouse record rooms. After fifty years of research, my mother has recently started compiling it all into biographical works. Her aim wasn't to list the dry facts of her ancestors, but to bring them to life by striving to understand how they lived.

This was especially true when talking about her mother, my grandmother.

Grandma worked as a computer operator in the 1940s, advancing in her career. Then, a soldier returned from the war, and she was tasked with training him. And then he took her promotion. That soldier turned out to be my grandfather. Grandma had to quit her career to focus on raising her family and maintaining the household. She never vocalized a complaint about what could have been, but it makes me wonder. In the "what if" alternate universe, where Grandma kept her career at the university, how would her life be different?

Well, there would be no me, so I'm selfishly glad things worked out the way they did. That doesn't mean I can't mourn the loss of what could have been for her. You can be perfectly happy with your life, but still entertain thoughts of how it could have been different.

I see it all over my family histories, women who are absorbed into their husbands. The husband dies, and she remarries immediately because, well, that's what had to happen back then. Each man wants seven of his own children, even if the woman already had five from her last marriage. I felt filthy re-reading some of the dialogue in this book, but it's likely pretty accurate, which is even grosser.

The Widdershin Widow blossomed from this. From women trapped in their expected role. History loves to repeat itself and it takes a defined act to break the cycle.

One

The dock advertised a ferry, but I ride to the island at the bow of a puttering fishing boat. It wheezes to crest each swell, though the day is mild. The island bobs over the horizon, a clump of soaring pines and maples standing out against the endless ocean. After almost an hour on the boat, stinking of long-dead fish and her pilot in desperate need of a bath, I yearn for the fresh air ahead.

The engine pops and backfires, yanking my attention back to the black smoke belching from the stack. Mr. Farlow—loath as I am to call him a captain—waves his hat at the oily plume. He doesn't seem alarmed, so I breathe out my gasp and will my fists to relax. My nerves are frayed after my long flight, but relief will come soon enough.

Beyond him, nearly lost to the boat's soot, the Chatham lighthouse stands sentinel over the Cape and shoals that claimed the lives of countless sailors.

"Just another few minutes, Miss," he yells over the engine. His coat and hat are black, but the smudges across his face and hands tell me the fabric may once have been lighter. Grime coats buttons that had been a handsome silver or brass.

"You're lucky to have found me," he continues. "No one else would go to the island, especially not with a storm coming."

I glance at the blue sky. There isn't a cloud in sight. He was right on the first part. I'd asked three other sailors before finding him. The others made the sign of the cross and walked away.

"Because of the legends?" I ask.

"Aye, but even more, the currents. The water doesn't move right around here. The eastern cliff has taken more ships than we may know. They used to say to sail Widdershin was to turn your back on God." His gaze moves past me, unfocused on the island to my back.

"Don't you fear God's anger, Mr. Farlow?" I try to keep any mirth from spilling into my question.

His jaw tenses, but he does not answer.

"Why didn't they build a lighthouse on the island, if it's so dangerous?" I ask.

He snorts. "Who would man it? Only a madman would build and stay on a cursed island." His gaze shifts to me with a frown. "Sorry, Miss."

I shrug and turn from him, toward the isle. The trees grow taller, though the dock poking a gnarled finger into the Atlantic looks no nearer.

As I have whenever a spare moment presents itself these last six weeks, I take the folded scrap of paper from my coat's front pocket. I committed the words to memory long ago, but I still find comfort in reading them, giving solidity and reality to my absurd plan, quickly coming to a head. My fingers trace along the familiar creases of the linen paper and long-dried ink smudges of the delicate, looping script.

My dear Miss Primrose,

You shall forgive the imposition, I hope, from one who may be little more than a name to you. I was a long-standing acquaintance of your late father and mother—both of whom I held in the highest regard—and it is in their memory, and with sincere respect for your reputation, that I write to you now.

I find myself charged with the affairs of Widdershin House, a rather singular estate located upon the island of the same name off the Cape of Massachusetts. The house contains a most impressive—if regrettably disordered—collection of books, journals, and manuscripts. It is precisely for this reason that your particular interest in the cataloguing and organization of literary materials is of keen interest to me.

You would find your needs amply provided for:

the pantry is well-stocked, the house well-furnished, and though it must be said the island enjoys a certain solitude, you will want for little in the material sense. I regret that my own visits shall be infrequent, if at all, but I am confident you will find the peace most conducive to your work.

It strikes me as just the sort of engagement well suited to a capable and independent young lady such as yourself. However, I do hope the isolation will not delay any future opportunities to become happily settled, if you pardon the familiarity.

As the estate is preparing for eventual sale, time is regrettably of the essence. A modest commission based upon the value of the collection shall, of course, be yours upon completion of the task.

I do hope you will consider this opportunity with both generosity and haste.

Yours sincerely,

Laurence Sparrow, Esq.
Finch, Finch, and Sparrow, Boston, MA
Executor of the Widdershin Estate

Overlooking the errors in the lawyer's knowledge regarding my life and recent events, I wrote back to him the next day.

Several correspondences later, I had yet to correct him and had no intention of doing so.

The dock comes near enough to make out the details, looking repaired a hundred times from what abuse the ocean rails against it. Weathered and patched, but still serviceable. I grin as I see myself reflected in the wood silvered by salt and wind. It, too, goes on fulfilling its duty on this tiny, forgotten isle, as would I. Mr. Farlow navigates the choking craft near and tosses a frayed rope to the tie points, expertly nestling the boat against the dock. He heaves my luggage up, jumps onto the wood with confidence I would never grant it, and offers a hand to help me across the gap.

"Welcome to Widdershin Isle," he says without warmth.

A narrow stone path leads from the dock to tall iron gates held ajar with rust. Beyond, an overgrown garden sprawls before the manor house in the style of Greek revival. Six columns, wrapped with splendid green ivy, rise to frame the two-story façade. Trees taller than the home surround and shade it, yet none are so close as to obscure the blue heavens directly overhead. The circle of sky is too clean, as if the trees have stepped away from the manor house, unwilling to come any nearer.

The ferryman clutches at his elbow, pulling his long jacket tighter as if to warm himself, despite the promise of spring in the Massachusetts sea air. His thick, drooping mustache mirrors his frown while his eyes dart between my shoes and the Widdershin House.

"Are you sure you won't wait for your husband, Miss Violet?"

Had I a dollar for every time he or another asked me that very question, I would have no need for the work which brought me here.

"You needn't worry about me or him, Mr. Farlow," I say and gesture to the single piece of luggage beside my leg. "Between what I have brought and what supplies Mr. Sparrow promised, I have everything I need for my stay." I hope, for my own sake, that my words are true. I hadn't told Mr. Sparrow I would be arriving early, but the timing was too perfect.

"My mother would turn in her grave, knowing I left a young woman as fair as you on this island." His focus moves to his shoes.

"You're a good man to worry, but really, I will be fine."

"When will your husband arrive? He hasn't yet booked passage."

Nor would he, God permitting, but the ferryman refused to let me step onto his boat without a promise to the Almighty that I would not be alone long.

"As I told you, his business in Salem will be done within a few days, a week at most. Then he'll be on the next coach here," I say. "He insisted I start my work without him." The salty sea air tugs at the hem of my long wool dress, chilling my legs and shivering up my back.

Mr. Farlow feels it too. He shudders and steps to the edge of the dock, putting too much trust in the ancient wood's edges. A worrying impulse calls me to grab for his jacket and pull him to safety, but I resist.

"I smell a storm on the wind, Miss. Best you get inside and settled before it gets dark. Or I can take you back to the mainland, no extra charge. Your employer here can't fault you for waiting for your husband."

His eyes flick to the gray clouds appearing out of nowhere to obscure the blue. The captain might be correct about his weather forecast.

I smile and adopt the tone I always do when men try to protect me unbidden. "That is a kind offer, Mr. Farlow, but I really will be fine. My husband would be cross if he found me lounging about the tavern when there's work to be done."

Mr. Farlow grunts his acceptance and understanding. "I won't be the one to cause your marital problems. The telephone in the house worked, the last I knew. If you run into any issues, call the Chatham lighthouse keeper, and he can direct aid."

"Thank you," I say. His eyes speak of worry when he finally raises them to meet mine. I fold my hands before me, hopefully conveying that he is free to leave.

He glances once more at the sky and steps into his boat, tossing off the ropes as he does. He takes his place behind the wheel before looking back at me.

"Beware the White Rider," he says, almost to himself. "Shut your eyes tight and do not follow him."

His whispered words draw me a step toward the dock's dubious edge. "A White Rider?"

He wipes a soot-stained hand through his mustache and shakes his head. "Don't whistle thrice. It's a warning for sailors coming around the cape, drawing ships to their doom on the rocks and sand. They say the Widdershin Witch cursed him. Mayhap he rests here between storms. With one on its way, he'll soon be mounted."

"You speak in riddles, Mr. Farlow."

I maintain my soft smile, though only barely. Since receiving Mr. Sparrow's letter, I read everything I could find regarding the island, as sparse as the details are, from newspaper clippings to a book of local folklore. Even William C. Smith's rare *History of Chatham, Massachusetts*, an otherwise verbose four-volume set, left out Widdershin Isle, almost to the point of seeming suspiciously purposeful. What I did find tells a rich history for such a small parcel of land, though some seems more fiction than fact. A fire that killed four children and their nanny. A suicide on the foamy rocks below the eastern bluff. And of course, there was the witch who gave her name to the island, or the other way around.

At last, Mr. Farlow putters away in a cloud of choking smoke. I return his wave and watch him until he is far enough into the sea that I'm confident he won't rush back to rescue me.

When the lapping of waves overtakes the engine, I turn back to the house. What seemed a grand estate at first glance begins to sour the longer I notice the details. The flaking paint, a broken window on the second floor, the sagging roof. The garden is more than overgrown; it's completely lost to thistle and choking vines. It would take a small army a week to wrestle some control over it. The manor and grounds appear to be twenty years neglected, but Mr. Sparrow stated that the previous residents had been gone a fraction of that time.

The sagging roof worries me, but the rest can be fixed with a bit of effort.

Though that is not an effort I am here to supply. I am here to catalogue a literary collection worth over a hundred thousand dollars. It seems impossible to imagine such a treasure would exist within the rotting husk of Widdershin House, but I know better than to judge a book by its cover.

My shoes crunch on the path's broken stones as the garden rises around me, blocking all sight of the maples and pines beyond. The house fills my world, leaning over me while I ascend the creaking stairs to the front door.

My shoulder cries for relief, and I set my case down beside me, raising a hand to knock on the solid door that may have been planed from the ancestors of the trees surrounding me. My knock echoes once.

Thunder threatening in the distance is the only response, and I laugh, bending to find the brass key ring in my case. At twenty-four, this is my first time using one, always having doors unlocked and opened for me by my father and, quite recently, my husband.

The tumbler clicks with a satisfying finality.

This is it. I enter Widdershin House, a woman traveling with her life condensed to a single piece of luggage, without her family's knowledge or her husband's consent. After Mr. Sparrow's stipend, a generous five percent, I will have all I need to escape either West or across the ocean. Perhaps to Paris. In a few weeks, I will be free. Free to live my life as I choose.

Free of *him*.

I release the key, and the door swings inward on hinges that sigh, rather than creak and moan. Perhaps they know my story and choose to welcome me gently. A stale breeze greets me next, issuing from the dark maw of the entry foyer and the deepest recesses of the house.

Thunder rumbles again, closer.

"Well, House," I say, lifting my luggage with the other arm. "I'll be in and out before you notice, but I hope we can be friends."

Two

Just inside, I run a hand over the smooth, dark wainscoting, searching for the light's toggle switch. The chandelier overhead hums to incandescent life, though half the small bulbs are missing, shattered, or burnt out. It illuminates a double staircase, lined with a floral rug, drawing my eye to the second floor's overlook. The hallway disappears in either direction, its striped wallpaper faded, but otherwise undamaged from what I can see of it.

Mr. Sparrow had given me a basic layout of the house. A kitchen at the back would be well-stocked with canned goods, and a hatch to the root cellar containing yet more. Up the stairs, to the left, I would find the library, where most of my work would be done, beside a serviceable bedroom and a lavatory. Mr. Sparrow suggested that I avoid the rooms to the right entirely, though he did not elaborate as to why. Straight ahead of where I now stand, French doors lead to a small vegetable garden that he promised was better tended than the front. Though it is too early in the season to expect anything from that. A short walk would take me to the eastern bluffs and a breathtaking sunrise.

The same bluff and shores, Mr. Farlow said, were the doom of so many sailors.

I have no intention of honoring Mr. Sparrow's suggestion that I avoid the southern wing on the second floor. If my job here is to catalogue all things literary, that job would be un-fulfilled without a thorough search. I will collect everything into the library, stacked and sorted. That meant opening every cobwebby drawer, searching under every dusty mattress, and pawing through boxes of moth-eaten clothing in the attic. The house is not as immense as I imagined, so how difficult can the task be?

The thought of scouring the large estate thrills me. I had always been under someone's watchful eye, unable to explore my adventurous nature. Do I have an adventurous nature? How would I know? I itch to uncover every hidden mystery of the estate, so I suppose I do.

I close the door behind me, shutting out the chilling whip of wind through the trees looming over the house. The sounds of the manor are no more comforting. The groan of a foundation still settling after more than eighty years, the sighs of siding bracing for the coming storm, the smack of loose shutters, and the low whistle of wind through a broken pane.

Thunder rolls, and the house responds by dimming the lights overhead.

I can start a fire for warmth, if needed. At least, I have seen it done enough times. And the days are getting longer, giving more light to work by. But in all my planning, I never considered what to do without electricity on the island. My father had it installed at home when I was young, making us the talk of the town and the envy of our neighbors, and I could scarcely imagine my life without the simple comfort. Light with the constant risk of setting your book aflame? How did people live like that?

The lights fade again and come back to full, warning me not to place too much trust in the comfort.

I lift my bag and stare up the long set of stairs with a sigh, but I can't stop my grin. Mr. Sparrow and Mr. Farlow are the only two people in the world who know where I am. The lawyer knows nothing of my husband's existence, and there is no reason a person would ask the fisherman about my whereabouts.

The thought of total anonymity and freedom is as exhilarating as it is terrifying.

I grip the banister carved into the form of some great, long sea beast, and let my fingers settle into the space between its scales as I climb. Small portraits in embellished gold frames line the steps, mixed with a few photographs. Exhaustion begins to overtake me, stealing any curiosity to inspect them more closely. I would be in the house for at least a few weeks. There would be plenty of time and better lighting to see everything.

Three hours by train from Portland to Boston, another six to Hyannis, and nearly two on a coach to Chatham. Finding Mr. Farlow and the ride on his stinking boat took another three hours. It's no small wonder that by the time I reach the top of the stairs, my legs are wobbling beneath me. I want to see the library, but my constitution is fading rapidly when I spy the door to my left, which must be the bedroom I am to use.

By the last light of day coming through the tall, Western-facing windows, I'm greeted with a four-poster bed with no canopy, a worn carpet with a Turkish design, and a cold hearth. The curtains match the red and black embroidery on the bed's duvet. There is a dresser without a mirror facing the bed and an armoire, both heavily engraved and lacquered. The stack of wood beside the fireplace will be enough for at least two evenings, and the bookshelf beside a chaise in the corner confirms my suspicions. I would have to search the house to find and collect every book of any worth into the library.

I set my bag down and collapse, face-first, onto the mattress in a puff of dust. The bed sinks, slowly enveloping me, wrapping me in an embrace that makes me sneeze. I should arrange myself with my head on a pillow, or at least take off my shoes, but the comfort is too immediate, too complete. It must be the stress of a long day's travel or the culmination of my scheming coming to fruition, because there is no way a broken mattress has any right to draw me in so completely and wonderfully.

My mind drifts toward nothingness, but some nagging remembrance keeps me from succumbing to oblivion.

I crack an eye and note the light from behind me spilling in the doorway, from the chandelier in the foyer. Should the lights burn out, I have no means of replacing the bulbs suspended ten feet over my head. With a curse on my lips, I push from the bed, which tries its best to reclaim me, yet I manage to wrestle myself free.

I try each of the switches on a panel at the top of the steps. One lights the sconces along the upstairs corridor, giving me a clear view of the southern wing, which I am to avoid. It's just more ornate doors nestled in the deep, rich wood. Most of the switches do nothing, but notably, none turn off the lights in the foyer. One casts a spotlight onto a portrait at the head of the stairs. A mother and father stand behind their seated daughter. The father's hand rests on his daughter's shoulder.

Not rests.

The daughter's dress has a sweeping neckline, leaving her shoulders bare to be tickled by her auburn ringlets. The artist had been deliberate in showing how the father's fingers pressed into her skin, gripping her. I move closer and reach out to feel the brushstrokes there.

Thunder rattles the roof, and I hop back, as if scolded by nature.

The man's face draws me past the girl. His cold, black eyes so like my own father's stare directly back at me. His cheeks and chin, dark hair graying at the temples, all leave me with the impression that the artist wanted to finish with him quickly and move on. The mother stares vaguely to the left, unfocused.

By the women's dresses, I place the painting from fifty or more years ago, possibly not long after the Civil War. That might align with this being the last family to live here, or maybe those who built the manor before the war. This is no happy family, but one with all power channeled to the man standing behind his two women. No matter who they are, I cannot fathom why anyone would choose to display such a grotesquery.

The question answers itself. The man saw his power in the portrait, so he chose to hang it in the hallway. He didn't see the women's silent pleas; he only saw his own posture. I know it all too well from my own homelife, and a husband who thinks himself the center of the world.

With a shudder, I turn to the long stairs down to the checkered entrance.

Even as I do, I feel the father staring at my back.

Lightning flashes, and the thunder comes with little delay. A gentle drone of rain pelts the roof far over my head.

I barely remember ascending the stairs a few moments ago, but now I feel each one creak under my weight. The smooth black and white tile is slippery. I turn the locks on the door and put a hand on the light switch.

The chandelier dims again, as if asking for the night's rest.

I press the switch, plunging the house into darkness.

Darkness, save for the light directed on the family portrait at the top of the stairs.

The father stares at me, judging me, disapproving of me.

I curse again—I will have to go to confession for my language if I keep this up—and grip the textured handrail.

The father watches me.

The daughter pleads for someone to notice, to offer succor.

I squeeze my eyes tight and take a deep breath. Then another.

Without raising my vision above the carpeted stairs, I rush upwards, pounding up the steps faster than I ever have in life.

I turn the corner, giving no mind to the portrait or pausing to switch off their light. The house would be a better place if the spotlight over that portrait were to burn out.

I slam the door behind me and lean against it, plunging the room into darkness that my eyes strain to understand. My heart pounds in my chest, in my ears, and no amount of careful breathing calms it.

Lightning illuminates the room, and I cross to the bed between flashes, pulling off my shoes before I allow the mattress to envelop me again.

"Just a few weeks," I say, crawling to place my head on the downy pillow. "Just a few weeks, and I'll be free."

The wind shifts, and rain slams against the tall windows in sheets. I focus on the quiet cacophony of the old house standing up to the storm while just trying to survive, and soon, the darkness takes me.

Three

I awaken, refreshed despite a night in an unknown bed surrounded by unknown sounds. No night of feverish terrors.
No trembling, no tears, no bracing for the worst before I even
open my eyes. The peace unnerves me, a hollow space where my
anxieties should live. I lie there, doing nothing except listening
to a lone dove cooing on the other side of the window's thin
pane. She gets no response.

The bed is less possessive in the morning, and I roll to its
edge and out, landing on stockinged feet from which the plank
floor immediately leaches all warmth. The library door is visible
across the hall from where I sit, but I know once I set foot in
there, the day will be lost to me. No, the sensible course is to
see to my necessities first. I arrived a week early, so will there be
food in the cupboards or the basement's cold storage? After last
night's rain, the island's cistern should be overflowing, but what
is the state of the indoor plumbing?

I stand, step into my shoes, and heft my case onto the dresser. I can unpack my things after finding breakfast, but I have never liked clutter on the floor.

Well... One thing, first.

I take a silk pouch from an inner pocket of the bag and extract the gold ring from it. A symbol of love without beginning or end, the priest said as Edmund slipped it on my finger. Holding it at arm's length, the morning light isn't enough to make it gleam.

I drop it to be lost at the bottom of my bag under my stockings.

The room's tall window opens onto the veranda across the front of the great house. Venturing out, I hug my arms across my chest against the morning's chill and step to the spindly iron railing. Fog hangs across the garden below, giving the vines and hedges the look of some great tentacled beast cresting the sea. I squint against the gloom and can barely make out the iron gate and dock beyond. Any sight of the cape or lighthouse is lost to me.

The constant little reminders of my solitude are already growing wearisome, but this would be my life, God willing. I will be alone for a while here on Widdershin, then alone for as long as I choose afterward. My father entrusted me with the care of his great library, then his patron's, which led me to my fledgling career. Whatever mess awaits me across the hall will be well within my purview.

Movement in the fog pulls my eye back to the garden, drawing me to place my hands on the veranda's iron railing and scour through the mist curling in lazy eddies, shrouding the world below. Something small screams its death, quick and violent, and the world is again silent within a breath. I suck in a gasp, unable to release it as I frantically search for the victim.

Then, I see it by the gravel path. It is already watching me. The predator. Pale, golden eyes pierce the thin cloud, observing me, judging me with disinterest.

I've always adored cats, and I had one until my husband forced me to give it away when we got married.

"Cats are for children, spinsters, and witches," he said.

Sobbing, I gave Toby to a neighbor who promised I could visit him whenever I pleased. When Edmund found out, Toby disappeared. When I asked him what happened...

I rub the ribs on my left side. I am still young, and the pain should fade with time, as the doctor told me. If he suspected anything more about why I came into so many household injuries those first months after being wed, he never spoke his mind. A cracked rib. Bruising around my wrist. A broken finger. The nurse in the room said nothing. I said nothing. But we all knew the truth.

A cat will always win a staring contest, and I concede, stepping backward into the bedroom. The world beyond Widdershin Isle may be lost to me while I reside here, deep in the fog, but at least there is other life besides a lonely dove.

In the hallway, I hold up my hand to block the family portrait. Though I cannot see him, I feel his cold eyes staring down that sharp nose, glaring at me, evaluating me. Disapproving of me. It burns my cheek as I pass and flee down the stairs. The house is gray and dull with the misty morning light, but the creaks and groans are less. Maybe those were its way of greeting me last night. Or, a warning. And now that it's said its peace, it will not repeat itself. I can respect that. I don't like repeating myself, either.

At the back of the house, windows look upon a stone patio with chairs for relaxing and planters for small vegetables. The fog devours the world beyond another ten feet, lost to the tangle of pines and maples. The kitchen is large enough for three cooks to work on a feast without bumping elbows. Why a full party of guests would come to this island and stay for a dinner invitation is beyond me. The image of men in tails and women in their grandest frocks, studded with glittering jewels, choking the dilapidated dock and the wild garden, brings a smile to my lips. I see them gathering to drink and dance to the screech of an out-of-tune string quartet. Perhaps the builder had grand intentions that never saw fruition.

The first cupboards I open hold only dusty dinnerware. Bone china with delicate floral inlays. I would be fine with a simple tin plate and cup, but the kitchen holds nothing I would consider appropriate for everyday use. Everything is nicer than the set I received as a wedding gift.

There is also no food, nor supplies to make any. No flour or powdered eggs. Not even a satchel of dried fruit. I will starve to death on this little island because I failed to message Mr. Sparrow, telling him I would arrive a week early. I wanted as few things as possible to trace my whereabouts.

My heart leaps when I find an old coffee tin, but I frown into the stale grounds when I pull back the lid. Mr. Farlow said I could call the lighthouse with problems, but it seems silly to ask the operator to connect me, asking for a picnic basket, barely ten hours from my arrival.

Then I remember the mention of a root cellar, a cold storage.

I scan the snug wood planks of the floor and see nothing out of place except for a thin rug before the stone oven. I toss that aside, uncovering the square door cut into the wood. I flip the latch where a lock might go, but the iron ring resists its rusty slumber, and I grip it with both hands. It takes nearly all my strength, but I manage to pull the portal open on screaming hinges and let it rest against the stone. Beneath, stairs cut away from the kitchen, through the manor's foundation, swallowing the morning light with unnatural efficiency.

A lone bulb pokes from the stone masonry beside the second step, and I reach to pull the chain, casting light down the slender stairs, until it's lost to the room at the bottom.

My stomach grumbles, considering what food might be down there. But what else would there be, besides dried apples and rolled oats?

I remember the death cry from the garden and the cat's piercing gaze.

Another image comes to me, of descending into the darkness, only for a stray breeze to blow the hatch shut. I could barely lift it. I would never be able to push it open from the inside, especially if the latch flips down. The same action knocks something heavy on top of it and shatters the light bulb, leaving me buried alive in some mockery of a Poe tale.

"Stop this, Violet."

The quiver in my voice does little to reassure me.

"You're alone here, and any wind that would knock this closed behind me would knock the whole house down, which would make for an expedient death."

Worries of a languishing, starving demise assuaged, I descend the steep stairs.

At the bottom, another naked light with a tarnished brass pull chain reveals a room about seven feet on a side. The rough-hewn stone walls are interrupted by two flimsy white-washed doors, at total odds with the house above's intended opulence.

I try the first, opening into a long, narrow room with two shelves running the length on either side. Blessedly, yet another bulb illuminates the room that smells of onion, salt, and something a little sour. Burlap sacks are piled along the floor, and I note the printed labels for flour, salt, and oats. As long as they haven't turned, I would not starve here. A familiar label calls to me from between a cloudy jar of pickled eggs and a tin of ground chicory: a stone crock stamped with blue letters of Berrymore Farmhouse Creamery. Pulling it forward, I peel back the sealing wax paper. The butter had split along its top, but it smells fine. Better than fine. Berrymore Farms was only a short carriage ride from our house when I was a child. Mother always kept a crock on hand for her pie baking. I ate it for years, but I cannot remember if I actually liked it. It could be nostalgia, a familiar icon so far from home. I take it off the shelf.

Butter's butter.

With the crock tucked under my arm, I peruse the shelves stacked with cans and jars with drawings of vegetables stuck to their fronts. Jars of preserves with long-faded, hand-written labels, another of crystallized honey, a crate of some root that tried, and failed to quest for earth, tiny white arms sprouting from between the slats. "Eggs" is stamped across a crate in the back. I stare into the sawdust filling it for a moment, again verging on some morose thought about what might be hidden in the dust. The larder seems devoid of vermin, but that doesn't mean a lone rat didn't fall in twenty years ago, to be mummified.

I shake my head and brush the sawdust aside, taking two eggs.

Tins marked for coffee and tea call to me, but I can make a second trip.

I switch off the light and leave the storeroom with breakfast and dozens more meals accounted for, but the other white-washed door piques my curiosity. It would be better to know the full layout of the house I will be living in over the next few weeks. Balancing the eggs atop the crock, I pull it open, and am greeted with the scents of decaying florals, mildew, and vinegar. The light from the bottom of the stairs reaches the first wine rack, enough that I can see that most of the bottles are missing. I step in, avoiding the shattered remains of a bottle and the red crust long ago soaked into the hard-packed dirt floor. The bulb in here sparks to life, revealing another two racks, similarly empty. What remains is dusty, cobwebby, and unlabeled.

I have no head for wine, so no interest in this room, yet I stand at the back, beside the smashed remains of a fourth wine rack. The light falls in shadows across another whitewashed door. Except, a kitchen chair is propped under this one's handle. A heavy chain spans it, secured through iron rings set into the stone walls. Two beams, possibly salvaged from the wrecked wine rack, are nailed across the frame.

There is no earthly reason to lock a door in such a manner. I tell myself that whoever did this was silly. Or insane. Why should anything be locked so thoroughly in the back of the wine cellar?

I clap a hand over the butter crock shaking under my arm, but an egg topples free to shatter across the floor.

Something is scrawled deep into the wood spanning the door, and I edge nearer to improve my angle with the poor lighting.

I tell myself the chill down my spine is simply nerves as a breeze works through the door's old slats, smelling of wet earth and wildflowers, enough to overpower the wine.

Run.

No. What are those words, hastily etched deep? I move nearer to better see.

"Don't whistle thrice, don't call her name"

I know the rhyme, but the rest of it escapes me. It's the last line of something the children sang about Deliverance Black.

Deliverance Black. The Widdershin Witch. I dismissed the island's place in local folklore until Mr. Farlow mentioned the White Rider. He'd said part of this verse, too. Now I stand before a barrier inscribed with a children's rhyme mocking the witch.

Not a witch, a woman. Mistreated in her time and remembered cruelly by history.

Water drips behind the door, and the breeze pulls back as if the locked room breathes. I shift closer. It wouldn't be much effort to move the chair and unbar the door. The house has been empty for years. Whatever was locked away can no longer be a threat.

The floral bouquet is enough to make me gag now that I'm near enough to trace fingers into the scrawled rhyme. There's something more beneath it, another scent that the flowers mean to cover up.

Something heavy slams overhead. The naked lightbulb flares and pops, plunging the room into darkness. The light at the bottom of the stairs outlines the door, but it surges and cuts off when I'm barely halfway through the wine cellar. Something grabs my ankle, knocking me against the door frame. The butter crock and remaining egg smash to the floor, and I run for the darkened stairs.

Four

Mercifully, the crash was not the cellar hatch slamming down to entomb me below. I race through the kitchen and hall, up the stairs, and barely breathe until the sunken bed's thick comforter is safely over my head.

"It's nothing, Violet. You're being silly."

The thick cotton and down swallow my whispered words.

I know there is nothing to be frightened of; that this is my first time alone, and my imagination is running amok. The part of my mind that knows this is at odds with the part that will accept it, and by the time I pull back the sheets, my stomach reminds me I haven't yet eaten.

I scrounge a piece of jerky wrapped in linen from my bag, one of a handful I had the foresight to bring, and tear at it from the bedroom doorway. Glancing toward the steps causes something to tighten in my chest, making it difficult to breathe. I'll stay upstairs for now. The door at the end of the hall to my left is, I confirm, the restroom.

A single bulb buzzes to life in the room with no windows. Everything feels darker than it should as light hesitates to spill onto the simple tub, toilet with a pull chain, and pedestal basin. After splashing cold water on my face from the clamshell sink, I look up at where a mirror should be, but there is only a lone hook above in the peeling wallpaper. I remind myself yet again that I'm being silly about all of this. There's nothing sinister about this house or the island. Even if there were, I don't believe in those things. That should, in all fairness, offer me some immunity.

I use a musty hand towel to pat my face dry and push through the medicine cabinet beside the door, hoping for some clue to the age of everything. It's bursting with dubious herbal remedies. Doctor This and Professor That claim they have the cure to any malady, but other than the dust and a bit of fading on the paper labels, they might have been stoppered five or fifty years ago.

With a deep breath, I stand before the library door. After the disrepair elsewhere in the house, I can only imagine the worst for what I am about to walk into. My future relies on the funds Mr. Sparrow promised upon the completion of my work, and the sooner I start, the sooner I will finish. The sooner I have the security to move on with my life.

The heavy door swings inward but stops abruptly, blocked by something on the other side. Through the crack, the library is dimly lit with the gloomy daylight mostly blocked by heavy drapes hanging from floor to ceiling across the far wall. Leather and cloth-bound tomes are heaped on the ornate desk by the windows and scattered across the floor. Bookshelves line the walls and reach the ceiling twelve feet up, but the contents, I can tell at a glance, are a jumble. It looks like someone dumped wheelbarrows full of books, then tossed the rest in, slamming the door before they could spill out.

Pushing a shoulder into the wood, I squeeze into the library, careful not to step on a tome, and press the light switch just inside.

Nothing happens.

I press it off and on again, this time with more force, but to no avail. Perhaps a fuse blew in the surge that knocked out the lights in the basement. I'd have to search for the cause of that later, once I could descend the stairs without a panic attack.

No matter, I can work by daylight until I find the fuse box.

The curtains rain dust into my hair when I toss them aside, exposing grimy panes looking out over the back patio and the forest beyond. Fog that should have burned off hours ago still chokes the world. The upward slope leading to the island's eastern cliffs is more evident from a higher vantage point than it was from the kitchen. When the fog clears—if it clears—I should make an effort to explore the island out to those bluffs. While I have little desire to see the rocks where countless sailors lost their lives, I still imagine the view would be spectacular.

With my back to the windows, I take in the full size and state of the library. From the door, I might have thought it was a rectangular room approximately the size of my bedroom across the hall. Now I see it wraps around what would be the end of the hallway outside, forming an enormous L across the house's north face. The shelves threaten to spill their crushing burden and bury me forever in a dusty tomb.

At a glance, the room, with its dark corners and ladders to reach the high shelves, could hold at least ten thousand books. The shelves are a third empty, made up for by the stacks and heaps on the floor. I am to catalog and organize the collection, verifying titles, authors, publisher information, and checking for clues as to the edition. I must inspect each one for the quality of binding and paper, and note any damage. I must scan through each, looking for annotations and ensuring nothing is tucked between the pages. I have done this work before, for my father, so I know an ordinary book might take two to five minutes to mark down. More complex or rarer works might take ten or more to inspect.

Also, at a glance, I can tell most of the collection falls into the second category. Rare and obscure.

Luckily, arithmetic is a strong skill with me. If I average seven minutes per book and assume I don't find a sizable number elsewhere in the Widdershin House, I am in for over a thousand hours of work. Months of work. Months and months and months.

The air thins with my reality, and I brace my palms on the desk to catch my breath. If Edmund stays away the full duration of his three-week business trip, as promised, he will come home to an empty house. I know him well enough to know he will not write off my absence, never to think of me again.

He will pursue.

Maybe this work will not be so daunting. Maybe I can finish in record time. Maybe a pattern will emerge, offering a shortcut. What else have I to do in the creaking, dusty house but this?

First, I need to clear the pile of books that has toppled against the door so it can open fully. The stale, dusty air, far worse than anywhere else in the house, is not suitable for the old tomes.

***

On the third day, still without the aid of artificial light, I swipe the dampness from my brow and survey my labor's result. The library's floor is clear to the desk, where I set the ledger used to mark the collection. Nothing is organized yet, but I have cleared enough space on the shelves directly next to the door, so I might start placing things once I'm ready. My life has been nothing but the bedroom, bathroom, and library. I gnaw on the last piece of jerky and know I cannot put off the inevitable.

I must pass that awful family portrait at the top of the steps.

I must explore the rest of the house in search of more to add to the collection. The other bedrooms. The attic.

There is nothing I need to prove to Mr. Sparrow. It may be nothing more than silly pride to think he would care, but I don't want to leave this job without having given it my full effort. That means not just marking down every book in the collection, but leaving them well-organized in the library. For that, I should gather everything first.

In just three days, the daunting task and pressing time schedule flowed seamlessly into an overwhelming desire to excel at my work, returning me to my time at the Portland District Library. I had yet to crack a tome, but the act of structuring how I might organize the library makes my job feel achievable.

But I've run out of food between the three rooms. Bodily needs necessitate that I venture back to the cellar, where I would be wise to gather everything I can carry. I can locate the fuse box and repair what I can while I'm at it. In a house this size, the electrical box must be massive, and the library surely cannot be the only room with a burnt-out fuse.

And just like that, my plan to leave the North Wing becomes a full event, as if I am planning tea for the mayor's wife or an expedition into an untamed jungle.

Thunder rumbles in the near distance, and the pale light coming through the library's dirty windows dims noticeably. The weather comes fast and hard out here alone in the Atlantic. A spider web of lightning crawls across the clouds, reminding me that my little mortal plans are nothing compared to its power.

I step into the hall and roll back my shoulders. Past the stairs, the dark wood on the walls devours all light in the other wing, leaving it an inky mystery.

The father's penetrating stare seems less accusatory without the spotlight focused on it. I still avert my eyes as I pass, keeping a guiding hand on the smooth banister. The entryway's chandelier flares to life, fighting back the shadows, and I cross to a small, jeweled door handle popping from the striped wallpaper under the stairs. Pulling it open reveals a dark landing at the top of more stairs stretching into the nothing below. With a cellar below the kitchen, I did not expect another basement. The space smells strongly of mildew and faintly of rot, telling me whatever was down there was not dry.

I tug the chain dangling in the middle of the cubby, and the naked bulb overhead shines on a metal box, a foot tall and half again wide, mounted on the wall. Red letters are painted on with a stencil, contrasting starkly against the dull metal.

Franklin Electrical Co. - Lowell, Mass
Model 6-A Safety Fuse Panel

The light does nothing to reach down the basement stairs to my left. I try not to look, lest I begin imagining things moving down there. Yet, not looking is doing a worse job. The basement's wall is cracked, allowing a steady stream of rainwater to enter. Rats, as long as my arm, swim through the pool. They climb atop broken shelves and boxes, masters of the dark kingdom, away from the cat prowling the garden.

I shudder and focus forward, casting out the image.

I pull the fuse box open, the door squealing on rusty brass hinges.

Thunder shakes the planks under my feet.

A knife switch controls the main power with eight ceramic fuses neatly lined up beside it, with space for another half dozen. A small paper label is above or below each.

Kitchen / Dining
Library
Bedrooms N
Bedrooms S
Attic
Back Cellar
Drawing Room / Parlor

Hall

One of the spaces without a fuse has a curled bit of paper below it. I carefully flatten it. Boat House.

Thunder rumbles again, accompanied by the scrabbling nails of any small things on the other side of the wall.

No, that is just my imagination again.

I hope.

The glass on the front of the library's fuse is darkened with soot, as are those for Bedroom S and Attic. I pull out the small drawer at the bottom of the fuse box, which holds exactly four identical ceramic fuses, along with a lot of grime.

Thunder shakes the walls again, and whatever I'm imagining clawing behind the walls squeaks with fright.

I clap a hand over my mouth to hold back my own.

With fingers suddenly trembling, I unscrew the spent fuses, dropping them in a pile in the corner, and replace them with those from the drawer. I think of adding the fourth to the empty spot labeled Boat House, but decide better of it. If another fuse blows before my work is done, there is no reason to risk the limited supply on places I never intend to visit.

At least not at any time but the full light of day.

The claws, squeals, and splashing in the basement's standing water are not elements of my imagination. I can no longer convince myself of that comforting lie. They grow louder and more distressed with each boom of thunder and deep shake of the house.

I yank the chain, returning the rats' domain to its eternal darkness. Thunder masks the slam of the door and the rush of my feet up the stairs.

Five

A t least I had the mind to switch off the foyer chandelier as I passed it, but now I lean against the library's closed door, huffing to catch my breath. The library's sconces glow a soft yellow, bathing the room in subdued light that pushes back the darkness I was becoming accustomed to. I exhale slowly and realize my failure.

My hands are empty. I went downstairs with the intention of gathering food and supplies, and didn't make it halfway to the larder.

No matter. I can go a day without food. In the morning, after the storm breaks, I can venture from my triangle of living quarters and journey into the dark back cellar again.

Light radiates from the dusty leather spines, welcoming me to trace my fingers along them while walking the library's length. I reach the end of the shelves lining the wall along the hallway, where the room turns sharply to the left. I haven't been through here yet, being too worried that the mess would overcome me. The warm light emboldens me, and I glance down the stacks running along the house's north face.

At a glance, it's more of the same, except there are no windows. Books are stacked to the ceiling on both sides, with a shorter rack running through the center. The islands of wood, free of texts, where I might place a foot without treading on a tome, are more frequent, allowing me to carefully, if still slowly, make my way to the far end. My eyes are in constant motion, searching for any covers or spines with titles or authors. Most seem, at a glance, to be on topics in mathematics or law, leading me to hope the section may have some order. Though perhaps not. I duck around a ladder set into the rails nine feet up, and spy a book of children's rhymes. A rider in white atop an equally pale horse is painted across the cover. Did anyone read all these, or were they just collected for the sake of a collection?

My fingertips never leave the books, tracing between leather and cloth, feeling the age and sensing the effort they contain. Authors, surely most long dead, are immortalized here by the words they left behind. It seems an awful waste to have them locked away on an island, never to be read. Hopefully, whoever purchases the Widdershin Estate from Mr. Sparrow's efforts will take the collection away to be enjoyed.

The room again cuts to the left, where it must wrap around the bathroom beside my bedroom. The library takes up what would otherwise be three bedrooms. Whether this was by original design or later modification, I might never know. The space is free of book clutter on the floor. A single, massive leather chair sits before a cold fireplace, but the knit throw tossed over the back of it looks cozy. The shelves are positively neat, dotted with a globe here, a glass sculpture there. Trinkets, I can imagine, collected on a previous owner's travels.

This was their sanctuary, I'm sure of it. This dark corner with a chair to relax into, covered by a heavy blanket, warmed by the fire. The small table beside the leather chair could hold a snifter of brandy at easy reach. In fact, I notice a few glass decanters holding amber or darker liquids scattered between the books.

This could be my sanctuary. Surrounded by literature, science, and tales of fancy and romance. The Widdershin collection holds more than I could read in a lifetime. If the matter of steady food were settled, I would be quite comfortable here.

Reality worms into my fantasy. I am a woman on the run, soon to be hunted, if I'm not already. Comfort and sanctuary are not luxuries I can risk.

My eye passed over the details a dozen times while I tried to take in everything about the nook, but now I can see nothing but it, and I stagger back with a gasp.

A skull is mounted, at least three feet wide, above the great stone mantle. Not a skull of some great beast from the Western plains, but a thing from the pages of Dante's *Inferno*. Horns, textured like a goat's, spiral away from deep, empty eye sockets. The fangs, as wide as my hand, curve toward the center. I cannot take my eyes from the grotesquerie. It must be an artist's carving, not a trophy from a grisly hunt to the eighth circle of hell. No such creature could exist on God's planet. Realizing that does nothing to explain why a person would want to defile their quiet sitting space with it.

The longer I stare, the more the initial horror fades into fascination. Some might have fat cherubs guarding their bedroom or an angel draped in mourning over a loved one's gravestone. Why not a demon keeping station over them while enjoying a book in silence?

Without noticing my crossing the room, I stand before the great hearth, staring up at the beast, the warm light of the sconces shining upward, giving its shadows greater detail. My father, and certainly my husband, would scold me for looking so closely at a work they would deem evil. The craftsmanship is astonishing. I want to touch it, to know if the teeth are sharp. Is it carved directly into the chimney, or is it installed over the top of the stone?

I stand on the hearth and put a steadying hand on the mantle that is just taller than my head. The longest fangs are nearly in reach as I stretch, pulling on the mantle to lift myself the last few inches—

Something slips under my fingers, and I topple back, landing hard on my backside. Thankfully, the thick rug with a simple geometric design softens my fall. I hadn't noticed that before, either.

I look down at the scrap of paper in my fist. I had blindly put my hand on it on the mantle, something I now immediately recognize as a page torn from a journal. The paper is wadded and creased, as if it had been violently torn from its notebook, but despite its wear and foxing, I can tell its quality. The blotchy yellow was probably once a pristine cream with fine printed lines. The handwriting is tight and efficient without a single extra frill.

October 16th, 1842 – Boston

Today, at The Anchor's Rest tavern, I overheard something strange.

Two sailors spoke of an island they wouldn't dock at—not for gold nor God. Widdershin, they called it. One said the winds there run counter to the tide, and that a woman once fled there, never to return. A witch, he claimed.

They laughed, but I did not. My son, Nathaniel, would have believed it. He believed in trees with memory. In rocks that "hummed."

I asked where it was. The older man made the sign of the cross and said, "You don't want it, sir."

But I do.

"EV" is stamped in gold in the bottom-right of the page.

Even over eighty years ago, sailors feared this island. I wonder who EV is—was—but also wonder about the rest of his journal. One torn-out page implies others, or an entire bound collection of un-torn-out pages. Would I need to run my hand over every high surface in the house, in the hope of finding a lost page or trinket?

I stand on the hearth again and walk from the right edge, brushing my hand blindly on the dusty mantle. Another piece of paper flutters down directly beside where the journal page had been, but there are no others.

This page is a newspaper trimming, barely holding together after the better part of a century at rest on the mantle.

Boston Evening Recorder – June 3rd, 1843

Wealthy Widower to Build Home on "Witch's Isle"

Erasmus Vale, prominent shipwright and gentleman of leisure, has reportedly purchased the land known locally as Widdershin Isle—an uninhabited islet off the coast near Chatham, long spoken of in tones of superstition.

Despite murmurs among seamen and townsfolk of "curses" and "witch hauntings," Mr. Vale appears undeterred. Sources say he intends to build a full-time residence there—Widdershin House, as the papers filed in Barnstable County refer to it.

When asked why he chose the location, Mr. Vale replied simply, "I go where echoes last the longest."

His household staff will reportedly remain in Boston, save for one hired man to deliver supplies.

"He's a lunatic or a visionary," said one Chatham

merchant. "Either way, I don't fancy his odds come
winter."

I chuckle at how quickly and neatly God answered my unspoken question. Though... I glance at the demon's skull. Maybe this nook is shielded from the eyes and influence of the Almighty.

Erasmus Vale, E.V., who had at least some degree of madness, built Widdershin House. Knowing him would help me to know this place. Was that him with a wife and daughter in the portrait in the hallway?

The wife... I shudder away a chill as I remember her. The artist captured her lost in some internal dread, leaving her un-focused, staring away into nothing. I know that feeling and that look. I could barely look away from the father, as much as I wished to, when I stood before the painting, but I remember more of the wife and mother in my memory's eye.

"Don't whistle thrice, don't call her name"

That was the line scratched into the wood barring the door at the back of the ruined wine cellar and whispered by Mr. Farlow. Yet, it returns to my mind when thinking of Erasmus Vale's wife.

Mr. Farlow's other warning returns to me, and I give the demon a last look before retracing my steps.

Once clear of the alcove, the storm beyond the outer walls returns in force with booming thunder quaking the floor and lightning spearing across it from the windows ahead of me.

I find it easily enough—the book of children's stories with a man in all white atop a glorious steed on its cover. It has only a dozen pages, and I brush through them, ignoring how the light from the wall sconces flares and dims in time with the storm. Towards the center, I find it. The right side has the same picture as from the cover, except the rider is now holding a lantern high with a storm darkening the sky behind him. The left page has a simple, typed rhyme.

> On Widdershin Isle, the wind don't sleep,
> The rider comes when fog runs deep.
> His coat is white, his boots are red,
> He seeks the wife who struck him dead.
> Don't whistle thrice, don't call her name—
> Or you'll be caught in the rider's flame.

A boom shakes the library, tossing precariously perched books to the floor. They clatter around me, and the lights wink out, plunging me into complete darkness.

"This is nothing. Just another blown fuse."

My heart pounds in my ears, but I focus on my breath, trying to control it through the shaking. A hand on the shelves helps to ground me, but I can feel the house tremble with every rattle of thunder.

I retrace my steps, waiting for lightning to cast long shadows just quick enough for me to spot the next safe place to step. I worry again about what will become of me and my work here without artificial light, but also about where the day went. It must have been before noon that I repaired the fuses, and suddenly it's as dark as midnight outside. The windows, clouded with grime, never let much light in, but this was more than the dark clouds of a storm. I've lost hours staring at a demon skull.

No.

I shake my head, knowing that's yet again being silly. I must have woken late, and it was far later in the day than I thought when I went down for the fuse box. There are no clocks in the house. At least none I have encountered yet in my limited travels.

Rain beats against the windows by the time I finally reach the hall. It beats the roof and every outer wall, hitting the house from every direction at once. With my hands extended before me, I move by memory to my room, feeling along the carved wainscotting and pushing the door open. On a surge of optimism, I try the light switch.

The small lamp on the bedside table flares to light, and I exhale a long breath. It's just another blown fuse. I make a mental note to unscrew half the lights in the library before replacing the fuse a second time. Unless there is another drawer, there are no spares. If it blows again, I will have to start disconnecting power from other parts of the house to prioritize the library. I know I should see to the lights again, or, knowing the rest of the house has power, test my bravery in the cellar in search of breakfast, perhaps for more fuses. But the bed... The cream linens sag into the center, forming a nest that fits me perfectly.

I heard somewhere it's unsafe to mess with electrical boxes during a storm, especially so close to the standing water in the basement. The standing water full of rats and mice, assuredly. I can deal with it all in the morning.

I step out of my shoes and roll into bed, coming to a comfortable stop in the middle, and the mattress gives, sinking downward to embrace me.

Wind slams the rain against the glass panes in a slow, hypnotic rhythm, lulling me to oblivion.

Six

I wake as I have every morning since coming to the island: refreshed and well after the sun has risen. I could never sleep this late at home, what with Edmund requiring his coffee, eggs, and toast, which he usually leaves untouched, before departing for the office. He didn't eat them, but unleashed hell if I didn't have them ready. I wanted to sleep in, or at least wake when he did, but he demanded his shirts be pressed that morning, not the night before. His shoes might get dusty if I polish them before going to bed. Why did he invest in that juicer for me if I fail to make him fresh juice every morning from the fruit I bought at the market the day before?

On top of his innumerable other sins and abuses, the man is exhausting.

I imagine Erasmus Vale's wife had it worse. After reading one entry from his journal, I know that man belonged in an institution. Edmund is at least in full command of himself. He may be cruel with his words and quick with his hands when he thinks I need reminding, but there is no madness. He's a

God-fearing man who leaves bruises where only God may see them.

Edmund isn't insane. At least, not how it's generally understood. He sees and understands his cruelty. That quiet control behind a face that never breaks is why he terrifies me so.

What we have between each other isn't love, and never was, but what choice did I have? My father died suddenly without a will. His lawyer was hellbent on finding the next male kin, which turned out to be some distant cousin who had never heard of Thomas Primrose until he moved into his house. My house. Mr. Calvin Searcy seemed kind enough, offering to let me keep my room until I could find other arrangements, but his wife, Celeste, didn't care for how he looked at me when he thought I wouldn't notice. I don't hold a grudge toward her for demanding I leave, remembering the sadness in her eyes as the taxi drove me from my childhood home. If anything, I envy her. She told her husband something she wanted, and she got it.

I only hope she sees and appreciates what she has.

I could remain in bed forever—or at least another hour—but a task that never starts is one that is never finished. My mother had a quote to that effect. She said it to me most mornings, yet it slips my memory.

Like yanking out a child's loose tooth, quickly and unexpectedly, I jump from bed before another stray remembrance pulls me deeper. I step into my shoes, smooth the wrinkles from the dress I slept in, and am in the library within a few heartbeats. I stop at every other sconce on the wall to unscrew the bulb, but pause before rounding into the alcove with the comfortable chair and demon's skull. Whatever light was in there may remain, and I don't want to lose half my day again to whatever mystical force stole my yesterday.

Hoping fewer light bulbs drawing power means less chance of a blown fuse, I pile the loose bulbs in a small wooden shipping crate in the corner, brush off my hands, and move on to my next task.

The library's fuse is the only one burnt out this time, and I replace it with the last spare from the drawer.

Another task done. Today is turning out to be quite productive, considering it started so late.

Fog curls around the trees at the back of the house, as it always seems to on this island, but I pay it little mind as I turn into the kitchen. The dark maw of the cellar door beckons without any of its prior malice. Malice... I scoff at myself and roll my eyes. It's a dark staircase down to some moldering goods and an unknown door. Something startled me the other day. I tripped over a broken wine rack and fled, hiding under the covers.

I seriously hid under the covers, like a terrified child.

I descend without pausing, pulling the chains on the bulbs as I pass. The shattered butter crock and egg are exactly where I dropped them, unmolested by what swims in the front basement or skitters in the garden. All of my dread for the place is just...gone. It could as easily be my pantry back home. The wine cellar and its boarded-over door sing to me, promising a mystery easily solved if only I can find a length of sturdy metal thin enough to wedge in and free the door.

My stomach sings louder, reminding me that I haven't eaten in a day. The mystery of the door and what lies beyond it isn't going anywhere. As I turn from the larder to the stairs, a shadow slides across the steps. My heart leaps to my throat, but I swallow it down, recognizing the gait as it slinks away. It's just the cat from the garden.

I return to the kitchen a few moments later with a jar of pickled eggs and oats that I might make into a porridge. The stove, to my delight and surprise, is gas, and I find a striker in a drawer to light it. Within a half hour, I am eating a filling, yet disappointing late breakfast, over the wide country sink. Anything other than just chunks of over-salted jerky is an improvement, but I also long for the toast, eggs, and bacon of my recent past.

I stare without seeing out the window over the sink, watching the fog shift and swirl, forming tiny congregations and moving on as quickly. It feels random at a glance, but the longer I gaze, idly chewing on oats soft enough for an infant, a pattern emerges. The fog is slowly dispersing as it shifts away from the house, channeling along a path through the trees. It resolves as I watch, gray pavers bright against the dark earth and verdant underbrush, inviting me to follow it into the forest.

I haven't left the house in days, haven't opened the windows with the sudden rain. If I don't go now, I never will once the library's work absorbs me again.

The wide, French doors from the back hall open without a complaint, and a wisp of cool, moist air tickles my ankles. It's not enough to go back for the sweater in my bag, and anyway, I'll only get warmer with the exercise.

The breeze brings a hint of wildflowers, though I can see none. Just a dense bed of growth between the maples. Ferns, and... I'm not familiar with plants, but the undergrowth is thick. I move with the fog, following that narrow, but clear, path. After a few steps, I can barely see the house behind me. After a few more, the path takes a steep incline. The maples turn to pines around me, then suddenly, just as I begin to feel the exercise, they end, leaving me a few feet from the sharp drop to the water below. I edge closer, as close as I dare, leaning to see foam splashing over the rocks jutting from the Atlantic, perhaps fifty feet down. Sea spray washes over my face, cool and refreshing after the sudden exertion. I squint into it, thinking I can make out a bit of ship hull against the rocks.

My shoes' smooth soles slip on the slick stone beneath me. I scream, cartwheel my arms uselessly, and fall hard on my bottom. The momentum over rock, still moist with morning dew and ocean spray, carries me forward another foot toward the edge, but I stop there. My feet hang over the deadly void in a way that might be whimsical, were it intentional.

Slowly, yet as quickly as I dare, I push back from the abyss with my palms ground into the stone and my heart racing in my throat. I don't risk a breath until I'm seated on the packed earth.

Minutes or more tick by while I watch a ship cut across the horizon, perhaps bound for Provincetown or Boston. Finally, courage builds within me enough to push up to standing. My dress is a wreck, covered in grass stains and mud. The lace at my left wrist is ripped, and the top button at my throat is missing. At least it isn't as though anyone will see me in the near future.

Almost a week in the house set me on a course to malnutrition, but leaving it immediately almost kills me. Time to head back.

The downhill trek back to the house is slower with my left ankle complaining. I hadn't noticed an injury when I slipped, but perhaps my body was waiting to know I wasn't dead before airing its grievances.

Moving slower and without the fog's guidance, the trip takes thrice as long, but the stone path is clear under my feet. Just as the first hint of Widdershin House pokes from between the trees, I note a cleared bit of ground to my left. A low, rusted iron fence surrounds the square parcel of land, fifteen feet on a side.

Sore ankle forgotten, my feet don't wait for my mind to decide, and I step over a break in the fence a moment later. Brush and weeds choke the space, but not enough to completely obscure the small stone monument in the center. I stub my toe on another object hidden in the overgrowth on my way to it, this one a fraction of the size, but with an unmistakable rounded shape: a gravestone. A half-dozen others glimmer from their resting places with no semblance of neat rows.

I bend to inspect the one I inadvertently kicked, pulling away the vines and brushing off lichen. If anything were written on it, the weather long ago washed it away. After checking the other side, I inspect the next, and the next. I move last to the center stone, scraping off the moss over where "Lavinia Vale - 1875" is scratched. Erasmus Vale mentioned his son Nathaniel, writing as though he were already dead in 1843. How many children did he have? Was Lavinia the girl in the hallway portrait, with the father's fingers digging into her shoulder? I should search for the rest of his journal. If I can find it, it might help to piece together the history of Widdershin House. Perhaps I could deduce who else is buried around where I now stand. Is Deliverance Black, the Widdershin Witch herself, buried right here?

Who would have been left on the island to bury her?

No...

My fingers fall from where they were tracing the deep scratches.

The history of the island and its residents is not my work. Learning their history will not bring me closer to the goals that brought me here and will only serve to delay my future. Not only that, but these idle distractions also put me at risk. Every moment I spend looking out to sea or rummaging through ancient graveyards is a moment not spent on Mr. Sparrow's work. Time not spent on work pushes my timeline back. It's another moment I am exposed to the risk of being found out. Or simply found.

I abandon my curiosity with a frown and cross through the back patio smelling of wildflowers. Inside the main hall, I place a hand on the carved banister. Why is it that when I'm tired, there seem to be more steps to climb?

Banging on the front door makes me jump. My ankle gives out, tossing me forward onto the steps.

Perhaps if I don't make a move, they'll go away.

The banging, knocking, perhaps, starts again.

"Miss Primrose? Are you in?"

I don't recognize the voice, but at least it isn't Edmund. I could flee to the library, or to the rats swimming in the basement.

The brass door handle shakes with the scrape of a key.

It's too much. I rush up the stairs, limping when my ankle complains with the sudden effort. I barely round the corner and peek back to see the door burst open. Daylight outlines an older man wearing a straw hat, tweed suit, and huge, round glasses.

He looks directly at my hiding place, and a toothy grin splits his trim, white beard.

"Ah, Miss Primrose. There's no need to hide, my dear."

Seven

There's no point in hiding. He's seen me. He knows who I am. He knows my name.

"Or, I assume, Miss Primrose," he says, setting his briefcase down beside his foot in the doorway.

I smooth back my hair and step into full view of him with the family portrait at my back.

"Who is asking?"

"Laurence Sparrow, esquire." He tips his hat. "Estate lawyer of this, Widdershin House." He sweeps a hand to indicate the foyer and takes a handkerchief from his inner breast pocket to dab his forehead.

"Yes, of course." My shoulders relax, unknitting a knot between them. I put a hand on the carved railing, bracing myself. "It's a pleasure to meet you in person, but I'm surprised to see you here, Mr. Sparrow."

"The pleasure is all mine, I am sure. The surprise is mine, as well, Miss Primrose. I arrived exactly when I said I would, prepared to open the house as I promised, only to hear that you, or at least a young woman matching your description and intentions, had already gone ahead of me."

I told Mr. Farlow that my husband would be following me soon, but Mr. Sparrow believed me to be unwed. I certainly hope they never had reason to discuss the matter of me. Who else would pilot the lawyer to the island he called God-forsaken, and what else would the two discuss on their journey?

"The timing presented itself, so I thought I might as well get started," I say.

He tucks his handkerchief away. "Well, Miss Primrose. You've put every man within fifty miles in a sore spot, leaving a maiden alone, defenseless, on an island in the middle of the Atlantic."

"What do I need protection from, out here alone on an island?"

His brow crinkles. He doesn't understand the question.

I barely control my smirk. "While I like hearing that chivalry is not dead, we're hardly in the middle of the ocean. I can see the Chatham lighthouse from the dock on a clear day. And you can call me Violet."

"Are we so familiar?" He pauses to consider his question. "No, Miss Primrose. Not yet. How about a cup of tea?"

By asking for tea, he was, of course, telling me to make it. I work in the kitchen, descending to the cellar for a tin of loose leaf, while he is elsewhere in the house. He returns just as I pour water from the kettle into his mug.

I lean against the kitchen counter and let the tea's heat leech into my fingers. "You were going to open the house, meaning what, Mr. Sparrow? Did you bring some fresh bread or fruits?"

His thick glasses make him look like a goldfish, and they steam over as he blows across his tea.

"Your dress, my dear. It's in tatters. What's happened?" he asks.

I look down and gasp at the state I'm in. Grass, dirt, ripped seams.

"I slipped in the garden. I was going up to change when you arrived."

"How horrible." His tone doesn't deliver much sympathy.

"Yes. And if you cannot call me by my first name, I would thank you not to call me your dear."

His eyes widen, and he snorts. "Very well. To answer your question, I had every intention of bringing fresh things with me, Miss Primrose. Then I arrived in town and heard that you had arrived and had already gone ahead of me. I chartered the first boat over."

"Was that difficult? Finding a captain willing to come to this island?"

He almost has the mug to his lips, but lowers it with a confused twist in his brows. "Should it be? Why should the captains of the sea have their boats, if not to take people across the water?"

Of course, it shouldn't, for a man. The first few captains I asked didn't want to deal with a lone woman, and Mr. Farlow thought he'd have some fun in frightening me.

"I've made some decent progress already," I say. "The sheer number of volumes…" I pause, not wanting to give him my time estimate. Then I pivot to a more pressing topic. "Who in town told you I'd already come through? Did you talk to anyone about me?"

"I dropped my things at the Chatham Bars Inn and went in search of a drink. It's no vice, you see, but traveling is dusty work. One table over was occupied by some fishermen, one of them talking about having taken some young lady to Widder-shin. Except, he was certain that you were married and awaiting your husband here."

My heart seizes in my chest, but Mr. Sparrow's bushy eyebrows imply confusion, rather than suspicion.

"As you said," I say into my tea, "you met him in a bar. He must have confused my story with someone else's. It's as simple as that. Was he the only one?"

My question seems to startle him. "No. I came straight over. Most of my things are still at the hotel. I was in the middle of the ocean before I remembered the telephone here. Though if you were tending to the garden, you won't have heard it."

"I see. Good. So you aren't intending to stay?"

"Certainly, I do! I won't sleep a wink knowing you are alone on this island. I can make do with what I brought a few days, then I will call the ferryman to either bring the rest of my luggage, or I'll make a round trip one afternoon."

"You should make a day of it. Chatham seems like quite the up-and-coming town."

He hums thoughtfully. "A question has plagued me. I offered you this position by post, thinking it would be a nice distraction, but I am left unsure of your motivations. Why would you come early, without notice, just because fortunate timing presented itself?"

"I rather enjoy the work, and the offer felt generous. I came early because I was excited to get started."

"Money? That's why you're here?" He leans back and shakes his head. "I don't understand why a young woman would willingly accept the burden of finances. Wait and let your husband take care of you."

"And while I wait for him, I should be able to afford to buy a sandwich. I can sign it all over to my future husband, and he can give it back as I need it for groceries or a new hat."

He hums again. "I suppose that's fair."

It's already too late in the day to expect Mr. Farlow, or whoever brought Mr. Sparrow here, to make another trip. I'll be stuck with the lawyer for at least a night.

"I know it's a ways off, but what were you making for dinner?" he asks.

I have to get rid of him. "I've been eating jerky for days. Breakfast was porridge and a pickled egg."

His nose crinkles. "I'm surprised there isn't anything better in the pantry. I'll make sure a good stock of groceries is brought over along with my things."

"You aren't intending to stay the entire time it takes me to sort through the library, are you? That wasn't your plan in your letters. I'm sure I'll be fine here on my own."

He frowns. "If you're worried that I'll get in your way, know that I can find other things to occupy my time. I have a meeting in Boston in a few weeks, but otherwise, yes, I'll stay. Your parents, God rest their souls, would be furious with me if they knew I left their little girl here unescorted."

"My parents. I wanted to ask you about them. How did you know them?"

"Why, your father used to work for me." His tone shifts to match his distant stare. "He talked about you all the time, how his little girl just loves to read."

"He... My father owned a stationery supply store. When did he work in a legal firm?"

"Ah, my dear. Miss Primrose. Thomas Primrose was, before all that, a great salesman. He helped to revolutionize the process at Finch, Finch, and Sparrow. He sold us typewriters, ribbon, and paper. Your mother trained the young girls who would become our copyists and secretaries. They were a powerful pair."

"Wait..." I set down my tea to consider the timeline. "My father opened his shop when we moved to Portland when I was seven. Are you saying you worked with him before then? Sixteen years ago?"

He nods. "That sounds about right."

"He never really worked for you, just made a big sale to your firm." I know that one big account provided my parents with the capital needed to settle in one place, but I never inquired further about it. Why would I? I was a child. "And you kept in touch afterward?"

He slowly shakes his head. "Alas, not as often as I would have liked. I would stop by his shop when in town, which wasn't too often. Then one day I was browsing the obituaries, as one does at my age, checking for old friends, when I saw your mother, and not too long after, your father. Tragic."

The lawyer's opening letter to me made it sound like he was a dear friend of my parents, not just a client who purchased from them. "How did you know about me, then? That I would qualify for this work?"

Mr. Sparrow's smile returns. "I told you, my d— Miss Primrose. Your father told me at length about how you love to read. I bet on that passion transferring to what was needed for this job, and look, I was right!"

"I grew up around books and all the things to organize papers. I worked at the Portland District Library for two years before..." I stop myself from mentioning when Edmund came into my life. "My mother never directly taught me how she organized the business, but I learned a lot from watching her."

"You did?" Mr. Sparrow's eyes grow impossibly huge behind his thick glasses. "What grand luck! You must have been beside yourself with delight on first seeing the library upstairs. No wonder you rushed here."

I stare at him for a moment before I realize my jaw is hanging slack. He didn't offer me a job organizing the books at Widdershin House, even though my resume is ideally suited to it. He hired a seven-year-old girl who loves her dime novels and penny dreadfuls. He likely didn't intend to offer me a job, but rather thinks of this as a harmless diversion for a young, unmarried woman. Something to keep my mind busy while searching for a husband, not what I intended to be my career before Edmund swooped in and dashed away all my dreams. I am a favor to a friendship that exists only in his mind.

"As you say." I dump the remainder of my tea into the sink. "I'm going to get back to work."

He stares at my mug on the counter and stifles a yawn. "Travel does me in, especially as much as I've done today. I'm going to lie down for a bit. Did you take the bedroom in the North Wing? I'll find a suitable one on the other end and see you at dinner."

Mr. Sparrow tips an imaginary hat, having taken his off when he entered the house, and is gone before I can process his full meaning. He intends to wander the house, doing whatever would make him look busy and useful. He'll come into the library at lunch and dinner to ask what I'd like to eat, and a few other times a day, saying we should have tea. My task is already daunting, with a tight and unknown schedule, and he will only delay it. In the moment, I can think of no way to be rid of him completely, but perhaps I can dispose of him for a night while I think.

I run after him, reaching the bottom of the stairs as he is about to disappear into the South Wing.

"Mr. Sparrow!"

He turns, stifling another yawn. "There's no need to shout, Miss Primrose. We are the only two for miles."

"Mr. Sparrow," I say in a low voice. "Could you call the dock to send someone back for you immediately? I'll be fine tonight, and I thank you for checking in on me. I, we, could use some bread, apples, and fresh milk for the coffee and tea."

He waves me down, yawning again. "Tomorrow, dear."

"I'll call right now. I'll wake you when they arrive."

He rolls his enormous eyes and grins. "I don't know if I'll ever get used to the young ladies of this new world. It's as though you don't want a man to care for you."

He doesn't hear the irony in his words.

"What will people say with the two of us alone here?" I plead.

"How do you mean?"

"A young, unmarried woman alone with an older gentleman?"

He snorts a laugh. "Older is right. I'm old enough not to bother with foolish girls."

"Think of my honor, Mr. Sparrow."

"Don't be silly."

Heat flushes my neck and cheeks, and I reach a bracing hand for the banister. "Very well, Mr. Sparrow. Enjoy your nap, and I'm sure the smell of warm porridge will wake you for dinner. I insist you call for the boat at first light tomorrow."

My fingers clench around the wood when he flashes that grin of condescension, the one that says, "That's a good, obedient girl." Then he goes down the hall.

Eight

Mr. Sparrow grumbles about the strong wind the next morning. I notice nothing, but he claims it's grounds to not bother calling for a boat. He has a headache the next day. His mumbled complaints about how I brew coffee or fry an egg are loud enough that he must intend that I hear them. I ignore it all. If he has something to say, he can very well say it to me directly.

At least he stays out of the library. I hear him shuffling about, coughing constantly. When he isn't coughing, he's grunting to clear his throat. No matter where he is in the house, no matter what he might be doing, he may as well be sitting behind the desk in the library. It's as though all the sound in the house channels to this room.

Storm clouds build during the afternoon, and I hear the first distant rumble of thunder while I stand over the stove, stirring yet another terrible pot of porridge for an early dinner.

"Is that all that's down there?" Mr. Sparrow asks between coughs.

"What's wrong with porridge? My mother said that clean food makes for a clean body and clean spirit. I think that's quite lovely." My mother never said anything of the sort. She loved gin and cigars, but made me promise I wouldn't tell my father, who already knew. He had his own vices that he swore me to pointless secrecy about. It was a silly game between them.

"Well, I won't be the one to contradict your mother, Miss Primrose. Say, have you been in the South Wing bedrooms? Or to the attic?"

"No. Should I?" I ladle flavorless glop into a bowl and hand it to him. His nose curls with disgust, and I have to turn so he can't see me biting back a grin.

"Perhaps you should. The room I selected contains a book-shelf bearing some interesting tomes. And there is a bible and what seems like a journal in the nightstand."

I whip back to him. "A journal? Whose?" I had all but forgotten my interest in Erasmus Vale's journal since the lawyer's arrival.

"I wouldn't know," he says and lets a spoonful of porridge drop into his bowl. "After I leave for my things and the groceries, you are free to clear the room of its books. If you run across a feather duster, the mantle and desk could use a woman's touch."

"Which room are you staying in? Is it Eras—erm, Mr. Vale's?"

He shakes his head. "I wouldn't know, but I think it was a guest room. The first on the right. The stationery in the desk's drawers is too neatly stacked to have been regularly used. Mr. Vale's mind was a whirlwind. He rarely left the library."

That might explain the state of the room when I first entered it.

"You must have known him well," I say.

"Not at all, only by reputation. I know what you're about to ask. I represent the Widdershin Estate, not the estate of the late Erasmus Vale. His will was... complex."

"What can you tell me about him, then?"

Mr. Sparrow pushes his bowl away, less than half eaten. "He was a particular man. Peculiar. I'm sure you've noticed there are no mirrors in the house."

I hadn't, but nor had I explored most of the manor. The empty hook in the bathroom told me there had once been a mirror there, but one missing mirror is not enough to form a pattern.

He tsks and shakes his head. "Tragic life. He buried three wives and twice as many children, then he died here six years ago, in the library, a day before his one-hundredth birthday."

"He died in the library?"

Mr. Sparrow nods. "Working, as always. It wasn't messy, I hear."

"Which was Lavinia? Wife or daughter?"

He folds his arms and leans back. "Why ask me when you know so much? Lavinia was his daughter, his favorite. She was the longest-lived, making it to seventeen years old. That's her at the top of the steps, along with his fourth and last wife, Sara."

I count off the relations on my fingers, working out the timeline. "That means Erasmus was born about one hundred and five years ago, about 1820, and built this house around 1843. Lavinia was born about 1858... What about Sara?"

"What about her?"

"Is she still alive?"

"Oh, no. She passed last year in Rhode Island."

"Why not here? Wasn't this her home for at least seventy years?"

"Yes, but she was an elderly widow. She was in no shape to inherit. Not that women should take on the ownership, the burden, of large houses."

"A woman can inherit, Mr. Sparrow. I'm sure she would have rather spent her final days in the house she called home."

He chuckles. "Sara Vale left Widdershin when her husband died. She probably couldn't stand the emptiness without him. It was left abandoned since. But anyway, why should she wish to control an estate as well as their duties of keeping it fit?"

"It's 1925. Women are getting the power we deserve. We can vote now. We should have property and rights."

"Hmph, I have my opinions about that. I know those opinions have fallen out of favor, so I will keep them to myself."

His civil tone belies the cruel words and meaning behind them.

He has a coughing fit, but I make no move to pat his back as he hacks into his fist.

"This salt air generally does me well. I sleep like the dead here, but it gets into my lungs. Maybe it's the dust. If this storm passes quickly, I hope tomorrow will be pleasant enough that I might call for the boat. You could come with me, my dear. A day on the town might do you good. You look quite flushed."

"I'm not your dear. Call me Miss Primrose." I clutch the counter's edge. "Thank you, but I'd rather stay and work."

"Quite the worker bee, you are. If you change your mind, I know you would do better in picking out the best fruits at the market than I."

***

Thoughts of having the house to myself fuel my evening. I have the bottom shelves closest to the door empty, up to the height I can reach without a ladder, and have made the first entries in the ledger. There is no point in organizing the collection, regardless of my original plans. I'll catalog it and note where I put each tome, but once it's gone—once it's sold to someone else, whether in part or in full—it'll be their problem to group similar subjects together.

An Index of Infernal Climates, Rev. Jonathan Carruth, 1st London Printing, 1824. Occult weather phenomena. Red leather, warped and water-damaged.

Little Dreadfuls: Nursery Rhymes for Unquiet Children, Multiple Authors, hand-pressed chapbook, unknown date. Children's literature. Softcover stitched with blue thread, illustrations in ink and blood-red wash.

Beasts and Their Vices, Sir Alfred P. Merrow, Private Press, signed by author, 1913. Moral philosophy. Thick, cracked leather, with gilt-edge tooling shaped like claws.

The Widow's Almanac, Clarinda Bell, Tenth Colonial Reprint, 1791. Herbal remedies, folk wisdom. Blackened calfskin, barely legible script on the spine.

The last book, small enough to fit in an apron pocket, catches my eye for a moment longer than the others. Clarinda drew the delicate pictures of herbs and petals more than one and a half centuries ago. She was likely alive when this country declared its independence. So much had changed since then, yet so much was the same.

I flip through its pages, tracing a finger down the paper's rough edge. The illustrations are brilliantly detailed and annotated to mark how one might identify this or that plant against other similar ones. Near the center, a page comes loose. My heart jumps, then I realize it was tucked into the book, not a part of the binding.

I hold it to the light and clap a hand to cover my giggle as the purpose of the handwritten recipe card becomes obvious.

To dull the flame in a man's belly, that he may seek neither pleasure nor conquest.

3 pinches of dried hop flowers (to subdue restlessness)

1 sprig of rue (to blunt virility)

A shaving of willow bark (for cooling the blood)

4 black peppercorns (to ward away curiosity)

2 crushed juniper berries (for bitterness and clarity of mind)

A spoon of honey (so it may pass the lips unnoticed)

A single drop of laudanum (if peace is preferred over conversation)

Steep the herbs in warmed vinegar for the span of

a Psalm. Strain through cloth touched by no man's hands. Store in glass, buried beneath stone, until needed.

I wish I had Clarinda's strength to simply drug her husband for a restful night. Edmund might be more bearable if he took the correct herbal tincture, mixed into his morning coffee or evening brandy. Or his afternoon tea. Or with his every beverage every day.

I turn it over and fumble it, almost dropping it in my shock at seeing what is on the other side. This was not Clarinda's recipe, though she may have benefited from it. The back, or rather the original front, of the paper is a church's handbill, printed before the first newspaper in the state. Delicate swirls fill the corners of the stock paper.

A Joyous Union on the Eve of Winter

On the 14th day of November in the Year of Our Lord 1689, Mr. Absalom Black, esteemed trades-man and landholder of the township of Beechfield, did take to wife Miss Deliverance Ward, the only daughter of the late Reverend Thomas Ward of Plymouth Colony.

The ceremony was held at the Beechfield Meeting-house under the guidance of Pastor Josiah Withers. A modest supper followed at the Black homestead with kin and neighbors in attendance. Miss Ward is praised for her upright demeanor and learned habits, particularly in letters and herbal practice.

Let us pray the Lord shall bless their house with virtue and increase.

Deliverance Black again. If the recipe were hers, with instructions like that, I have little doubt why she was branded a witch and forced to flee her home.

With respectful reverence, I place the single sheet in the desk drawer along with the page from Erasmus Vale's journal and newspaper clipping. If I can find more about either or both of them, it would be wonderful, but not at the risk of delaying my timeline. Widdershin House feeds me information at a pace that keeps my interest piqued, so I have no doubt another interesting bit will come forward on its own on the morrow, or the following day.

Near-continuous thunder and rain slamming against the library windows mask Mr. Sparrow's constant coughing from elsewhere in the house. He hasn't pestered me since leaving most of his dinner untouched on the kitchen counter. Assuming, hopefully, he leaves tomorrow, I will rush about, collecting all the books and journals. Then, when he returns, I'll have even less reason to encounter him. Those fantasies will have to play out tomorrow.

If he leaves tomorrow. He'll surely blame the storm for the reason to stay another day. Perhaps the rain will make the ocean too wet.

The wind is steady, blowing away from my bedroom window, so I leave it wide to let in the breeze and fresh air. As I lie cocooned in the broken, dusty mattress, staring at the cracked and flaking plaster ceiling, a low whistle reaches my hearing. I wonder for a while if it's the wind through the trees surrounding the house, then decide it's a distant ship's fog horn. That still isn't quite right, but I don't come up with another idea before sleep claims me.

Nine

I awaken as refreshed as I have every morning in the Widder-shin House. A glance out the window shows the grounds, as usual, choked with fog. I can only hope that Mr. Sparrow doesn't use that as an excuse to, again, not call for a boat.

I dress and go downstairs, knowing Mr. Sparrow will want his coffee first thing. Starting the day on his bad side is no way to get rid of him.

His hat and luggage are tossed by the front door. That is a good sign.

Upon entering the kitchen, the first thing I notice is that the cellar door is closed, and a heavy block from the hearth is pulled over it.

Curious.

I make coffee, just as I have the last few mornings. I pour mine, then leave Mr. Sparrow's on to burn for, as Deliverance might have put it, the span of a Psalm. A drop of vinegar, a dash of salt, and it's ready.

Slight movement across the hall catches my eye. I have yet to enter the dining room, but there, sitting with his elbows on the table and his fist clenching his hair, is Mr. Sparrow. Taking up his mug, I cross to him. The dim light in the dining room casts deep shadows into the corners, but even in the gloom, I can tell it was once grand. But I could say that about anything in this house. The long table has easy seating for fourteen with a moth-eaten runner spanning its length. A hearth at the far end sits cold beneath a painting of some ancient, bloody battle.

He brings shaky fingers to his lips, and I smell the cigarette smoke before I see the red glow of its tip as he inhales. A tin lay open on the table before him with a half dozen stubs smashed to nothing on one side.

I pull out the heavy chair beside Mr. Sparrow, and he doesn't acknowledge me even as I sit and slide his coffee toward him.

"Did you not sleep well, Mr. Sparrow?"

He runs both hands through his hair, heedless of the ash dropping onto his head.

His words come quickly and whispered, as if he's trying to get them out before the house can overhear us. "I called for the boat first thing, but it can't come soon enough. We have to get away from here."

I chuckle and lean back to sip my coffee. "I can't leave yet. I have a job to do here."

"What job is worth your life? Your sanity?"

He whips his head to me, and I gasp, cringing back. His eyes are red-rimmed and bloodshot over heavy bags. He looks ten years older than he did last night.

"She called to me all night. Screamed and wailed," he says, turning back to stub out his cigarette and take up another. His hands are shaking too hard to manage the lighter.

I set down my coffee to help him with the flick of flame.

"You had a bad dream."

"No! She wants me. Wants me dead like she killed her husband."

"Who?"

"The Witch!"

"No, Mr. Sparrow. Maybe you heard the wind or a foghorn, but there is no witch."

"You're wrong. The Widdershin Witch was real. As real as you or me. Maybe more so, as her curse still haunts this island centuries later."

"Her name was Deliverance Black, and she was just a woman, the same as me." A woman willing to regularly drug her husband. "She didn't kill her husband; she fled here to get away from him."

He chokes out a snorting laugh. "Don't tell me what did or didn't happen, young miss."

I watch him in profile for a moment, the hunched posture, the rumpled suit jacket. Some noise in the night was all it took to wreck this man's dignity. Perhaps I can press on that.

"What happened in the kitchen, Mr. Sparrow? Why is the cellar shut?"

He shakes his head and drops it to his elbow, folded on the table.

"Fine. Let's go to the dock. I'll wait with you and see you off."

"No!" He knocks his coffee mug away in a rush to grab me by my forearms. "You can't stay here." His breath reeks of his cigarettes. He sees himself as a grand white knight champion protector, despite being terrified of the wind and a stormy night's sleep.

He won't let me go. Rather, he won't let me stay without him.

I glance at his coffee splashed across the table, then down at his hands on me. He follows my gaze and slowly releases me.

"Maybe we need something stronger to calm our nerves," I say. "I saw some whiskey in the library. I'll just run up for it and grab my bag on the way back down."

"It's a bit early for liquor, but..." He nods, shakily. "That's a good girl. Yes, thank you."

Upstairs, I get my bag, but put nothing in it. In the library, I round to the darkened cubby with the demon skull over the hearth and perform the sign of the cross, staring up at it. "Forgive me." I pour two fingers of what smells like whiskey from one of the crystal decanters.

I stop in the bathroom for a glass vial I saw amongst the medicines the other day.

Mr. Sparrow is waiting for me, standing beside the open front door with his briefcase in one hand and his hat in the other. I hand him the drink, and he tosses it back without a breath of hesitation, leaving the empty glass on the small side table beside the door.

The empty glass vial feels like a stone in the folds of my dress.

He leads us to the dock, not uttering a word, moving quickly over stone still slick with the morning's mist through the tangled garden. His footing is failing him a bit too easily, with a toe or heel catching on the vines at the edge of the path by the time we reach the rusted iron gate. The water opens before us, with the Chatham lighthouse standing out as a flashing beacon near the horizon. A smudge of oily smoke is approaching us.

"I see the boat, Mr. Sparrow."

"Did you not hear it, Miss Prim..." He falters and swallows. "Primrose? I spoke the words of Isaiah aloud. And when she stole them from my memory—when I could no longer recall even the rhythm of the psalm—I opened the Book. I read by shaking hands until the wind died. It was all I could do to keep her from taking me."

"What if she had taken you? What would the Witch have done?"

"Don't tempt such fancy." He slides to his right and grabs for the gate to steady himself, and uses the other to pull his jacket tighter.

"I need to finish my work here. I need the money you owe me, Mr. Sparrow."

"What?" He steps away from the gate, stumbles, and reaches for it again. "What, no. It isn't safe. The Witch."

"Isn't safe for whom, Mr. Sparrow? I've been here a week with no problem. She came for you on your third night."

I step close and cup a hand on his cheek as he struggles to focus on me so near. Maybe I put too much in his drink.

"The Witch has no interest in me. I'm safe here, but you are not."

The boat chugs close, and I'm glad to see it isn't Mr. Farlow's fishing dinghy.

I drop my hand and quickly move down the dock to meet the lone man on the small vessel.

"Thank you for coming so quickly," I say as he steps onto the dock, tightening a rope to the posts with effortless skill. He's a younger, attractive man with wild black hair peeking around the edges of his captain's hat and eyes as green as sparkling jade.

"Everything okay? He made it sound like a real emergency, even offered an extra ten dollars to get here quickly."

"How noble of you, Captain..."

"Carver, miss. Asa Carver." He tips his captain's hat and flashes a warm grin. "What were you two doing out here?" His focus shifts past me to the lawyer, who is struggling to keep his feet under him.

"Nothing the Lord would frown upon, I promise you. He hired me to tidy up the house before the estate sells. Please, Mr. Sparrow needs your help."

The young captain frowns at the lawyer, now holding onto the gate with both hands, yet still swaying on his feet. Mr. Sparrow is mumbling something, punctuated by shouted words at irregular intervals.

"He said it would be the two of you," Asa says.

"No, just him. He's confused. He..." I lower my voice to a conspiratorial tone. "He drinks, and I don't think that goes well with his medications."

"Come on, old timer. Let's get you back to town." The captain slips an arm under Mr. Sparrow's and helps him down the dock. Twice, they nearly spill into the water.

"Wait! Wait..." The lawyer flails his arm, nearly knocking Captain Carver over a third time while stepping onto the boat.

He looks up at the young man, as if seeing him for the first time. "Stars, you're an infant. Are you old enough to pilot this thing?"

"I'm twenty-five, sir, and I assure you I'm more than qualified."

"She's coming," Mr. Sparrow slurs. "You're coming too. M iss... You can't with the Witch."

I step back with my hands neatly folded before me. "We talked about this, Mr. Sparrow. I must stay and work. I will telephone when I am done, and we can arrange for my payment."

The captain looks back at me with wide eyes, as if begging me to join so he isn't alone with the drunken old man.

"You can't," Mr. Sparrow starts and collapses backward onto a seat along the edge of the boat. "Tell her you..." He loses his words, staring down at his open palm.

"He has a room at the Chatham Bars, but I don't mean for you to see him all the way there. Please make sure he drinks plenty of water," I say.

"Will you be alright here alone, Miss...?" Asa asks.

"For a while, yes. There are enough oats and pickled things in the cellar to keep me going."

A line creases his brow. He opens a box attached to a post near the controls and offers me two red cylinders.

"They're flares. You should have them in case of an emergency," he says.

I push them back, and heat rushes up my neck when our fingers touch. "Thank you, but I'll telephone if there's an emergency."

The crease in his brow deepens, but he nods and unties the moorings. A moment later, the ship is a stone's throw away, but

I can clearly see Mr. Sparrow slumped back in his chair. He's still holding up his hand, so I know he's alive. I didn't take the time to read the medication's suggested dosage.

Once I can no longer see his face, I reach into the folds of my dress, taking out the vial. I rub a thumb over the faded label.

> *Dr. Winterthorn's Soothing Chlorodyne*
> *"For Nerves, Nightmares, and Nuisances of the*
> *Flesh."*

Deliverance and Clarinda may have had a different reason to drug their men with laudanum, but it was just as effective for me.

I arc my arm back and throw the vial as far as I can into the Atlantic Ocean.

Ten

I wait as long as I can stand it, not wanting the dashing Captain Asa Carver to look back to see me sprinting toward the house. Mr. Sparrow would spend the day in bed and nurse a hangover tomorrow, but what about after that? Surely, he wouldn't make any wild accusations against me, that I drugged and confused him with tales about the Widdershin Witch. If he rushes back, demanding I vacate, I would need enough evidence of my hard work to prove that I should remain. If he forces me off, I should be able to reasonably demand payment for the services I have rendered to that point.

That sounds like a legal battle that I am ill-equipped to take on and would never win. He would only need to point to the lies I have told to have the case thrown out. That is, if Edmund allowed it to get that far.

When the boat is an inky smudge, and I can no longer make out their forms, I turn and run as quickly as I dare on the rickety dock, then through the tangled garden. I fairly fly up the stairs, more pulling myself up the banister than letting my feet beat on the carpet. I scowl at Erasmus as I pass him, and am at the first door on the right in the South Wing one ragged breath later. I allow myself to take that breath, and a dozen more, before pushing the door open.

The room is about the same size as the one I have used for a bedroom this last week. The bed is unmade, the dresser drawers askew, and the desk is a small disaster of loose papers. An inkwell is spilled over it all, still glossy and wet.

If he hadn't fled, I have no doubt Mr. Sparrow would have concocted a reason that I should come and tidy the room within another day.

Actually, he had. Something about me finding a feather duster while he went to town.

The lacey curtains flow in a breeze, and I track the movement to a broken window pane. Wind flows over the glass in bursts, whistling as it goes, and I wonder if this is the cause of Mr. Sparrow's distress. It wasn't a foghorn or witch's cursed wailing, but a broken pane.

As described, a squat case of books sits beside the window, just as haphazardly filled as the library. At a glance, it seems to be all dime novels, nothing of interest, but I should still collect everything into one place.

A massive leather-bound tome on the floor beside the bed immediately grabs my attention as I turn to scan the room. "The Holy Bible" is etched deep into the hard leather, and I pick it up, shocked by the weight. It must be at least a foot long, ten inches wide, and seven inches thick. Along the spine are "Holy Bible References", "Bible Dictionary and Cities of the Bible", and "2000 Illustrations". I flip it over and ensure the pages will lie flat before setting it down on the bed. After only a cursory flip through its pages, I can believe the claim of two thousand illustrations. Every page has several sketches with astonishing detail that draw me in more than the history and geographic lessons beside them.

A few pages in, under the delicate, illuminated text "THE FAMILY", is a hand-drawn family tree. Erasmus Ambrose and Sara Evangeline (Hathorne) Vale take up the center. Three names are written at the side in a block of their own: Nathaniel, Thomas, and Mary. The same steady hand drew a line from Erasmus and Sara to "Lavinia (1858)". It continues to the right, but grows fainter and shakier as it does. "Elias (1861)", "Ruth (1863)", "Augustus (1866)".

The family tree does not continue downward.

I can't stop myself. I rushed up here to work frantic hours, yet I flip through the thin pages, pausing to brush my fingers across yellowed newspaper clippings glued into the Bible. Happy announcements cram the pages, but the obituaries stand alone, as if the Bible needed space to grieve.

Barnstable Patriot – August 15, 1865

VALE FAMILY BEREAVED

Ruth Vale, youngest daughter of Mr. and Mrs. Erasmus A. Vale, passed from this life on the 9th instant following a brief but grievous fever. She was aged 22 months. Services to be private.

Barnstable Patriot – November 21, 1866

STILLBIRTH AT VALE HOUSE

Word reaches us with sorrow that Mrs. Sara E. Vale was delivered of a stillborn son on the 19th instant at Widdershin Isle. Mother and father are said to be in seclusion. May the Lord comfort them in their losses.

Barnstable Patriot – June 20, 1868

CHILD LOST IN TRAGIC ACCIDENT

It grieves us to report the loss of Master Elias Vale, son of Mr. Erasmus A. Vale and wife Sara E. Vale of Widdershin Isle. The child, aged 7 years, suffered a fatal fall into a disused well upon the family's property. Despite every effort, recovery was not possible.

Mr. Vale and family request the community's prayers and privacy in their time of mourning.

Barnstable Patriot – September 25, 1875

LAVINIA VALE PASSES AT SEVENTEEN

*After a long affliction of frailty and nervous com-
plaint, Miss Lavinia Vale, eldest daughter of Mr.
Erasmus Ambrose Vale, was called to her rest on
the 22nd inst., aged 17 years.*

*The family history being known to many, no vis-
itation is planned. Private internment is expected
upon the Isle.*

Four children died on this little island, three in his house, and
that is without the rumored nursery fire, which took another
four. Lavinia's obituary is the final article added to the Vale
Family Bible, as if they gave up. The weight of it all presses on my
chest. The death, the curse, the misery of this island. I wonder
if Lavinia kept a diary to record her "frailty", but I know that is
well beyond what I should be doing.

Mr. Sparrow said there was a journal, along with the Bible.
He clearly meant this monstrous tome for the second, and
dropped it from the bed in his fright. I yank open the barren
nightstand drawers, comb through the papers on the desk, and
try each of the drawers in it. I look across the spines on the
bookshelf, but none seem like a journal. Finally, I drop to my
hands and knees to pull up the bed's dust ruffle.

There, beside a scrape in the dust, is a single sheet of stiff
paper. I reach for it, noting the dust around it, but how neat

the paper is. Perhaps it fell from the Vale Family Bible and slid under the bed.

It's a pamphlet, or perhaps a religious tract. Block letters across the front spell out "Of Shadows and Memory in Maritime Landforms", but the rest is a rambling mess. It speaks of soil that echoes, trees growing crooked from sorrow, and wind that names the dead. After more flowery, mostly incoherent chaos, a narrative forms, describing the writer as standing in the center of a storm, of a place forgotten by cartographers and cursed by fishermen. It doesn't speak of horror, but of recognition and stillness.

A chill wraps around my spine and works its way to the base of my skull. I can guess who wrote this and what he wrote it about, even before the last line and sign off.

> *I do not wish to tame the island. Only to listen.*
> *-Erasmus Vale, 1852*

The man was insane, or at least he wrote as if he were. A space on the back might have been left blank for an address and postage, as if he had sent copies of his work.

I empty a wheeled cart I found in the library and fill it from the guest room's bookshelf. Within an hour, I feel confident that neither Mr. Vale's journal nor any other book remains hidden in the room. The bathroom across the hall has a few magazines and a Sears catalog. Two more bedrooms are neat, if dusty, and I clear them of everything vaguely literary.

The last room, I have no doubt, once belonged to Lavinia Vale. The room feels warmer than the others, almost inviting.

Faint bouquets of roses and violets bloom on the pale pink wallpaper. A plush fainting couch near the tall windows is perfectly aligned to watch out the drapes drawn open a few inches, as if Lavinia lay there, watching for someone's return through the garden. The canopy bed is draped in faded lace that falls apart at my touch. A silver brush set sits on the white vanity table, as if set down mid-use.

Lavinia died fifty years ago, yet the children's ballet shoes resting on a shelf are pristine. The dolls beside them are not, staring at me from empty eye sockets with cracked, porcelain faces and grimy clothes. There is no in between. Everything here is immaculate or rotted. Time wasn't sure what to do in this room.

I cringe away and move to the white vanity. The mirror—the only mirror I've yet to see in the house—is warped and spotted with age. Mr. Sparrow had made some comment about there being no mirrors in the house, yet here is one, sitting in the open. No matter.

A dark walnut box with mother-of-pearl inlay tracing a vine sits in front of it, beside the brushes. I note the tiny crank on its side and flip the rose-shaped clasp on the music box.

A small porcelain dancer stands on the spindle, clad in a pink tulle skirt gone brown-edged with age. One of her arms is missing—snapped clean at the shoulder. Her remaining hand reaches out, perpetually mid-spin.

The first notes stumble out—a tune once sweet, now dragging, each note just a breath behind where it should be. The melody warps at its edges, like a lullaby remembered in fever dreams. One gear catches slightly every fourth turn, causing a faint mechanical gasp between phrases. The dancer turns to her, barely recognizable, *Greensleeves* melody.

I look up from her to myself in the mirror, not remembering sitting down at the vanity, and frown at the sight of my hair. I only had my compact mirror this last week, which proved wholly insufficient for long-term use. My cheekbones seem more pronounced, and my lips thinner, as if my diet of empty things from the cold storage has affected me after less than two weeks.

I pick up the silver brush and run it through my hair. The simple act is nothing at first, just a basic routine. I can imagine Lavinia sitting in this very spot with her mother or a maid brushing her hair every night as the music box fills the room with its sweet tones. When did I last allow myself a quiet moment given fully to myself? This evening, I can prepare a finer meal, not the porridge I have been making for Mr. Sparrow. In the morning, I can wake when I choose and make coffee the way I like it.

I grin at the woman in the mirror as I imagine her future drawn out before my eyes. She's financially independent and in control of her life and all her decisions. Waiters ask her what she'll be having for dinner, rather than looking to the man at the table to order for her. I run the brush through my hair, humming along with the music box and wishing it were a violin playing on the corner of a Parisian street as I sit before a cafe, sipping espresso.

A spring snaps in the music box, silencing it forever, leaving me in the dead air that smells faintly of wildflowers. It grows staler with each breath, drawing me back to the abandoned room of slow decay.

There's work to be done, and my gamble with drugging Mr. Sparrow will only have a chance if I have a sizeable contribution done when he returns. If he returns.

I stand and turn, but lock eyes with the beast in the doorway, and stumble back a step. The cat from the garden. It stares at me from where it sits in the hall, a mangy gray beast. I pat my chest, willing my heart to go back to its usual place, rather than in my throat.

"Do you enjoy lurking around, watching me from the shadows?" I ask it, but it says nothing, as expected. It only stares, unblinking. "Do you not want me in here?" The air has grown thick to the point of being difficult to breathe, though it may be my nerves.

Will it attack me if I try to sidle past it? Best not to risk it, if I can avoid the encounter.

I glance around the room, remembering I haven't yet checked it for books. A sketchbook and a book of poetry sit on the nightstand, but there is no shelf like the other bedrooms have. I quickly pull out the vanity drawers, finding plenty of brushes, hair clips, and makeup tools. But also, in the top drawer, I find a silver letter opener that might be better called a knife. I hold it up, admiring the stamped handle that catches the light and reflects in Lavinia's initials at the end.

Never knowing when I might need a knife in my work in the library, I pocket it and look back at the doorway. The cat has left.

Seizing the opportunity, I grab the books from the nightstand and flee Lavinia's room.

The late afternoon light from the open door behind me hits across the wainscotting and illuminates the brass handle beside me at the end of the hall. Without thinking too long on it, I grasp the handle, pulling open a cleverly concealed door and the dark stairway beyond, twisting upward. The air drifting down smells of old things, dusty and forgotten, mixed with bird droppings.

The attic. I assumed there would be one. I knew there was one from the fuse box labels. But had I eaten yet today? I woke up to coffee, then poisoned a man before snooping through dead people's things. I should eat and organize what I have gathered from the bedrooms.

I push the door closed on silent hinges with a satisfying, soft click of the lock.

I am about to close Lavinia's door, but notice the gray garden cat lying on the foot of the bed. Its paws are tucked under its chest as it considers me with those pale, golden eyes.

"You want to sleep in here? Go right ahead."

I leave the door open and push the cart back to the library.

Eleven

My mind keeps returning to Mr. Sparrow and the sight of him slumped in a seat on Captain Carver's boat. I convince myself that if something happened to him, someone would call and arrive at the dock to tell me. Likely with handcuffs.

My work continues with renewed vigor, emptying four shelves haphazardly crammed to neatly fill three. I take to browsing Sara Vale's Bible while I eat or rest with tea or coffee. The illustrations capture me more than the words, depicting the saints and prophets in dynamic poses as they bless a sinner or proselytize a crowd.

On the third morning, still with no word from Mr. Sparrow, I reach the center of the Bible and the folded pamphlet shoved deep against the binding. I open the delicate paper stiff from decades of preservation. It is mostly taken up by talk of the upcoming church social and the three weddings to follow, but the article at the bottom of the last page definitely belongs with this house.

The Plymouth Colonial Circular (1693)

Notorious Beechfield Accused Vanishes Into the Wilderness

March 7th — Deliverance Black, long suspected of witchcraft and misdeeds in the town of Beechfield, has fled her homestead in the dead of night, leaving behind no trace but her husband's coat upon the threshold and an open Bible turned to Psalms.

Mr. Absalom Black has been reported as grievously wounded, though no details have been disclosed. He claims his wife was spirited away by shadowed forms in the trees, though no witnesses support the claim.

Some whisper she joined the witches at Gallows' End; others believe she took flight to the sea. The town remains divided—some cry relief, others, dread.

Her name shall be added to the list of absconded suspects, to be dealt with should she return.

This was Sara Vale's Bible, and she deliberately hid mention of the Widdershin Witch within it. The more I learn about Deliverance, the more I see myself reflected in her. Or, at least

I want to. We both fled our husbands to Widdershin Isle, but the author of this article seems to think Deliverance attacked her husband first. I just boarded an early train after Edmund left town. Had she been found, they would have hanged her or burned her at the stake, or something equally brutal. My plight feels petty by comparison. Edmund would drag me back to Portland with him. He would never divorce me; he's too proud for that. Would he beat me? He threatens to do it more than he does. The trauma of a threat causes scars that can sometimes sting more than physical ones, living on needles, never sure what will set him off.

I find a long, narrow box, the kind used by printers. The cardboard lid's corners are ripped and worn, as though it had been torn open and jammed shut a hundred times by careless hands. Within is a handful of fresh copies of the rambling tract by Erasmus Vale, the same as the one I found under the bed beside the Bible. The rest of the box is full of hastily opened letters from two dozen libraries and universities. I glance over a few and classify them as rejection notices. Mr. Vale intended to develop "Of Shadows and Memory in Maritime Landforms" into something much larger—a full reference book, perhaps a series—and was searching for sponsorship to support additional research. Every letter politely declines further interest. Some request that Mr. Vale not contact them again in the future.

I log the box as spare copies of the pamphlet, with related correspondences, and move on.

The library contains the things every private library should: The complete works of William Shakespeare, John Milton's *Paradise Lost*, several editions of Dante's *Divine Comedy*, some graphically illustrated, and Chaucer's *Canterbury Tales*. But also works from Plato, Aristotle, and Thoreau. Beyond the staples of any decent private library, the Widdershin Collection leans heavily into the occult and natural philosophy. I recognize only a few of the authors, but many knew Erasmus Vale personally, signing the books to him, often with elaborate and verbose messages of thanks.

To Erasmus Ambrose Vale,

Whose unwavering patronage and keen mind made these humble theories manifest in ink. Friend to seekers, confidant to visionaries—without whose discerning encouragement, these pages would have remained shadows.

In all gratitude,

Prof. Alastair Greaves
Cambridge, 1854

To my esteemed fellow, Mr. Erasmus Vale—whose correspondence, questions, and not-insignificant funding allowed this work to cross from laboratory to library.

Ever in pursuit of the unseen, your fellow student

of Twilight

Dr. Victor R. Calder
Edinburgh, 1851

To Erasmus Vale—one of the rare few who knows
that wisdom worth having is wisdom worth fear-
ing.

In the bonds of quiet brotherhood,

Henry Palgrave
London, 1856

By the fourth inscription, it was no longer a coincidence. These books with obscure titles that mean nothing to anyone but an expert on their topic had passed through Erasmus Vale's hands long before they ran through a printer. He had not merely read them. He had brought them into being. It creates the wonder of why his book went unpublished, despite helping so many others.

A bell rings somewhere in the library, and it takes several minutes to trace it to a telephone set on a low shelf in the corner. I hadn't known there was a telephone in here, but even after weeks of hard work, I barely had much progress to show for my effort.

I pick up the receiver and hold it to my ear.

"Yes?"

Crackling static is the only response for several long breaths, then a voice rises through it, distorted like the dying music box.

"Miss Primrose?" It's Mr. Sparrow.

I release a long sigh, grateful that it's unlikely he is calling me from the grave. "Mr. Sparrow, is that you? How are you? I worried after you, when you left looking so ill."

"I'm sure you did, Miss Primrose." He pauses to cough into his end of the connection. I hold my side away from my ear until he's done. "I have found a buyer."

"A buyer? For the books?"

"Yes. Well, perhaps. A German fellow with definite interest, but he needs to know more, first."

"Of course." I pause, hoping Mr. Sparrow will continue, but he doesn't. "Meaning what?"

"Send me a list of titles and authors. With Mr. Vale's reputation, this buyer is extremely interested in the entire collection."

"The entire collection? I've barely begun to organize things."

"What have you been doing all this time, Miss Primrose?"

"Working, but the collection is massive."

"Are you not up to the task?"

"I am. I certainly am. I just... I have been working methodically without a deadline. I can amend my strategy."

He sighs, which starts a brief fit of coughing. "Then just a list of the rarest, most unique tomes with a focus on... What's the best way to put it... On alternative sciences and religious doctrines."

"The occult?"

"That, yes."

"Send them to you where? You aren't in town?"

"I had to return to Boston. Between my health on leaving Widdershin and work piling up here, I couldn't stay."

I want to say my sorrows for his ill health, but think it better not to continue on that point. "I don't have much money. Can I hire Captain Carver on credit? How much will postage to Boston cost? And I should pick up a few things while in town."

"Captain Carver was more than handsomely compensated for his job. What he has been paid should cover another dozen trips."

"And the postage and foodstuffs?"

He groans. "There is a small sum under the mattress I slept on. I know the exact amount. I expect receipts and a detailed list of expenditures."

"Yes, Mr. Sparrow."

"That's a good girl. Get the list to me as quickly as possible."

"Yes, Mr. Sparrow. What is the address in Boston?"

I wait several breaths for his response, but then realize he's already gone. I replace the telephone and walk to the ledger open on the desk.

This buyer doesn't care about the incomplete encyclopedia collections, the works of John Locke, or an illuminated copy of Cervantes' *Don Quixote*. No, he wants all the books with grotesque drawings of human internal anatomy, or the ones bound in leather that don't feel quite right. This buyer wants to know what Erasmus Vale knew, and the signed inscriptions in so many of the tomes would only add to their value, as if the late occultist personally vouched for their contents.

A laugh rises from my belly, and I do nothing to stop it. I can skip the mundane titles, targeting first the obscure things of fantasy most likely to be touched by Mr. Vale, searching for what the buyer most wants. My months' worth of work might now be reduced to just weeks. I will send Mr. Sparrow a list of the best titles I've found, with a promise of more of the same, or perhaps even better, and the buyer will sign the deal. Mr. Sparrow will give me my share, and I'll be free.

All of that must start with a complete account of every piece of the Widdershin Collection. That requires a trip to the attic. I quickly consider the water-logged front basement, but the squeaks, scrabbling claws, and moldering stench are enough to convince me that nothing down there can have enough value to risk my nerves.

But first...

I pick up the telephone and wait a moment through the hissing static.

"Operator." Her gum chewing smacks in my ear.

"I need to speak with someone at the Chatham Lighthouse, please."

The static changes and pops. After a moment, there's a scratch and blast of noise that I guess is from someone fumbling the receiver on their side.

"Chatham," the gruff voice barks into the line.

"Good afternoon. I was hoping to speak with Captain Carver."

"Who?"

"Captain Asa Carver."

The line crackles for a moment. "Call the docks."

More scratching, then steady static.

I sigh and hang up my end to start again.

"Operator."

I'm sure it's the same gum-chewing woman.

"The Chatham Docks."

"Stage Harbor?"

I hadn't considered that there would be more than one dock in Chatham, but being a fishing town right on the ocean, it makes perfect sense. Where had the coach left me when I arrived? I'll just have to hope that Mr. Farlow doesn't answer. "Stage Harbor, yes."

She doesn't respond, just turns me over to the pops and buzzing of switching lines.

"Stage." This man sounds a fraction of the age of the lighthouse keeper.

"Good afternoon. I'd like to speak with Captain Asa Carver."

"It's your lucky day."

I can hear his grin through the receiver.

"Captain Carver! This is Miss Violet Primrose. We met on Widdershin Isle a few days ago when you came to collect Mr. Sparrow."

"Miss Primrose, I thought I might never get your name. Your friend was not kind to my boat. I've never seen a man vomit so much in my life." He ends with a chuckle.

"I do apologize for that."

"Nothing to apologize for. It mostly went over the side." He laughs, but abruptly stops. "Where are my manners, talking to a lady like this? Why do I have the honor of your call, Miss Primrose?"

I'm laughing along with him. "I was hoping you could come pick me up. I need to come to town to mail something."

"Gosh, who knew there would be such business in ferries to Widdershin? I'm really sorry, but I can't come today. Will the first thing tomorrow be alright?"

"That might actually be better. It'll give me time to put together what I'm sending."

"What about after? Are you staying in Chatham, leaving town, or going back to the island?"

One night in town would be a much-deserved treat. Eating a few good meals prepared by someone else and stretching out on a bed that doesn't smell like dust sounds like a brilliant idea. But after that?

"I'll need another ride back to the island," I finally say. "In a day or two."

"Understood. If you need a local guide..."

His sentence lingers on the line for a long moment before I realize it's an offer. I'm a married woman, unchaperoned, two hundred miles from home. But he doesn't know most of that.

"That's an alluring proposition, Captain Carver." My face flushes.

"Call me Asa. Think about it. I'll see you in the morning, Miss Primrose."

"Violet."

"Violet..." His voice trails off, as if my name reminded him of a distant memory.

"See you tomorrow, Asa."

I jam down the receiver before I start giggling like a schoolgirl. Too late.

I bite my thumb, recalling how very green Asa's eyes are.

Twelve

Any guilt I feel for preening over how Captain Carver said my name stems from the repeated thought, "I'm married." As if that is some distant, ephemeral concept, I never think of Edmund. At least, I try not to. He worms into my fantasies like mildew into silk—unwelcome, stubborn, and impossible to wash out. I see myself at the bow of Asa's ship, leaning back with my face turned up to the warm sun and the kiss of ocean spray cool on my neck. Asa pulls off his captain's hat to rake strong fingers through his wild crop of hair. Then, Edmund arrives as a literal black cloud, backlit by hellfire, reeking of brimstone, churning the seas, and tossing thunderbolts.

I know I won't sleep well tonight, and there is plenty to do before I try.

The label in the fuse box implied there would be lighting in the attic, but I still find a candle before opening the concealed door at the end of the hall. Dark oak stairs, worn low in the center from use, curl upward in a lazy spiral. They open onto a short hallway running parallel to the one below. The flickering candle shudders in the faint breeze issuing from beyond its reach. There are two doors on my left, one on my right, and inky darkness straight ahead where the hall opens to a vast room that devours the candlelight. A sconce beside each door buzzes to life when I press the light switch on the left wall. I try the doors on that side first, keeping the candle lit in hand, in case Widdershin House decides it doesn't like my snooping.

The first room is the bathroom with pinstriped wallpaper peeling in the corners. The running water in the sink faucet works, but the tub, stained with a dark ring, isn't even plumbed. A stepstool beside the sink hints at the children who once used this room.

The next chamber features a single, thin bed pushed against the wall, with a narrow window overlooking the garden. The table beside the bed is stacked with a mix of children's books and a few that make me blush. *A Duchess by Mistake*, *The Eligible Rogue's Tea Scandal*, and *Love & Lace in Limehouse* were certainly not published by what I would consider a reputable company. I tuck the books into the satchel slung across my shoulder, which I found tucked in a drawer in my bedroom.

The standing armoire reeks of mothballs and contains a few simple frocks. A plain pair of shoes at the bottom is coated with a thin layer of dust. Behind that is a crystal decanter with a glass tipped over the plug. I tuck my dress against my knees and bend down to take the decanter, set the glass aside, pull the cork, and gag at the whiff of cheap gin. I immediately put it all back.

Pivoting in place, I survey the simple room. Obviously, a servant lived here, and by the books, I guess the nanny. Erasmus and Sara Vale certainly had need of one, with all the children they had.

I cross the hall, but pause with my hand on the warm brass handle. Hadn't the other been cool to the touch? I push it open.

The scent of lingering smoke strikes me, and a story about the house slams back to the forefront of my memory. A fire in the nursery claimed the lives of four children and their nanny. I thought it was folklore, along with the Widdershin Witch and the Rider in White. But here, wooden furniture, smashed and cracked from flame, is piled against the blackened and curled wallpaper. Enough for four tiny beds. I feel heat from the floor, from the walls. If I squint, I can see the embers smoldering in the corners. If I close my eyes and hold my breath, I can hear...

I slam the door behind me, breathing hard into the hall's cool air. I feel heat from the nursery door, and cringe from it, knowing it must be my imagination.

That night unfolds before me in crystal clarity.

The nanny, having gotten the last child down, allows her smile to drain away as she crosses to her room, limping on a bad knee. She pours a measure of gin, takes off her shoes, and stretches out in her simple bed. She has no other furniture, and Master Vale has warned her against coming downstairs. A few pages into her book, she smells smoke and turns her nose up at the cheap, cow tallow candles. But none are sputtering. She smells more smoke. Is that... Is that the children calling out? She rushes across the hall. The brass handle scorches her hand, but she pays it no mind.

The room is an inferno, something lifted from Dante Alighieri's depiction of hellfire. The children are calling for her, pleading for her to save them, but the flame and shadows turn her around. She... She...

No.

It's a folktale. It must be. Who were the four children? Why had I found nothing in Sara's Bible about such an event? There had been notices of each of her children, but not of four dying at once. The room clearly had a fire, but it hadn't been terrible enough to consume the house. It was controlled, and they ignored the damage, as they did not need the rooms in the attic.

There had been a fire. News reached the mainland, and with how secretive the Vales were about everything else, a rumor circulated and grew with each retelling. After ten or twenty years, the rumor became fact, though no one could back it up with evidence. It wouldn't even take much effort. Based on the children's obituaries, the townsfolk held some strong thoughts about the family living on this island. It would have been assumed that the nanny and faceless children were buried on the island.

I push it all from my mind, continue down the hall, and am delighted to find another light switch that works. Incandescence flares to life over the portraits lining the walls, each shrouded in white linen. The room is massive, almost as wide as the floor below, and runs the length of the house, except for the space reserved for the rooms behind me.

I tug off the first sheet, exposing a gaudy gold frame and a portrait not unlike the one at the top of the stairs. Erasmus looks the same, standing in the back, staring down his nose with the curl in his lip that may as likely be a smirk as derision. The woman seated before him is, I assume, a much younger Sara, holding a swaddled baby in her arms. Mr. Vale's hand rests on her shoulder with no hint of his later violence.

The child is older in the next painting, and then another child joins them. Some also show a gray cat, just like the one stalking after me. Sara ages, her focus moving to the distance, yet Erasmus remains the same. I would assume him to be a vampire or Dorian Gray, had I not already heard of his unaging vanity. The artist was commanded, or understood, to paint Erasmus the same every time, but capture the other accurately. Eventually, Lavinia is the only child, and she takes her mother's seat.

With all the portraits uncovered, the rise and fall of the House of Vale surrounds me. Though the work is unsigned, the style and brushwork appear the same to my untrained eye. One artist captured Erasmus Vale's unwavering essence and his wife's slow retreat into herself.

No woman could blame her. I read—or tried to read—a few things written by Erasmus Vale. Unless he wrote as a character of himself, he must have been exceptionally challenging to live with. By the books inscribed to him, he clearly attracted his kin. It paints a very different picture of the dinner parties, where everyone is dressed in bizarre costumes, sipping drinks that billow smoke.

Even by the time we said our vows and left the church, I knew Edmund would never make me happy. He let his polished veneer slip more than once, showing the gleaming cruelty at the core of his being. But what choice did I have? My mother wanted me to wait for love, but my father wanted to see me married before he died, as if anticipating the apoplexy that took him.

Sara Vale had the same, I'm sure, but worse. So much worse. They were married before the Civil War, when her life would have been entirely consumed by Erasmus. Her husband would legally own anything that Sara had. She had no chance of inheriting by implication and didn't even have custody of her own children. Her life was only what her husband allowed it to be. Any assertiveness or interest in education would have branded her as hysterical.

I, at least, could vote, though I hadn't yet, being too young for the last election. That didn't stop me from marching with my mother, both sporting our oversized "Women for Cox!" buttons. Mr. Sparrow said Sara Vale only recently passed, narrowly missing her chance to have her voice heard on a national level.

I was familiar with inheritance woes, but only because of an overachieving lawyer who didn't try to hide how he loathed women. He and Mr. Sparrow would get along.

Like the endless tide, pulling back to the same dark shore, history repeats and never progresses. On the surface, perhaps, but would there ever be true equality?

Time slips from me, and I have no concept of how long I've been standing in the center of the hall of portraits, lamenting the past and fretting for the future. I note another door at the far end, opposite where I'd entered the attic. A storage room? An altar for Erasmus to conduct arcane rituals? A treasury laden with gold bars enough to sink a ship?

I hover in place, not stepping forward because... I don't care.

Widdershin House is a monument to the greatness of Erasmus Vale, and I don't want to be a part of that. To be just another woman to aid in the remembrance of a madman. Who would remember the Saras, Lavinias, Clarindas, or Deliverances of the world if those like me refused to?

Within a few months, the library will be packed and on a ship bound for Germany. A few portraits may hold interest for the buyer, but only because they contain Erasmus. The rest will be sold at auction for pennies of their commission cost. Sara's life will become nothing, a footnote to her husband with no children surviving to continue the line. Lavinia will be completely erased.

No, Erasmus discarded his old portraits to this room, covering them so that they would never be viewed again. He wouldn't have come up here, past the nursery for unknown children. The room at the other end of the house was not for him.

I open the door to a space not much larger than a closet. A simple plank desk sits against the wall facing a window looking out to the front garden. On it, a fat tallow candle long ago burned down to the silver holder, leaving a puddle around its cup. Beside that, centered beside an old inkwell sprouting a feathered quill, is a note written in slow, patient letters.

"I will remember you."

I pick up the yellowed paper, revealing the sheet beneath it. It's yet another handbill, like the one with the notice of Deliverance's escape.

Beechfield Town Register

Local Wife Stands Accused of Witchery

Beechfield, January 3rd — Mistress Deliverance

Black, wife to Mr. Absalom Black, has this week been named in declarations of suspicion by several townsfolk as one consorting in acts of unholy craft.

Amongst the charges laid before the council: the unseasonable withering of Brother Josiah Pike's cornfield following an argument with the accused, a red fox found lying dead upon the Black doorstep, and the continued ill-temper and feebleness of Mr. Black himself, for which no physic has availed.

Mistress Black, known to walk the woods at dawn and record dreams in long-hand, was taken in for questioning this past sabbath. She denies all charges.

A special meeting of elders is to be held upon the morrow to determine if further examination is required.

Apart from a local historian, I may be the only person alive who would care about the notice. History may repeat itself in an endless cycle, but perhaps there is a subtle forward movement if one views it from a sufficient distance. For me, seventy-five years back to Sara Vale, or two hundred and thirty to Deliverance Black, shows that things have improved, but there is still so much farther to go.

I take the quill from the inkwell and give no mind about why it isn't long dry until after I've scrawled a line beneath Sara's.

"I will remember you both."

Thirteen

M r. Sparrow called it a small sum, and he was not exaggerating. I pulled forty-two dollars in small bills from under the mattress, enough for an indulgent few days of respite in town. By the time he returns to the island, he will have the interested buyer at his side, and this stack of money will be forgotten. If not forgotten, hopefully, he will owe me far more than this, and it won't be a problem.

But now, to prepare for tomorrow's trip to Chatham.

I prepare a list of the two dozen most titillating titles I've found so far. I try on every one of Lavinia's dresses, pleased to find we are about the same size. I debate which to wear by considering whether I can get them aired out in time, but I realize they're all decades out of fashion. I should remember to bring these with me when I leave, in case I'm ever invited to a costume ball. So, I pack the dusky blue dress that I nearly ruined by the cliffs with the hopes of having the hems repaired and the thing cleaned while in town. I leave that, along with a few essentials, in my bag by the front door.

Like a child on Christmas Eve, sleep eludes me. Insects drone in the garden, wind plays in the trees, and an owl hoots in the distance. All the pleasant, gentle sounds should have lulled me away within moments, but hours pass with nothing but staring at the flaking plaster. I follow the cracks to the corners as best as I can by the moon and starlight, hoping it would have a similar effect to counting sheep, but my mind wanders to Chatham. I barely saw the town before, stepping from the coach at the harbor and talking to only the few other captains before Mr. Farlow.

Finally, the sky begins to lighten, and the solitary dove cries. Planted before the mirror in Lavinia's room, I pull my hair into a plaited crown and try on all of the jewelry I found in the drawers below the music box. I settle on a simple string of pearls and wonder if they're real. I dab perfume on my neck and sit on the veranda outside my bedroom. There is no chance of focusing on the book on my lap, with my attention split between straining my ears for the telephone ringer and squinting into the slice of ocean I can see through the trees, waiting for a smudge of smoke coming directly toward me. Would he call ahead or just arrive?

The harbor is busy this morning, with vessels crisscrossing on their own routes. After what might have been a few minutes or two hours, one definitely has Widdershin Isle as its destination. I fly down the stairs and rush through the garden, only to have to wait for almost half an hour before Captain Carver's ship glides up to the dock. I hadn't noticed the name before, *By Cod's Grace*, and now bite back a smirk. Where is the line between humor and blasphemy?

Asa appears from behind the wheel, all smiles, and pulls off his hat in a sweeping bow.

"Your chariot, Lady Violet." He offers a hand to help me across the watery gap. "I'm sorry I kept you waiting."

I keep my eyes pointed at my feet, watching as I step onto the boat, rather than meet those shocking green eyes just yet. "You didn't," I say. "Besides, you couldn't be late. We didn't agree on a time, and there are no clocks in the house."

"No?" He pulls his gaze from me to frown up at the manor. "I can't imagine you staying alone in that ghastly place. There are a thousand rumors about it, I'm sure you know."

"So I'm learning. What's your favorite?"

"Anything about the White Rider. The very idea of him, of a man being murdered with such rage that the sea can't forget... He must have really had it coming."

I settle into a seat beside Asa as he works the controls to pilot us away from the island. The ship responds with a rumble under my feet and issues a plume of smoke from the stack, but starts a slow turn back out to sea.

"You almost sound as though you believe the White Rider is real," I say.

"Oh, I do! I've seen him. Or, at least what they say is him. When the fog and moon are just right at dusk as a storm pulls in, I've seen his lantern swinging out on the waves. I'm sure there's an explanation science can provide, but it's nothing I know. So I do what the old timers do, and stay in when the conditions are right for him. Even though I don't believe in spooks and ghosts, why risk it? Let him have the sea and those foolish enough to be out with him."

"You don't believe in legends, yet you abide by them?"

He shrugs. "Like I said, I can't explain it, but why risk it?"

"Who was he? This murdered man?"

Asa cringes and chuckles. "I shouldn't be talking like this with you."

"Like what?"

"About murder and ghosts to a... You know."

"A woman?"

"Ah gee, you make me feel like I've become my father, saying it like that."

"Like what?"

He opens his mouth to respond, but shakes his head. I have a feeling the pink flush of his cheeks has little to do with the rush of salty air. "I'm sorry I said anything at all. What are you doing in town?"

I gestured to the bag at my feet. "The post office, a seamstress, and the market."

"Where are you staying?"

The question strikes a nerve, as if he's asking for some un-gentlemanly reason, until I let the practicality of it sink in. "I hadn't thought about that yet. I'll have to find a room for the night."

"There's a boarding house right in town. Miss Morrow's House for Ladies, I think, is the name. It seems reputable. I'm fairly certain that Miss Morrow is a retired nun. She's the type who makes sure no men get past the lobby." His grin sours, and he added quickly, "Not that I've tried, mind you."

I hide my reaction by focusing on adjusting the hems of my skirt. There's an awkward wholesomeness to Captain Carver that hadn't had time to surface in our short meeting the other day as he lugged Mr. Sparrow onto the boat.

"I'm sure I'll be able to find it, thank you," I say. "I'm glad it was you who answered the telephone yesterday. Thank you again for coming."

"No trouble at all," he says, only a little distracted with his maneuvers. "I'm glad you caught me, too. A lot of the old timers wouldn't bother with a trip to Widdershin, no matter what you offered them. The legends and superstitions might be fake, but the currents, high sands, and rocks aren't."

We go in silence for a while, gliding toward the harbor with the Chatham Lighthouse to our right. That means we are going south, and not to the same port Mr. Farlow had taken me from weeks ago. The angle to the lighthouse is definitely different. I blow out a sigh of relief as my chances of encountering him plummet.

The shoreline bobs and shifts, giving the impression that it is moving, rather than us, and I look away before it plays with my stomach.

Asa speaks, jolting me from my reverie. "You really mean to go back there?"

"I have to. Mr. Sparrow hired me for a job, and I'll see it done."

"Just tell him you're finished. Would that drunk know any better?" He winks down at me.

"I'd know. I'm a woman of my word."

"You're a catch, Violet. Please tell me the race of men is unlucky enough that you haven't pledged yourself to one of us."

"That's rather forward of you, Captain Carver."

"That's why I put it so poetically."

I can't fault his charm. "Is there a Mrs. Carver clutching your handkerchief, gazing out to sea at the railing of her widow's walk right now?"

"I'll note that you didn't answer my question, but no. There is no Mrs. Carver other than my mother, grandmother, and two aunts. Have you helmed a steamship before, Violet?"

"I... No, of course not."

He's looking down at me with a wide flash of white that makes his jade eyes twinkle below the brim of his hat. He extends his hand in the same way as he had to help me across the gap and onto his boat.

I hesitate, not because I distrust what he might have in mind, but because it's yet another decision left entirely to me. My mind is immediately made up. I take his hand and let him guide me, but I grant myself the moment to relish such determination.

My fingers disappear into his, strong and calloused from a lifetime of wood and rope. I can't stop the encroaching thought of Edmund's hands as soft as a babe's.

Asa pulls me up and takes one step from the wheel, guiding me to take his place between it and him. My hands slip over the polished wood, and I grip tighter, feeling the tug when he lets go of it.

"That's it," he says close to my ear. "She likes confidence, but relax a bit. Not too tight. Give her some space to breathe."

I do as he says, letting the wheel shift, but not turn. My cheeks and neck are on fire, but I hope he doesn't notice from behind.

Asa's right arm grazes the outside of mine. He points to a bobbling globe set in the panel behind the wheel. "There's the compass, as I'm sure you can tell. We can see where we're going right now, out in the day for all of God to see, but that might be the most important thing to any sailor."

"Didn't you sailors—" I stop to clear my throat when my voice cracks. "Didn't you use to rely on the stars and sextants?"

"Sure. And now we have compasses and maps with no mention of sea monsters. Below that, you can see our speed, engine pressure, and fuel. More gauges than you'd want in a lifetime."

He's so close. What could I do if he attempted some advancement, out here in the sea? Though what could I do if he tried something while we were tethered at a busy dock, except scream and hope a Good Samaritan comes to my aid? I'm completely at his mercy, and my only hope is that he doesn't know it. His solidity fills the world behind me. What might it feel like to lean into him? The entire plot, which brought me to Widdershin, was to escape Edmund, not all men.

The ship lurches, stripping me of my agency and tossing me against Asa's chest. His left hand darts out to take the wheel, lacing his fingers over mine. His other is at my hip, holding me with a balance that no wave can upset. He is more solid at sea than any boulder on land.

We stay like that, with our bodies tight against the other's, his arms around me, for a dozen breaths, two dozen, but maybe they are just coming faster.

Finally, and too soon, he relaxes his hand away from my hip, but keeps the other over mine on the wheel. "Imagine that during a storm on the open sea. As much as you try, you never fully get used to it," he says. "The sea, she comes sudden and unexpected. You never know what might set her off."

"You could have fooled me, with the footing of a mountain goat," I say over my shoulder. I feel his breath on my cheek and quickly turn back to focus on the compass. "What's this do?" I touch the brass lever to the right of the wheel.

He brushes a lock of hair around my ear. All the effort I put into getting it just right is wasted by the sea air tugging at it. "That's the throttle. Forward to go faster, pull it toward you to slow down," he says.

The constant whip of salty air does nothing to cool the blistering heat. My back is on fire where Asa brushes against it. He doesn't need to be so close. He could back up an inch, so his chest isn't pressing into my back, but I don't want him to. He's fine where he is.

"I should get out of your way and let you pilot us into the harbor," I say and slip from between Captain Carver and the wheel. In another life... but I'm a married woman. Unhappiness does nothing to change that.

His chest swells, but he slips forward to fill the space I vacated. "The Harding Beach Lighthouse is just ahead. Not much farther. One more thing." He nods his chin to the thick silver chain swaying overhead.

I reach for it, unsure of what to expect, but his waggling eyebrows encourage me. I give it a tug, and the mournful bellow surrounds us.

Asa is biting his lower lip to, unsuccessfully, stop his smile from reaching too far. He pulls off his captain's hat, gently sets it on my head, and throws a hasty salute. "I relieve you of your post, Captain Violet."

Fourteen

I only wore the hat for a moment before returning it to the captain with both hands. He offered to hail me a coach or car to take me into the town at least five times, but I told him the half-hour walk would be good for my legs after the time on the boat. He let me go alone after a chivalrous number of politely refused offers of escort. Withholding information from Asa does not change the fact that I am married, and my unhappiness does not make the risk of infidelity any less of a sin in the eyes of the Lord. I countered his offer for dinner tomorrow night with a suggestion of coffee. The negotiation continued until we agreed on a schedule: him meeting me at the boarding house tomorrow, then lunch.

The town is growing to fill the space between it and its southern harbor, with both sides of Stage Harbor Road dotted with new construction, mostly homes. A few cars slow down and honk, the driver yells something about me needing a ride, but I plaster on a cheery grin and wave them off. I've spent the last few weeks alone, aside from the short stint with Mr. Sparrow, but I need just a little longer without people. Like a diver acclimating slowly after a deep plunge, I don't want to rush my reentry into society. I need time to think.

Can I finish the work to Mr. Sparrow's satisfaction such that he pays me?

He knows what I did to him, so what if he breaks the contract?

We didn't have a contract; we had an agreement based on a few letters.

My shoulder aches. I hadn't packed much; my bag isn't that heavy, but even a slow leak in the bathroom tap can add up before long. More than the clothes and toiletries, the plump envelope tucked between my grass-stained dress weighs down my bag. The cash isn't enough to start a new life—not by a long shot—but what it can buy me may not be too far off. I don't need a private villa in the south of France, I just need a ticket out of here. But before that, I'll have a night in a bed with turn-down service. Window shopping, where no one will tell me not to dawdle or sigh and check their watch. I'll be able to get a cup of coffee whenever I want and visit every bookstore in Chatham. Captain Carver, Asa, will be my local guide.

What if lunch takes us to an art gallery?

Then to coffee and dessert?

The weather is perfect for a carnival to be in town. What if there is one, and he wants to go? Fried bread and games of chance. He'll want to win me a toy creature.

Lunch will lead to dinner, then a drink, then...

What if Edmund finds me?

Grim reality slams over my gay delights. My husband has not arrived yet, but he will. I'm sure I left a trail akin to yellow silk ribbon tied to my shoe when I left Portland. I saw my chance and rushed away, but everything, including my clumsiness in hiring Mr. Farlow, has been a wild stab in the dark, unscripted and unplanned. But going forward, I have no excuse. I must act with care and intention. Two things I am woefully unpracticed with, and the stakes are too high to misstep as I stumble through.

Another car slows, honks, and I wave the driver off with a smile.

"He might find me. He probably will. Nothing I do in the next two days will stop him. But if, on the slim chance that everything works in my favor, why shouldn't I enjoy a few days? If the universe acts against me, and he's waiting for me on Widdershin when I return, ready to toss me off the cliffs in a fit of blind rage, I may as well go, having found some joy in my final days."

The macabre speculations succeed in lifting my spirits. Something about giving in to inevitability when there's nothing—or very little—I can do to stop it soothes my nagging worries.

It's a gorgeous morning in early May, with a perfect, cool breeze that hints at the heat to come in the afternoon. The sky is bluer than I have seen in weeks. The puffy white clouds look like they've never heard of rain or storms. The town rises around me with the scent of bread mere moments from ovens at Granger's Bakery and the sweet tune of a minstrel playing her violin outside of The Harbor Light Café. The towering white steeple of the First Congregational Church greets me at Main Street, along with a neat row of shops with finely dressed men and women going about their morning business. Families with well-behaved children on holiday clog the road, slowing the cars as they attempt to rumble by. Wickett & Sons General Store, Nickerson's Haberdashery beside Cape & Coast Millinery for the ladies, The Chatham Bookshop, three more restaurants, two cafes with white-shrouded tables out front, a barber, the post office, and Nickerson's Pharmacy. I wonder if the latter is any relation to the hat maker.

A few doors from the church, wide stairs lead to a porch in need of a good sanding and a coat of whitewash. A discreet brass plaque reads, "Miss Morrow's Boarding House for Respectable Women" in a delicate script. The lace curtains behind the windows on either side of the front door are yellowed at the edges from either age or smoke. Edmund would scowl and turn up his nose at that alone. No, he wouldn't see past the scuffed stair treads. He searches for any minor excuse to be upset. But Asa said Miss Morrow is reputable, and that's good enough for me. I can get a room, set my things down, and see to all my errands before noon.

And then what?

The concept of freedom in town, or at all, was a luxury at a distance, but now that I have arrived at it, it's quite frankly terrifying. Everyone in the street knows where they are going. So, too, do I—for the moment—but it's a foreign feeling to know the decisions are entirely my own. But this is what I want... right?

I climb to the porch that smells of starch and old tea. The six empty rocking chairs will, no doubt, be occupied by the respectable women of the house after dinner, enjoying the last moments of the day before retiring. A tired bell jingles overhead when I push the door inward. Lemon cleanser and rose water struggle to mask the stale cigarette smoke within. Stairs wrap the foyer, going halfway to the second floor before cutting to the left to finish their journey. To my left is a dining room with seating for a dozen. To my right, an ancient, rail-thin woman is pushing from one of the chairs in the sitting room. Her flowery housecoat may as well be hung on a hanger, for all it does for her skeletal frame.

"Room or delivery?" Her voice rasps with the strain of one who has spent their life smoking and coughing.

"A room, please."

She nods and opens a cabinet beside the stairs, producing a leather-bound ledger.

"This is a respectable establishment," she says. "Says so right on the door. Curfew is ten. Breakfast is at eight sharp. No men past where I'm standing. No funny business, or you'll be out on your ass so fast, you won't know what hit you. Got all that?"

Miss Morrow does not keep her reputation of respectability by running a loose ship.

My voice fails me, shocked by the juxtaposition, but I nod.

"I need a yes or a no," she says. "Your tongue works, so use it."

"Y-yes. I understand."

"Good." She shakes out a fountain pen and hovers it over the last empty entry on the page. "It's a dollar fifty a night, paid up front in cash. Will that be a problem?"

"No. I have money."

"Good. Name?"

My terrible—or complete—lack of planning will come to an end here. "Evelyn Bell," I say with a slight curl of my lip. As plain as grey wool and twice as forgettable. I only hope I can intercept Asa tomorrow before he knocks, asking after a Violet.

Miss Morrow slashes the name into her book. "How long are you staying?"

"Two nights, at least. Possibly three."

"Four-fifty." She holds out a weathered palm.

I buried and hid Mr. Sparrow's money deep in my bag for safety, but now I'm digging through it on the table beside the ledger. My untidily packed clothes are on display, and I'm all too aware of Miss Morrow's judging stare, though she's trying to make her prying eye look less obvious.

My blind fingers finally land on the envelope and remove a single bill. "Do you have change for a ten?"

"Of course I do." She snatches the money, depositing it down the front of her coat, in the safety of her brassiere. She waves at the mess in my bag. "All that, and you don't have a wallet?"

"I'm not used to carrying money."

Miss Morrow huffs and presses a key into my hand. "Second on the left. Washroom's at the end of the hall." She's shuffling back to her chair and game of solitaire before I can say a word.

Just like that, I have a room. I paid for it using Mr. Sparrow's money, but he'll soon owe far more than forty-two dollars, so this may as well be mine.

The room is nothing special. A flowery duvet over a narrow bed, a nightstand and a lamp with a massive green glass shade, a dressing table with a crack at the corner of its mirror, and a wardrobe sporting a few mismatched hangers. I brush the lace curtains aside for a wide view of the street below, still busy with pedestrians and the occasional automobile trundling through.

No, the room has one thing that is very special about it. I place my bag on the foot of the bed and cross to the door, where I turn the lock with a soft but satisfying click.

I flip it twice more, my grin widening each time. The flimsy lock would do nothing against a determined shoulder or kick, but no one alive wants anything from Evelyn Bell, the possible great-great-granddaughter of Clarinda Bell, illustrator of plants and keeper of a witch's home remedies. Only Mr. Sparrow knows I came to Chatham, to Widdershin, and now Asa is the only one to know I am at Miss Morrow's. If I disappear from here, who would be the wiser? If anyone checks the register, as Mr. Sparrow may, knowing I had to stay a night to complete my chores, his investigation will come to a dead end. Miss Morrow might be a testy old crone, but she doesn't seem the type to betray the women in her care by describing their physical attributes to men coming in off the street.

But thirty-seven and a half dollars is not enough to start a life any more than forty-two is. And that's on the hope that Miss Morrow pays me the change owed to me. I'm sure she will. Such a gross overcharge definitely classifies as funny business, which she does not abide.

I unpack quickly, hanging my blue dress to take to the fabric shop that I noticed by the millinery. With the letter addressed to Mr. Sparrow of Boston and ten dollars in smaller bills in my satchel, I tuck the envelope with the rest of the money into the nightstand drawer and lock the door behind me.

Fifteen

I avoid the sticky-fingered children running out of the sweets shop, but want little more than to go in past them once the whiff of chocolate and cinnamon hits me. The fabric shop has a stunning sundress on display, a lightweight cotton frock studded with tiny yellow flowers. It looks like it might be my size, but I wouldn't know without stepping in to inquire and perhaps try it on. It would only take a moment. I'd like to see how the fabric moves and billows when I twirl. I avoid those, but the bookshop nearly pulls me in, away from my task, with a sign advertising its selection of the newest releases and all the classics. Beyond the glass, warped by time and sun, books are stacked to the ceiling, two stories high. Catwalks and ladders grant access to every dark nook, each perfect for losing an afternoon to a good novel. No, I have mountains of books on Widdershin. The cafe, with the scent of bitter, earthy brew, is the last to tempt me before I reach the post office.

Without a specific address, the tired man working in the stuffy office assures me that writing, "The Office of Finch,

Finch, and Sparrow," will be enough to get the letter where it needs to be. He expects my mail to arrive in Boston by Saturday and be delivered to the law office by Monday's post. That will be the better part of a week since Mr. Sparrow called Widdershin House. I could hire a coach and deliver the letter to him this evening, but he hadn't suggested that. Maybe the idea hadn't occurred to him, either. Or maybe he doesn't want to see me after I poisoned him. Regardless of the reason, I should phone him tonight and tell him the task is done.

No, a telephone call would leave too much room for questions. "Where are you staying?" "Have you spent all of my money?" "Have you fallen for Captain Carver?"

I return to the man behind the counter. "May I send a wire ahead of my letter?"

He nods, slides a Western Union form across the counter, and I pen my message in clear block letters.

"Clarence Sparrow STOP High value appraisal to arrive Monday STOP Primrose"

I read it over, consider adding more, but decide on brevity. Every word past ten costs extra, and Mr. Sparrow will appreciate my frugality.

After paying, I give in to my first urge and sit at a table outside the coffee shop. The waiter comes, and I order my coffee with milk, not because I take it that way, but because I can. I hadn't thought to bring a book to read, but I would remedy that with a stop at the bookshop next. Though I shouldn't be buying books when I have more than I want on the island. Surely Miss Morrow's sitting room would have a small shelf with enough to occupy my time.

For now, the people of Chatham are my diversion. I sip my coffee and come up with a story for each family, couple, or solo adventurer. I begin dull, guessing which shop they will visit next. Then I develop backstories, tiny vignettes of these people's lives. That family is from Florida, scouting a home for the summer. That couple is celebrating their first anniversary. The longer I sit, the darker the tales become. The son is adopted, but they haven't told him. That couple, they're both cheating on the other, both know, but neither will talk about it. That older, well-dressed woman killed her first two husbands and is working on the next.

I force myself to stop and finish my drink. As diverting as it may be, pulling stories from my silly books, it feels wrong to put such darkness into the world.

The bell on the fabric store door greets me with a musical charm, the exact opposite of Miss Morrow's. The air is cool, carrying the scent of rosewater and fabric dried in the sun. Bolts, spools, and sample squares line the walls, but I cross first to touch the fabric of the sundress with the tiny yellow flowers. It's lightweight, almost slippery to the touch. Nothing like the stiff wool I'm currently wearing.

"Ah, *mademoiselle, bonjour*," rings a voice heavy with Paris from behind. She's a slight woman, shorter than me by half a head, with long, slender fingers that brush back a stray lock of hair the color of the sun. "I am Madame Solange. You are here for—how do you say—something new? Something..." she gestures vaguely at me, "...less tired, perhaps?"

"I..." I glance down at my gray wool. I really am as dull and forgettable as the Evelyn Bell I pretend to be. "I just came to have a dress repaired." I start to pull the dusky blue dress from my bag, but Madame Solange stops me with a hand over mine.

"Tut, tut, *non*. I see you gaze at this with stars in your eyes. Why not try it on?" She tugs me toward the one with tiny yellow flowers and pulls my hand to touch it.

"I really shouldn't," I say while feeling the neckline between my thumb and index finger. "I only came in to see if you could do something about the lace."

She takes the blue dress from me, her frown deepening and twisting to a snarl when she pinches it at the shoulders. "*Tes grand-mères*?"

"No, it's mine."

The sour cringe melts to pity. She steps closer, tossing the blue dress to a chair, her hands now on my shoulders, appraising but not unkind. "We make you... sharp. Fresh. You will look... mm... respectable, but not... ah... buried."

"Buried?" I choke back a laugh.

"Wool and lace. Gray and flat blue. *Non*. You are young, you are *vivante*."

I glance back at the dress in the window. Trying it on would only waste this woman's time. Though, she has no other customers at the moment, and she's ready to make me her sole focus.

She's fixated on what I'm wearing, a dull thing Edmund bought me. "*Non, non*, that cut—*c'est trop vieille femme*. We do better." Madame Solange circles me, humming and tutting as she goes. "*Mademoiselle*, your shoulders—beautiful, but we cannot see them, yes?"

My dress covers me from the throat to the wrist and down to almost the ankle. It's the same cut as the blue one I came in here to have mended, and essentially the same as every other one I own or have ever owned. Edmund likes my modesty, but it's also convenient for covering bruises and scrapes. What might it be like to wear something in public that didn't slowly choke me all day? Something with a sweeping neckline, like those of Lavinia's that I had tried on? Like the one with the tiny yellow flowers in the window?

I wave down her attention and circle to put myself between her and the door. "No. Really, thank you, Madame Solange. I only came to have this piece repaired and cleaned."

She glances at where she'd tossed the blue dress. "You wound me, Miss..."

"Violet."

I catch myself as soon as I say it. So much for anonymity here.

"Ah... Violet." She draws out my name, emphasizing the end. "A delicate *fleur, oui*? But dressed like... pfft—an ugly vase." Her fingers flutter at my skirt. "You are *belle*, truly, but your clothes—*mon Dieu*! They scream librarian who never laughs. Never smiles into the sun."

She isn't far from the truth.

"Thank you, but I can't. My budget's limited. I..." My gaze drifts to the dress with the tiny yellow flowers. Trying on a few things would cost me nothing. I would just need to retain my resolve.

"Tut, money. What is your happiness worth? A dollar? Ten? *Mille*? But *mon cœur*, you cannot put a price on happiness. If the dress makes you feel like the sun is inside your chest, you must wear the sun."

Even if something is lost in translation, the essence of the meaning remains. Her eyes bore into mine, pleading, and I stop my retreat to the door.

Madame Solange places a gentle hand on my shoulder, then squeezes my arm. Her words come as a hissed whisper, meant for only her and me. "The world—eh, the world is cruel. It forgets the quiet women. You must remind it, you must say: Look at me. I am here. I am alive. I am not his shadow. Not anymore. Let me have my moment."

She doesn't want to sell me a dress. She wants me to cast off my admittedly drab frock for something I no longer hide behind. She wants the world to see me as I see myself. Except, she seems to have a higher estimation of that image than I do. As a modiste spending her life in the confidence of women, she would know. Whatever my problems may seem to me, they are no different than every other woman who walks in here, just as I see myself reflected in Sara Vale, Clarinda Bell, and Deliverance Black. Our woes are the same, repeated across time. Her job, her calling, is to change the perception of her clients, external and within.

"I suppose it wouldn't hurt to try something on," I say, looking around the shop. The dress with the tiny yellow flowers steals my attention. "Money can't buy happiness," I say. "But I have a tight budget."

"Ah, I can guess. Your husband sent you off to occupy yourself while he drinks and plays cards." She takes my left hand in hers and rubs a thumb over my knuckles. Hiding my wedding ring in my suitcase was one of the few things I thought to do in terms of planning.

"Not husband," she continues. "No matter. Madame Solange will tell you a secret." She leans close, returning to her conspiratorial voice. "All women are on a budget because all money is held by men."

"That's dire. What about you? I assumed this was your business."

She rolls her sky-blue eyes. "Boston First Trust owns everything, except for maybe this chair." She stabs a finger at where she'd tossed my dress. "And that, my husband owns, though I have not seen him in a year. He stays in Paris. But you know what they cannot take, cannot own?"

Her thin eyebrows raise in anticipation of my guess, but I have none. My father controlled every aspect of my life until Edmund took over. It's no different through time, with the women of Widdershin. Even my mother, as independent as she seemed, could do nothing without Thomas Primrose's legal approval.

Madame Solange presses one palm to her chest and the other against mine. "They may take our hands, our days, even our name—but not this." She pulls back to tap her temple. "Mind. Heart. Spirit. No, no, no. These, they are for you. For God. For no one else. A moment."

She holds up a finger, retreats three steps, and disappears through the curtain leading to the shop's back area. I could use the opportunity to snatch my dress and flee, but I find I want a bit longer in the company of Madame Solange. I take the moment to more closely examine something I only then noticed: an in-progress wedding dress on a mannequin.

Where mine had closed around the throat, this dress sweeps low, but lace counteracts the openness. Mine was a shapeless thing from shoulders to floor, but this one follows the hips, hugging tightly. Yet a cape and train give it a silhouette similar to mine. The silk is as pure as fresh snow, but the embroidered flowers have cream petals with lavender highlights. The wedding dress screams of quiet protest, of following the letter of the law while breaking and bending everything else along the way.

Madame Solange emerges from the back room, a dark, frosted glass bottle in her hand. She thrusts it at me as she passes to lock the front door, flip the open sign, and pull down the shade. She snatches my hand and drags me along with her, past the curtain, to the space only meant for employees.

It's a chaos of fabric bolts, lace, and ribbons. The large table in the center is covered with scraps and things half-sewn. She snatches something else from a side table—two glasses—and pulls me to stop in front of a mannequin with what might be the most hideous dress I have ever laid eyes upon. Bright blue tulle over a purple slip, a low, asymmetrical neckline, too many ribbons and lace.

"What do you think?" she asks and taps a glass to the bottle in my hand. If she wants an opinion about the atrocity between us, I take a moment to pull the stopper from the bottle and pour out a few fingers' worth before answering.

"It's unique," I say. "Is this wine?"

"French brandy. A woman traded my sister a case of it for a hat. My sister, she does not drink." She holds out the other glass for me to fill. It can't even be noon yet. I should not be drinking. But... this is a vacation of sorts. I'm allowed to relax.

"Why did she trade for it, if she doesn't drink?"

"Neither did the woman who needed the hat. Neither wanted the brandy. One needed a hat. Trade, and one has what she needs. Two years later, my sister gave me the case for a new pair of gloves."

"I don't follow the logic," I say, restopper the bottle, and take the glass from Madame Solange. She taps hers to it and raises it to her lips. I follow her lead, letting the fruity alcohol warm my tongue. I wince once with the strength of it, but relish the sensation of it flowing down my throat.

"A man would need both sides balanced, or his side greater. They fight and wage war over it. Women are freer in that way," she says.

I scoff. "You make it sound like women are bad at business."

"What is better? That you end up with more, or that more get what they need?"

"Greed versus the greater good. I haven't considered it that way."

She shakes her head, dismissing the topic. "The dress, though. What do you think?"

The motion of the thick, maroon liquid in my glass is the most interesting thing in the room. "It's not my style, but I'm sure someone would like it."

"I make this one for a woman who never comes back. Now it lives here like a ghost—always watching me. Taking space. Sulking." She flicks the fabric and looks at me with a half-smile. "You wish your sad blue... thing... to be mended? *Bon*. I mend it. But you—you take this creature away from me. Give it to someone who deserves it. Burn it, if you are cruel. But do not bring it back."

"I... would it be so cruel to burn it?" I add a half-hearted chuckle, unsure if I'm joking. "You'll repair my dress for the cost of taking another from you?"

"*Oui*. I cannot bring myself to destroy it, so taking it is a favor." Madame Solange presses a palm to my cheek. "You are beautiful, Violet. Even in that." She nods down at my attire. "But I must work now. You come back tomorrow morning, *oui*? When the light is kinder—and I am less tired of people."

The day has barely started, yet she speaks as though she'd been open for twelve hours. To be fair, I know nothing of a modiste's schedule. I accept my dismissal and finish the French brandy in one go. She leads us back to the front door, unlocks it, and we exchange our farewells. As the noonday heat and light hit me, I stumble a step, forcing me to catch a hand on the shop's cedar shake siding. It wasn't much alcohol, but when one isn't accustomed to drinking so early, on such an empty stomach, it doesn't take much.

The bookstore will have to wait. I need to find a cafe for a quick sandwich, then a quick rest at Miss Morrow's until the French brandy is done swimming in my brain.

Sixteen

When I return to the boarding house, two blond-haired boys, about fourteen years each, are pushing around the furniture in the right-side sitting room. Miss Morrow watches from the corner, the red glow of her cigarette lighting her face with a long draw, tracing every wrinkle as it does. I wave, her eyes flick up to mine, but she doesn't react. She just goes back to watching the boys work. They might be preparing for an event, evidenced by the upright piano they're dragging from a side room, but I barely slept at all last night. I'm too tired to investigate. The day hadn't been too exciting—other than feeling Asa's hard body pressed against mine—but after weeks hunched over books in a stuffy library, even the most minor activity is an endeavor.

With the door locked behind me, I step out of my shoes and notice the piece of folded paper atop the dresser. The change owed to me by Miss Morrow falls from it with a clatter of coins on wood. The paper itself is a handwritten receipt for "3 nites, Miss Eveline Belle. No refunds." It's not how I might have spelled it, but this is even better. Any discrepancies can only help throw off my would-be pursuers.

Three nights are a waste, both in terms of the cost of the room and my time. Mr. Sparrow will have every reason and right to be upset with me for squandering resources, but I cling to the hope that none of this will matter. If the list I mailed to Boston fails to convince the German fellow to move forward on his purchase, I will have a great deal of work ahead of me. However, as there is no way to know the purchaser's intentions for days or weeks, I may as well make the most of my time.

I'll lie down for just a moment. The bookshop, along with all the other little stores along the main street, sings to me like a mythical Siren, tempting me to explore them without another instant lost. I'd love to see the beach and the lighthouse, and try something from every restaurant, but there will be time if I'm to stay for three nights.

The narrow bed doesn't embrace me in the same way as the one in Widdershin, but it doesn't matter. My limbs are heavy, and the sun is casting its lines deep into the room, through the gauzy curtains, when I open my eyes with no remembrance of the hours between.

I stretch, toss my legs over the edge, and stretch again. I've nowhere to be tonight. No one to expect me and no one to miss me. My time is mine to spend or waste as I please. An hour or three in the bookshop, a late dinner, then early back to bed with a book. A worn copy of *Northanger Abbey*, along with a few other classics, stares back at me from the short stack of hardcovers on the shelf beside the dresser. Perfect. The only things left are finding the market and securing passage back to the island. Nothing is demanding my attention.

Other than an innocent mid-day meal with Asa tomorrow, of course. And it will be perfectly innocent. We will sit across from one another at the cafe, then say our farewells. When he returns me to Widdershin the next morning, I will remain seated, one hand on my groceries and the other holding my hat in place. There will be no reason for him to stand within arm's reach of me.

Even as I think it, my mind simultaneously concocts a dozen ludicrous scenarios for us to end up much closer than arm's reach. He volunteered to be my guide, after all. What if he wants to point out something, and stands behind me to match our perspectives, and points beside my ear? My shoe may betray me over a loose cobble, but Asa catches me with strong arms, as he had when waves rocked his ship. Maybe without this captain's hat, a strand of wild hair will fall over his eye, and I won't be able to take him seriously until I brush it back. My mantra of "I'm a married woman" is only so good a defense against myself.

Muffled laughter reaches me, high and unfiltered, through the door, heard over a jaunty piano tune and murmured, overlapping conversation. Whatever Miss Morrow was supervising the boys setting up is now in full swing beneath me.

The clock over the mantle puts the time just past seven. I could stay in and read Jane Austen for the rest of the night. Such a long nap would make sleep elusive tonight. While not hungry, I am a bit peckish; the ham-on-rye sandwich from earlier didn't last long. If I'm quick and quiet enough, I could slip down the stairs and through the front door without being noticed, though that presents the later problem of how to return to my room. Maybe out the window to shimmy down a drain pipe?

I curse my lack of foresight for not buying a bag of apples to keep in the room for emergencies like this, and I notice the scrap of paper on the floor in front of the door. The handwriting is grand and flourished, but too quick for the pen to keep up. Some lines are thin and faint.

"If you're awake, come down and save me from losing. — C.A."

I stare at the bit of paper, then set it on the nightstand and take a step back, as if the distance will create meaning.

An invitation? In all of my scheming, it never crossed my mind to go down to see for myself what the music and laughter are about. Whatever social event is happening was planned before I arrived; therefore, it would be just fine without me. Better, maybe.

No. Those are the thoughts of Violet Bow, a destitute wife beholden to her cruel husband, whose life and personality were subsumed into his. They may even be those of Violet Primrose, the quiet, book-loving daughter destined for nothing. But here, I am Evelyn Bell, no matter the spelling, and Evelyn is an enigma. She has the iron will of Lillian Gish, long-suffering yet unbreakable. Like Jane Eyre, she's independent, demands respect, and holds a high moral standard. Evelyn, unlike Violet, would not poison a lawyer as part of a plot to make him leave her company. Evelyn would have gotten rid of the lawyer, sure, but in some direct manner, her chin held high the entire time.

Evelyn sounds like a lot of work, being so unlike the Violet I'm used to. But, what has being Violet gotten me? Twenty-four years with nothing to my name, no close friends, and terrified to go down to a party. I cannot go down to rescue C.A., whoever they are. I will remain in my little room reading Jane Austen. But Evelyn...

An image comes to mind, an implanted memory of a woman with the grandest hats, sprouting half an ostrich's plumage, gloves that reach past her elbows, which she would remove at the most dramatic moment, perhaps while singing, perched on the piano halfway through the night. Her eyes twinkle with mischief, and her smile can warm the sun.

My Great Aunt Samantha. She moved to Paris when I was young and died shortly after, so my memories of her come from my mother, who held her in great esteem, nearing reverence. She was never married, but somehow lived in a state of decadent, perpetual luxury. Dressing in the newest foreign fashions. Drinking wine and gin so exclusive, the bottles didn't have labels.

"*Mother hated her sister,*" my mother would tell me when my father was out with friends or associates. "*But she would never say it to her face, always acting fake and friendly with her. Nor did it keep her from sending me to live with Aunt Sasa for weeks at a time in the summer. I suppose that, as much as she hated her sister, she also resented having me around all the time. Aunt Sasa would buy me hats, dresses, and dolls, anything I showed the slightest interest in. My parents would scoff, grumble, and make me send it back to her, but Aunt Sasa kept everything, devoting a room to me at her home. It wasn't just that; it wasn't just buying me trinkets and clothes. I was her sole focus, pausing her life for me. She always had ice cream, would take me for long walks in the park to enjoy the air, and answer any question I asked of her. Nothing was off limits. Nothing made her blush. I've never been so seen as I was with Aunt Sasa."*

I always understood my mother's stories as whimsical and fun. She worshipped her aunt and so sincerely wished she had been around for me to know as well. But now, thinking back on how Mother only ever talked about her aunt when my father was away, I see it in a different light. Longing. Envy. Maybe a touch of regret. Great Aunt Samantha, Sasa, lived as any woman should want to: free to explore her own interests and live exactly as she wanted.

A peal of laughter cuts through my reverie. Someone downstairs is having a grand time and is not afraid to let the whole room, the whole house, know it.

I lack the mental stamina or agility to take on the persona of some great woman from stage or page tonight. I cannot create and be Evelyn Bell on a moment's notice any more than I can channel Great Aunt Samantha to guide me through this social outing. Yet, as the laughter finally fades, I wonder what Aunt Sasa, and by extension, my mother, would think of me hiding away in this little room while life happens at the foot of the stairs. Stay or go. The decision is mine to make.

My gaze drifts between *Northanger Abbey* and C.A.'s note

I can read one-hundred-year-old books anytime, anywhere, but here is a chance to see who I really am, or who I could be. Or, perhaps, who I'm not. No matter the outcome, I will return to bed having learned something about myself.

I turn to the full-length mirror and tidy the lay of the wool dress that I can only see as a dead, lifeless thing after Madame

Solange's musings. It's all I have, so it will have to do. Just as I must make do with myself. Being Violet has gotten me this far, and Violet's future is mine to decide.

What a difference a few moments of introspection can make, time I never allowed myself to take. Another crack of laughter seals my decision.

I snatch up C.A.'s note and unlock the door.

Seventeen

The laughter belongs to a woman with a shock of white hair wearing a floral muumuu. Pearls and her glasses swing around her neck as she slaps the table and tries to catch her breath. Seated across from her, another woman of similar age and style holds her glasses up with one hand and covers her face with the other, shoulders heaving with her barely-contained giggling. The other two women at their table are smirking awkwardly, but not entirely overtaken by humor, as the others.

The room has been rearranged to accommodate three small round tables, each seating four. An upright piano is pushed into the corner, where a woman in a pinstripe suit is playing a jaunty ragtime. Her fingers dance across the keys, barely touching them. Beside her, a woman in a long, glossy shift and a gold necklace reaching her waist claps in time, encouraging a faster tempo until the boogie hits a fevered, yet coherent pitch. Someone at the tables hoots, the musician hits a flourish, and crashes back to a reasonable tempo.

It takes me a moment to pull in all the details and realize what I have walked into. The cards, the drinks, the conversation interrupted by a gasp or an unrestrained cackle. It's a Bridge party, a sacred conclave of women, safe and free in each other's company.

My hand is on the banister, ready to flee to the safety of Jane Austen, but someone catches me by the elbow. Her dark brown hair is cut short, curling around ears studded with silver earrings.

"You must be Evie," she says with a grin that shows the slight gap between her pearly white teeth. I can't place her accent. British, maybe? Though I could never guess the exact sort of British. She's a few years older than me, but certainly not more than thirty.

"Evelyn," I say, but quickly correct myself. "Evie is fine."

"Clara Ames," she says and grabs my right hand in both of hers for a tight, curt shake. "You got my note."

The music and chatter have me dazzled for a moment before I remember the scrap of paper in my hand. "Yes. C.A., Clara Ames. It's a pleasure to meet you. How did you know my name?"

"I snuck a peek at the roster." She taps her nose and winks.

She drags me to a table with two women seated across from each other, pulls out one of the empty chairs, and pats the velvet seat. The girl in a conservative wool frock, not unlike my own, and a cloche hat pulled down to her ears, might be sixteen or seventeen, but the woman across from her has seen more winters than the three of us combined. Her wide-brimmed hat adorned with gold-flecked ribbons and a bow, her strings of pearls around her neck and wrists, and a practiced look of interested boredom scream old money.

"Evie, this is Miss Hester June Peltier and Mrs. Dorie Plum," Clara says, waving between the two others. "We have our fourth, so let's get this game started."

"Theodora Plum," says the old woman in a slow southern drawl. Her hands are a blur, shuffling a deck of cards. The soft electric light catches on her silver and gold rings set with diamonds, rubies, and sapphires. "But Dorie will do. Miss Hester June was telling us about her upcoming nuptials, but as she will have to start over now, we might as well hear something about you, Evie, darling. What brings you out to Chatham?"

The sudden attention disarms me, combined with the sparkling scrutiny in her clear gray eyes and the way she calls me *'darling,'* as if I were a niece she's known my whole life. I'm tired of the lies, but as much as I'd like to trust a den of women playing cards, now isn't the time to purposefully leave a trail. "I'm just passing through, on my way to elsewhere."

"Oh, child, Chatham ain't a *passing-through* sort of place. No one comes out to the elbow of the cape, where the sea wraps round you twice, because they're going somewhere else. You come here to be here." Dorie taps the deck once and tosses the cards out with the efficiency of a casino dealer. "But you keep your secrets, and we'll get back to you. Miss Hester June?"

The girl starts at the sound of her name. Her eyes flick up, then settle back on the cards spread in her hands, but she keeps her shoulders hunched to remain small. "I'm picking up my wedding dress." I have to lean closer to hear her small, high-pitched, nasal voice dripping with New York twang.

"From Madame Solange?" Dorie asks, tossing a Jack of Spades to the table's center.

Hester June nods.

Eyes turn to me, and I stare down at my hand. I've never played Bridge, but I know enough to follow suit, setting out the Six of Spades.

Clara confidently plays the Queen of Hearts.

"No spades?" Dorie asks.

"Oh, yes." Clara takes back her card and drops the Four of Spades. "I was thinking of the Portuguese rules."

"I think you were thinking of another game entirely," says Dorie. I don't have time to see what Hester June plays as the older woman sweeps the cards to her and plays a Queen.

"I saw your dress earlier today," I say, and follow suit again with no strategy. "At least, I assume I did. The cape is stunning."

Hester June's lips form the motion of "thank you", but the sound doesn't reach me over the piano music.

"Is she actually French?" Clara asks, taking the trick and putting out another heart. "Her accent is a bit muddled. I lived in Marseille and Paris for five months each. I know a proper French accent."

"Yes, yes. You've lived all over. You're the Queen of Doilies," Dorie says, rolling her eyes. "It's muddled from living here six years, but I assure you, she is French. Are you married, Evie, darling?"

"No."

Dorie leans back in her chair, gaze boring through me, and hides her ghost of a grin behind her remaining cards. "What an immediate and short answer. Before we continue, know that anything said in this room tonight remains in this room. If you cannot abide by that, I'll ask you to leave."

"I... yes, of course," I stammer, trying to hold her stare.

She maintains it an eternity longer, then sniffs and focuses on her hand. "If you're not married, stay that way as long as you can. My periods of unmarried life have been brief, but frequent. I gave up on husbands when I buried my sixth last year. Harold was the best of them, God rest his soul. The interludes between let me cruise the Greek Isles, go on safari, and all my other adventures, but the options for us dry up so quickly."

"I've done quite well without a husband," Clara says. "My brand is in dozens of shops down the coast."

"Miss Ames is the top supplier of lace doilies this side of the Mississippi, as she'll be delighted to tell you," Dorie says.

"That's wonderful. I've never met a woman who owns a business, and now I've met two in one day," I say.

Clara pats my arm. "And like you, I'm just passing through, on my way to Provincetown."

Dorie pushes the trick toward me, and I take the cue to toss down another card at random.

"I'm surprised Madame Solange isn't here tonight. She must be busy with your dress, Hester June." Dorie says, twisting in her chair to survey the room. "When did Mr. Sheppley slip in? Remind me later to ask him if that ointment I ordered has come in yet."

I follow her gaze and, sure enough, a man in a neatly pressed suit with a thin mustache is seated at the far table. He had to have been there the whole time, but my eyes moved right over him when I walked into the room.

Clara leans toward me. "Mr. Sheppley runs the general store. He's the safe sort of bachelor."

I don't grasp her meaning, but nod anyway. He seems perfectly at ease at the table, laughing along with the others and tapping a finger in time with the piano.

"I intend to die a spinster with every man within a hundred miles vying for my hand and fortune," says Clara, pulling me back to our table.

"And what will you do with your vast fortune, my dear?" asked Dorie. "Do you ever stop working long enough to enjoy it?"

"I'm enjoying myself right now." Clara raises her glass of champagne and drains it in one go.

"Have you considered investing in a local shop and settling down? Think of the good you could do."

"Not this again, Dorie. You have the money. You bail her out."

I arrange the cards Hester June dealt and draw in a deep breath. "Bail who out?"

"Solange," Dorie says while furiously arranging her cards. "Her husband died two years ago, but the bank doesn't know yet. When they do..."

"She told me he was living in Paris," I say.

"He's certainly *in* Paris, but he's most certainly not *living* there," Clara chuckles.

Madame Solange's exact phrasing escapes me, but I clearly made an assumption. With Clara and Dorie laughing about Madame Solange's husband's demise, I focus on the last member of our table. "When is your wedding, Hester June?"

"Next week."

"So soon. What's your fiancé's name?"

"Louis."

"Just like our good Mr. Sheppley," says Dorie.

"Hopefully not *too* like him," Clara snorts.

"Don't be unkind, now," says Dorie, her sharp eyes narrowing across the table.

I ignore them and keep pressing Hester June. I'm not sure why I care; I have no investment in these women and will likely never see them again after tonight. "Tell me something about him. What does he do for a living?"

Clara and Dorie turn to watch the younger woman's response, who shrinks under the scrutiny. "He's a businessman."

Clara laughs, and Dorie shakes her head.

"What's wrong with being a businessman?" I ask.

"They've never met, darling," Dorie explains. "Miss Hester June was telling us about the five letters she and her husband-to-be have exchanged. Now, mind you, arranged marriages can be quite successful. My second was arranged, and while dull, Correy wasn't offensive in any way. We were just starting to love one another when a boar gored him."

My jaw hangs open. "A boar... gored him?"

"Like some Scottish king of times old," Dorie says.

"All of Mrs. Theodora Plum's husbands have passed in similarly sudden and tragic ways, leaving their fortunes to her," Clara says, raising an eyebrow.

"I don't think I care for your insinuations, young lady," Dorie says, but her tone and expression remain even. "I have known great sorrow, but if you mean to imply I quickened anything, you're welcome to join me when I speak with St. Peter and Jesus before long, Miss Ames."

The two are catty, at each other's throats, but there's no real menace behind any of it. It's precisely the sort of relationship I have never shared with another woman. The game continues, still without a clear strategy and with seemingly arbitrary trick winners. Dorie calls out Clara for playing by the rules of some other nation twice more, but I get the impression it's to get her to play a different card in their version of table talk.

After the deal passes once more around the table, Miss Morrow shuffles in from the back rooms of the house with a tray of crackers and cheese to drop on each table.

Clara sets her cards down to spread brie on a tiny slice of rye bread. "I saw the lights on at Widdershin," she says with a hand covering her full mouth.

My heart jumps to my throat, and I hope snatching a cracker will cover any outward reaction.

"Curse that place," Dorie says. "I lost a husband to the currents around that horrid isle."

"Have you always lived in Chatham?" I ask.

"Do I sound like I was born here?" she asks, emphasizing her drawl. "No, darling. Just these past twenty years. More than enough time to know it's best to stay clear of that god forsaken place."

"Did you know Sarah Vale?"

"Why, you're just brimming with questions now." Dorie sets her cards down and pushes them to the center of the table. "I did, the miserable soul. Before her, I never imagined a creature so mistreated. She hated her husband, feared him more than she feared God, but was powerless against him."

"Why did she stay?" came the tiny voice from Hester June, pulling all eyes to her. "Why didn't she leave or... or do something?"

Dorie smirks. "Something like drug and murder him? I hear it's the thing to do on that island." She chuckles to herself. "No. Erasmus would have never allowed her to leave. He was powerful, connected, and until late in life, wealthy. But more than all that, he was frightening, insane. Violent and unpredictable. No, Sarah's only chance of escape would have been murder, and she didn't have it in her. She was a quiet, sad thing."

I think of Sarah's note in the attic, of her silent protest, not wanting the women of the past to go forgotten. She didn't want to be powerless, but never found her outlet.

"The day Erasmus died was the best day of her life. It freed her of that terrible place," Dorie says.

Of course. She didn't leave Widdershin to avoid caring for it, but to flee the memories of that place. It's obvious, but yet I still hear myself asking, "That's why she left for Rhode Island?"

"Better to die with strangers than to live with the ghost of a madman, surrounded by her children's graves." Dorie leans back and stretches her arms overhead. "I'm done in," she says. "You can't shake a flower all night and expect it to open with the dawn. Hester June, Evie darling, it was a pleasure. Do stop in before you leave town, Clara." She pushes from her chair, produces a cane, and makes for the front door, waving at Miss Morrow and the pair of old women who were laughing when I entered the parlor.

"Good night," Hester June says, and spryly jumps up. She's gone up the stairs before Clara or I can respond.

"How long are you staying here?" Clara asks while tidying our deck.

"Three nights. Maybe just two."

"If he comes asking, should I say I never saw you, or send him off in another direction?"

"Who?"

She taps the cards on the table. "Your husband."

I open my mouth, but the words aren't there.

Clara raises a hand to quiet me.

"How?" I manage.

"You have your tells, and I'm good at noticing them. You often touch your empty ring finger, as if making sure it's still empty. You answer some questions too quickly, while you deflect or delay others too long. But your face betrays you more than anything. Every time a husband or abusive man came up tonight, you followed the conversation with too much... investment. Don't worry. I would never betray you. What's his name?"

The game is breaking up, now that Dorie was the first to leave. If Clara is so good at reading people, my discomfort in the discussion surrounded by strangers must be as clear as if I wrote it across my plain wool dress.

"We can talk in my room," she whispers. "If you want to. Sometimes it helps."

I have read stories involving the catharsis that comes with the divesting of a secret. To share something huge and terrible, even with a stranger, even just to hear it said out loud, can bring immense relief to the bearer. I hope the stories are true.

Clara's room is decorated the same as mine, with the same amenities, but she has far more luggage, stamped with what I assume is her company's logo. She shuts the door, we sit on the end of the bed, and I blurt, "I'm working at Widdershin to get the money to flee my husband and start a new life."

From there, it tumbles from me. Clara never interrupts, except for the occasional clarifying question. I tell her about my father and Edmund, as well as Mr. Sparrow. Of Edmund's demands and his rage. His quiet, explosive fury, seen only by me. To everyone else, he is the sweetest man they've met. I thought that, too, until our vows were sealed.

"Your life is defined by the men in it," Clara says as I pause to sip my tea. "Your father was kind, but flawed. Your husband is cruel. Your employer treats you as a child."

It is a statement rather than a question, but it leads me to circle back to Jakob Vogel, my first love—the one who got away.

"And when you escape Edmund, is there another, or will you finally be able to know yourself?" she asks.

Asa. If he had been around instead of Edmund, and I had instead had to choose between Asa and Jakob, my life would be completely foreign to how it is now.

"The first," Clara says. "Be careful, Evelyn. Men can be fun for a distraction, but that's all they are. They'll slow you down and make you make mistakes."

"There isn't anyone else. I've stayed true..." I let my pitiful rebuttal die. "We can't all be single. The world needs couples."

Clara rolls her eyes. "What ten-penny book did you pull that from? Obviously, the world needs people to keep making people, or this whole thing we've spent thousands of years building comes to an end. That doesn't mean it's your or my obligation. Leave the work to those who really want it."

"What about being in love?"

"Sure, if that happens. Lust is far more common, and often a lot more fun."

"How can you be so jaded? You're not much older than me."

"We all age at different rates that have nothing to do with the world spinning around the sun. I'm not going to ask you to promise me anything, Evelyn, but consider doing one thing for me."

I lean toward her, anticipating her next statement.

"Love yourself."

"How do you mean?"

"I mean exactly what I said. The world is not kind. You are the only person you can rely on. If you don't love yourself, that's a void nothing else will fill."

"That sounds grim."

"It's meant to be grim. I've had a half dozen apartments across Europe, crossed the Atlantic five times, and been up and down the East Coast. I've been around, so I can tell you with all certainty that the only person worthy of your trust is yourself. But at the same time, that trust must needs be realized and allowed. Listen to your gut."

The concept of a solitary life, on the surface, is frightening. My first time being alone was when I arrived at Widdershin. Clara isn't suggesting a life without a husband, but rather one where I am the primary focus. One where I make myself happy. "I don't know…"

"It's only advice. Take it or not." Clara shrugs and stands, stretching her arms behind her back. "I've enjoyed this, Evie. One true joy of travel is the people I meet. I leave tomorrow evening. Hopefully we'll have a chance to talk more, but it's way past my bedtime."

The clock on the mantle puts it after midnight. We'd been talking for almost two hours. Well, I did most of the talking, but I leave feeling lighter.

Clara catches me at the door, pulls me into an embrace, and presses something into my hand: a lace handkerchief with a monogrammed "E" in a corner. It's almost enough to make me push back into the room and admit my false name, along with anything else I edited from her, but I manage just a smile and whispered thanks.

Eighteen

A rattle of thunder wakes me sometime in the night, and I pull myself from bed to close the window before rain finds its way in. Standing at the window, looking past the dark shops across the street, a patch of greater darkness is visible, likely the ocean. Ahead, the lighthouse sweeps its beam across the water. Had I left a light on, would I be able to see Widdershin House from here? Clara had commented about seeing my lights from the mainland, so I suppose I would.

Thunder rumbles again, but it already sounds like the storm is giving up, moving on. I imagine that thunder circling Widdershin, but finding no fun in tormenting an empty house.

The next time I wake, it's to muffled conversation outside my door, in the hall, and the smell of frying bacon. It's not yet seven, but despite getting to bed late, I can't risk catching a few more minutes of sleep. I'm just tired enough that doing so would only mean losing three hours, and then I'd have to rush before meeting Asa.

My heart sinks as I sit on the bed's edge, staring at the miserable, sad wool thing hanging on the wardrobe door. He saw me in it yesterday and didn't run away screaming, and it isn't as though I have much choice in what to wear. And why should I concern myself with how he sees me? This isn't a date. We're having lunch, and he might show me around town a little. It's the most innocent thing in the world. If my clothing is all the terrible things Madame Solange said about it, Asa will be that much less likely to tempt me.

Why is that my job? The question answers itself: that's how it's always been. It's a man's world, and the rest of us are just trying to survive in it.

Nevertheless, I would like a new outfit, if only for myself. Something that I pick out entirely on my own. Maybe not as fun as the dress with the little yellow flowers. That feels like a step above what I'm ready for. Perhaps Madame Solange will let me borrow something; she seems like the kind of woman who would help another. As I sit on the bed's edge, deciding over something with no options, the voices in the hall move away. I snag my ugly dress and make for the bathroom to freshen up before breakfast.

After only cold baths at Widdershin, my steaming shower at Miss Morrow's Boarding House for Respectable Women might be the longest and hottest bathing ritual in my life. Yet, despite the comforts of warm water, fresh linens, and the promise of a hot meal prepared by someone else, my mind drifts to the quiet and solitude of Widdershin, where I never had to wait my turn for the bathroom or anything else.

It's nearly nine when I descend the stairs. The boys are back, folding the tables and stacking the chairs, reverting the parlor to a tasteful sitting room. Miss Morrow is shuffling between them, carrying lighter things to their appropriate storage locations.

She glances my way with a jerk, looking me over as if shocked to see me. "If it isn't Sleeping Beauty. I was about to call the coroner. Have a good night?"

I prepare a witty retort, but she's already moved off, disappearing into the back of the house with a wicker basket of playing card decks.

The breakfast spread is picked over, with the platter of fresh fruit down to a single sad strawberry. But the rich, earthy scent of dark coffee is all I really need. Edmund would say something cruel if he saw me loading a plate with three strips of bacon for breakfast, so I take five. And a raspberry danish. And a sausage link.

A soft breeze blows through the small conservatory at the back of the house, bringing with it the roses, lilies, and loamy soil. The hot, bitter coffee, the crisp, fatty bacon, the bird song, and the bouquet of more flowers than I can identify. This is the definition of a perfect morning.

Except someone is crying.

It's just a sniff and the shaky catch of a breath, but I abandon my meal for it. In the back corner of the little arboretum, shrouded by the dark vines, and wearing a long jacket over what she'd worn last night, sits Hester June. She holds her head in both hands, her shoulders twitching with her mostly silent sobs.

"Miss Hester June?" I ask as gently as I can, nearly whispering.

She gasps and snatches a scrap of paper from her lap. I know the shape enough to recognize a telegram. She wipes at her face and plasters on a smile before looking up at me.

"Miss Evie. I thought you were already gone for the day."

"I had a late start. What's happened, dear?"

"Nothing. It's..." Her facade shatters with a single sob that won't break, leaving her breathless. "Louis died." She shoves the telegram at me and gives up all pretense of being quiet with her grief, wailing loud enough that they could likely hear her at the lighthouse.

"Chatham Ms HJ Peltier STOP Louis dead STOP Return home"

What monstrous callousness. She didn't know the man, despite being prepared to pledge herself to him, but no one deserves to receive such news in such a manner.

I still have Clara's handkerchief gift in my pocket, and I offer it to the girl. "I'm so sorry." I shift a pot aside to sit beside her. Whatever words I should offer are lost to me. She may want to be alone, but that thought dispels when she squeezes my knee.

Hester June draws a deep breath, and her face darkens as her grief morphs to rage. She spits out her words through a clenched jaw. "It was my father, I know it."

The air is suddenly too hot, too thick. Hester June has me pinned in place with no chance of escape. I manage to squeak out, "What about your father?"

"He killed Louis, I know it. He hated him. Hated that I'd want any man in my life, other than him."

"But, I assumed... Wasn't it an arranged marriage? Didn't your parents set that up?"

She shakes her head once, more like a twitch. "No. That's just what Miss Clara and Miss Dorie assumed. I was about to tell them how Louis and I started corresponding through the newspaper, but you came in, and I lost my nerve."

"I'm sorry about that."

Hester June snatches the telegram from me, shreds it, and tosses the scraps at her feet. "I'm sick to death of everyone saying they're sorry for my misfortunes. I know you don't mean it, but it only makes things worse."

I'm about to repeat the words she doesn't want to hear, but bite them back. "What will you do?"

"I don't have a choice," she sighs. "I have to go back. Louis was my way out, and he's gone."

The fear and dread in her hollow stare, as she gazes into her empty hands, belie a deeper meaning I dare not ask about. Her grief isn't just for a dead man she never met, but for a future that will never happen and a return to something terrible.

"Come with me," I say before I think about it.

Hester June doesn't react.

"I'm about to come into a sum of money. I'll have an apartment in Paris within four months. Come with me and start fresh there. Get away from whatever..." I gesture at the bit of paper on the floor between her feet. "Whatever you need to get away from."

Even as I say it, I'm ashamed to hope she refuses. I know nothing about this girl, and she could easily prove to be a liability. I can't lose everything I've been working for to help a stranger. But if I can't, what does that say about the type of person I am?

No. I am the Good Samaritan. I will help any woman I see in need.

Hester June holds the handkerchief to her cheek. "You can't save everyone, Evie." I have to lean in to hear her whispers as she continues. "It'll only be worse if Daddy thinks I tried to run. He might like it. It'll give him more of a reason to do what he'll do."

I don't want to ask, yet the words tumble out. "And what's that?"

"I wish I were so innocent." Her red-rimmed, bloodshot eyes lock on mine. She snorts, the start of a laugh without mirth, and shifts her gaze to just past my ear. "I know you're trying to help, but save that for someone not so far gone." She presses the handkerchief against my palm and squeezes my fingers around it.

Like me, she had everything planned, an escape to a brighter future. Any dim glimmer is a beacon in the complete darkness, and Hester June Peltier's spark has been pulverized.

She rises and stalks from the conservatory like a woman bound for the gallows. I have no words or assurances for her, nothing to draw her back. Nothing I can offer is guaranteed, as my own future teeters on a razor's edge.

I can only watch her leave.

Nineteen

The wadded, tear-stained handkerchief is my entire world for a long while as I trace the patterns in the lace with my thumb.

"*You can't save everyone,*" she'd said.

I didn't want to save her, not when I first offered to, but how quickly that changed when she told me I couldn't. When she told me that hope and salvation are beyond her grasp now that her betrothed is dead. When she looked through and beyond me with eyes that had no business having seen so much by her age. I could run after her and offer... what? More empty promises about returning to Widdershin, then coming with me once I make my small fortune? There isn't a single thing I can guarantee for her when I feel my own life is set on borrowed time.

Do I want to be attached to this miserable young woman forever?

I shudder at my wicked thoughts. How would I feel were I offered help, only to learn it was born out of reluctant obligation? I must be better. Like Clarinda carrying Deliverance's torch, or Sarah Vale's quiet letters, I must carry my own when and where I can, whatever that might look like. For starters, it's not wasting time in Chatham when I should be organizing the Widdershin Collection. That is my path forward. Maximize the library's valuation, because each extra dollar will get me another mile from Edmund.

A single, frozen image flashes in my mind, like a photograph, of Asa's easy smile under his wild mop of raven hair and eyes like pure gemstones.

No, he's a distraction. Not to mention a road to sin. A playful, gentle, easy-on-the-eyes road to sin…

Hester June is right. I can't save her. Clara Ames is correct that men are a distraction. I can't save anyone until I've saved myself. That means I have to collect my dress—and the hideous one she's forcing on me—from Madame Solange, visit the market so I don't die of malnutrition, and find a boat back to Widdershin today. No lunch or sightseeing with Asa.

The thought lights the fire under my backside, and within half an hour, I have my things shoved back into my case and am knocking at the plate glass of Madame Solange's shop door, right over the "Closed" placard.

The lacey curtain is shoved aside as I pull back to knock for the third time, and a very annoyed Madame Solange glares at me.

"What? What is the emergency so early?" she yells through the glass and shakes a stray curl from her face.

Early? "Apologies. I was hoping..." I pause, unsure of what I'm apologizing for. It's past ten on a weekday. "I thought you would be open."

Her gaze flicks to the placard, and her expression softens. She might now think I'm illiterate, but she unlocks the door. This is fine. She can pity me if it means I can get everything done and return to Widdershin sooner.

With a merry jingle from the bell, she opens the door, but raises a palm to keep me from wandering too far into her shop.

"Let me get your dress, Miss Violet."

She's gone in a furious click of her heels, leaving me alone with that dress with tiny yellow flowers and Hester June's wedding gown. The latter has a veil and gloves arranged over the back of a chair beside it. There might have been a fitting scheduled for today.

Snippets of French come to me through the heavy curtain. A few quick phrases carrying a clear tone of annoyance. Another, higher-pitched voice responds. It's pointless for me to eavesdrop, but I sidle nearer to the curtain. Perhaps I could pick out a phrase or determine if the annoyance is aimed at me.

Solange bursts through the curtain, and I jump back. Her eyes run over me, from head to shoes, but she says nothing about why I was so close to the back.

Madame Solange hefts the cloth garment bag slung over her shoulder.

"Your blue dress wasn't as bad as... this one. Nonetheless, I added a sparkle of life to it and took some from the other."

The other. How could I almost forget about that hideous thing that she showed me yesterday?

"I can't thank you enough," I say.

She shrugs. "You do me a service, taking this from my sight."

"Have you spoken with Hester June today? I assume this is for her."

"*Oui*, but no, I have not seen her today. She is a lively young thing, no? How do you know her?"

"She's staying at the same boarding house as I. We played Bridge last night."

"Ah, tut. And I was working."

"She... She received news this morning. It's not mine to spread, but you should speak with her soon."

Madame Solange leans back and brushes a finger through her hair. "Mysterious. Dire."

I want to say more about Hester June's father, how she thinks he had a hand in Louis's death, and my unease about the nature of the relationship between them. But these aren't my tales to tell. It would be no better than gossip. Hester June has enough on her plate without me, a random stranger she met at a card game, starting rumors about her. It's the same reason why I hold my tongue, so eager to ask details about the seamstress's husband.

Madame Solange's sharp edges soften over the next heartbeats, as I transform from someone who can't read a "Closed" sign to something more compelling. Someone capable of holding another's dark secrets.

She grins and holds the garment bag between us. "Why don't you try it on?"

"Now? I don't think I have time. I need to get to the market, then to—"

"Please. As my payment. I should like to see you as the budding petal you are inside."

With the rest of Mr. Sparrow's money in my pocket, I could pay her and be on my way, but what harm would another five minutes do?

The changing room is woefully insufficient for its purpose. By the time I hang the garment bag bulging with two dresses on the hook, there's barely enough space left for me to turn around. The me staring back from the mirror is everything Madame Solange described yesterday. Tired, frayed, dull. I should be in the happiest moments of my life, when I have my youth and health, yet I certainly don't look like it. Once all this is done, I deserve a week somewhere warm and sunny.

The muslin garment bag is stamped with the same logo as the shop's front door, and this close, the fresh lavender water spritz overwhelms my senses. As I wriggle out of my lifeless gray thing, wisps of the conversation in French return to me, sounding a bit calmer than before. Clara suggested that Madame Solagne isn't really from France, but her language sounds convincing to my untrained ear.

A button and ribbon tied into a neat bow hold the bag closed. When I pull it free, the gifted dress fairly bursts out, like a moth from its cocoon. Gone are the layers of lace and far too much tulle, replaced with clean, tasteful lines and tiny dots of yellow thread in the field of purple. Nothing about it reminds me of what it was yesterday, enough to make me wonder if it's not a completely different piece of clothing. It reminds me of the dress from the window that keeps pulling my eye, but in reverse.

My dusky blue monstrosity peeks from behind it, and while Madame Solange has done a masterful job at repairing the seams and lace, and cleaning the grass and dirt from the fabric, I can't ignore the rising repulsion toward the frock. It had been one of my favorites. Now it reeks of repression and missed opportunities, as if a garment could possibly convey such things.

By comparison, the new dress hangs to just below my knees, leaving my calves exposed for the world to see. Now that I'm wearing it, hints of its former life are visible, but subtly altered to create something new. It's something I've read in a dozen books. *Jane Eyre, Great Expectations, Cinderella*. The main character receives clothes or gifts that change the course of the tale. Now I count myself among those literary giants. Or perhaps a penny pulpback. But here, this overlooked and frowned-upon little dress will become the star of my wardrobe, the subject of an untold fable akin to the Phoenix, rising from the cinders of its past life in dull, gray wool.

A gentle rap at the room's wooden frame. "Violet, may we see it?"

I rip the curtain aside and am greeted with Madame Solange and a second woman of similar height and style. They both gasp, and the new woman shoots Solange a smirk.

"*Magnifique.* You outdo yourself just because you can," she says and claps. "Or is it to show off?"

Madame Solange waves off the mixed compliment. "My sister, Sabine."

"A pleasure to meet you," I say and twist my hips, letting the fabric flare. "You own the millinery next door?"

"*Oui*. If only I were a..." Sabine stops to snap her fingers. "*Cordonnière?*"

I can't guess at the word and look to Solange for help.

"Your shoes," she says. "Sabine hates your shoes. I agree, but am not rude enough to say it."

They are bad. Blocky, scuffed leather, an eyesore beside a new dress that lies so neatly against me.

Sabine scoffs. "You say such terrible things." She pushes her sister's arm and turns to me. "You are a work in progress, *mon petit chou*. One step at a time. I can look for what I have in stock, or order to arrive in a week, yes?"

Madame Solange steps in front of her sister. "No, Sabine. Violet is quite busy. She has no time for your upselling."

"Let the woman speak for herself."

Solange looks back at me, and her sister leans to peer around her, both anxiously awaiting an answer.

"She's right, I'm sorry. I'll be on my way today. Before lunch, if I can."

"Ah, tut, *non*. Not before lunch," Sabine laments. "You must eat by the harbor. And it is a full moon, so then you must come to Zora's seance tonight."

"Seance?" I look between them, searching for some sign of jest, but see only anticipation. "I'm a good Christian woman. I shouldn't. I... No, I shouldn't."

Sabine snorts, and Solange rolls her eyes. "It is a bit of fun, Violet. We are all good Christian women. Not one of us has suffered God's wrath in the three years since Zora moved to town."

"I'll think about it."

"Good. Come back if you decide yes, and I will give you the address and password."

A password, like an underground nightclub. How delightfully mysterious.

I thank Madame Solange, say a pleasantry to Sabine, snatch my drab gray thing from the dressing room floor, shove it into the garment bag, and rush to the door with my luggage case before they can invite me to something else. No one had asked me to do anything before Clara slipped the note under my door last night; now I'm declining things to stay on track and keep my focus. Edmund could show up at any moment, a tempest of cold, unrelenting wrath. But Edmund isn't here, so the danger feels a thousand miles away, easy to forget. I could almost forget it entirely for a moment and enjoy life.

Just not today.

Turning from where I lean on the shop's wood siding, I run into a wall. A wall of soft, navy blue wool and brass buttons. Firm, yet gentle, hands catch me at the shoulders, steadying me. He seems taller as I crane my neck to look up and up into eyes like cut gems.

"Asa!"

I jump back, but the garment bag catches under my heel. Asa's there before I hit the brick sidewalk.

How many times would I end up in his arms?

He's thinking the same thing. "I might get used to this if it keeps happening, Violet." He effortlessly raises me to my feet, then stoops to retrieve the garment bag I didn't realize I dropped. He slings it over his shoulder. "I was just coming to fetch you. Hungry?"

His black hair is combed and oiled, but I liked it more when it was untamed on the sea, flaring out around the edges of his captain's hat. I shift to hold my luggage with both hands, so there is something between us.

"No, I'm sorry, Asa. I shouldn't have agreed to lunch. I need to get back to Widdershin."

He deflates with a frown. "If I said something about having to wait for the tides, could I get you to stay for coffee?"

"Do we have to wait for the tide?"

Asa bites his lower lip.

"No. I only recommend against going out there in the dark."

He'd shaved and splashed on something woody and musky for our lunch. This clearly means more to him than he's ready to say out loud. It would mean the same to me, were circumstances vastly different.

"If the tides are as dangerous as you say, maybe we should wait until just after lunch. I was told to go to some place with a special by the harbor? And I need to visit the market."

Asa's frown lingers while he unravels my meaning, then it rises to crinkle the edges of his eyes. "The tides should be safe after lunch." He extends a hand to take my luggage, his other still laden with my drab dresses. On a surge of nerves, rather than passing over my case, I wrap a hand around his elbow. A voice in my mind yells, screams, about how unfair it is, both to him and to me.

He tenses, but relaxes within a breath before leading us toward Stage Harbor Road, back along the route I'd taken into town yesterday.

"That's a lovely dress. Is that new?"

My cheeks burn.

Twenty

A sa does all the talking for the next half hour, though it isn't his fault. His questions about my family and past are met with brief answers and my own thorough counter-inquiry. Each thing I ask him is met with a short silence before he speaks, though I have no reason to think he's slow. He's taking his time, ensuring he can respond without the story getting lost in tangents. At least, so I assume. He gives me every opportunity to take over the conversation, but I throw it back at him, and he gets the hint that I don't want to discuss myself.

His parents are still alive, though they are not very good parents. I don't press much on that, but I am left with the impression that alcohol was involved. His grandparents and an uncle raised him, affectionately known as Meemaw, Peepaw, and Uncle Timmo. His older sister married and moved west four years ago, and his oldest sister died of consumption when he was five. He says he doesn't remember much of her. Uncle Timmo gave Asa his boat, *By Cod's Grace,* when he was forced to retire after breaking both legs and the injuries not healing correctly. I feel prepared to write a pamphlet on the *Brief History of Captain Asa Carver* by the time I see the small market and a restaurant with a sandwich board that announces the day's special: fried cod cheeks with salt pork and potatoes. I'm not hungry, but this will be my last meal before returning to Widdershin, with its old eggs and canned beans.

Asa jogs ahead to hold the door open for me.

Photographs of schooners, displayed in brass, wood, or silver frames, line the wood-paneled walls of the Gull & Anchor. Nets and brass lanterns hanging from the ceiling give the impression that this place is decorated for tourists, but the clientele packing the small restaurant looks, at a glance, to be locals. The temperature noticeably jumps in the small space, bursting with a dozen overlapping conversations and the aroma of fried fish.

Asa points to an open table against the wall in the back, and I lead the way, snaking between the array of tables and patrons.

"Do you like cod cheeks?" he asks in my ear as he pushes in my chair.

"I kind of have to, growing up on the coast. But isn't that a bit heavy, all that fried food, if we'll be out on the water in a bit?"

"Uncle Timmo said you can't get seasick on seafood, but I've proved him wrong on that more than once." He starts to laugh, but quickly covers his mouth. "Sorry. That's not proper lunch conversation."

I pat his hand resting on the table. "It's fine. We're not eating yet. What is it that you do, that you can take yesterday to ferry me about and then spend the middle of the day with me today?"

He shrugs. "Charter fishing trips. Sunset excursions for tourists. Mail delivery. Pilot guide. Towing services. Ferryman to all the islands and beaches. You name it. I've been up to Nova Scotia and down to Jacksonville. When you own the boat, you own the business. My expenses aren't much. Just fuel and food."

"That sounds like complete freedom."

A short, older woman with her red hair tied back and wearing an apron around her waist approaches the table with a pencil and pad in hand.

"Cap'n Carver, good to see ya," she says around a strong Irish lilt and turns to me. "Aren't you a charming dear? What'll ya have?"

"Mrs. Tilley, this is Violet. Violet, Mrs. Tilley has run this place since before I was born, but she hasn't aged a day."

"Oh, shut it, Asa," she says, but I see the blush creeping around her neck.

"The special for me," Asa says. "But Violet's looking for something lighter. What do you recommend?"

"Oh no, don't do anything just for me. I'm fine with the special," I say.

Mrs. Tilley taps the pencil on her lips, nods, then shakes it at me. "Don't be fussin' over the menu, love. Every young lady should get what she wants. I've just the thing—cool tomato aspic, set up perfect, and a few water crackers to keep it company. Light as a feather, and no trouble at all to the kitchen."

An aspic is far from my favorite thing to eat, but I'd only had my grandmother's, who, I admit, with only the fondest memories, was a terrible cook. "If you're sure it's no trouble."

"None at all, and you'll feel grand after it."

"You're a treasure, Mrs. Tilley. Thank you," Asa winks, and she's gone.

"You've made quite the impression on her," I say. "You had her blushing like a schoolgirl."

"We go way back. And is that so wrong? She knows I don't mean anything with some harmless charm."

"How often do you do that, Asa? Harmlessly flirt with others?" I want to be more direct and ask if he's just flirting with me or if there's any actual interest, but I hold my tongue. I'm a married woman, as easy as that is to forget.

By how his jaw flexes, he catches my unspoken meaning. He leans forward, resting his forearms on the table. His voice is low, but it cuts through the noise around us clearly. "Since I took the drunk from your dock, I've barely gone an hour without thinking about you, Violet. You walk in my consciousness and dance in my dreams. Please, grant me this one grace and answer me: Why are you so bound to Widdershin? Why must you rush back to that awful place?"

His confession leaves me stammering for a moment. He thinks of me often?

"I told you. I'm working for Mr. Sparrow. Organizing the collection for sale," I say.

"Just a job? You tell me nothing about your past. That's fine. You owe me nothing. But you're hiding something."

"And if I am? Maybe it's with good reason."

He takes a deep breath and leans back, leaving his hands on the table between us. "Are you in danger?"

If I tell him, he may hate me for not telling him sooner. If I withhold, he will surely hate me even more later.

"I am," I say.

Asa bites his lower lip and nods, eyes drifting to the photographs on the wall beside us. "Is it money, or a person?"

He makes it easy, talking without specifics.

"A person."

Asa keeps nodding, and those brilliant green eyes return to me. He leans forward again and slides his hands, palm up, closer to me. "Come with me, Violet. We can go anywhere in the world. Whoever is after you won't find us in the Mediterranean or the South Pacific."

I stare down at those calloused, strong hands. I know what they feel like on my shoulders, at my hip, and can imagine how they'd feel brushing my cheek or holding mine as we drift to sleep. How long could we sail the world before I stopped checking over my shoulder for Edmund?

His offer, his wildly generous offer, sounds so much like what I'd said to Hester June a few hours ago. "Come with me and I'll save you," except I was relieved when she declined. Though Asa seems far more honest than I.

"I can't." My words eek out with a whispered sob, and I shrink back, expecting his reaction to be rage. How dare I refuse him when he has everything to offer me?

Instead, his shoulders sink and his hands reach another inch toward me.

"Is it that bad?" he asks.

How can I respond to this? I take a few breaths to brush the threatening tears from my lashes.

"I don't know. But I must solve this myself. It wouldn't be fair to get you involved."

"Fair to who, Violet? I want to do this. I'm offering it freely."

"Fair to me. I've lived my life, always holding someone else's hand, and I need to know I can do it on my own."

"Part of that means not being so prideful that you refuse aid when needed."

The heat rising in my cheeks has nothing to do with the restaurant's warmth and close quarters.

"How dare you?" I ask. "How dare you call me prideful when you know nothing about what got me here?"

He raises both hands defensively and sits back in his chair just as Mrs. Tilley returns with our plates. Asa's looks better, by far. The fish is lightly breaded and fried to a golden crisp. The potatoes are cut into neat cubes, glistening with oil and heavy with seasoning. By comparison, my tomato aspic is a wobbling, blood-red brick of congealed horror with bits of diced celery and a full tomato slice frozen in time just below the surface.

"There ya are, my loves," says Mrs. Tilley. "Put it on your tab, Asa?"

"Sure, yes. And could we get a couple of waters? Violet, would you like tea or a soda water?"

I glare at his smile. It's as if he forgot we were in the middle of an argument. Still, it's not lost on me that he asked, rather than ordering for me.

"Water's fine," I say.

"You look a little off, dear," Mrs. Tilley says. "I'll get you a ginger ale."

Asa's smile sours as soon as the kindly old woman leaves.

"I want to know you, but you tell me nothing. I want to help you, but you refuse. Meemaw didn't prepare me for this when she taught me how to treat a lady."

"If only more men listened to their Meemaws." I poke the aspic with a fork. Asa's meal pulls at my hunger, but the wiggle in mine quickly squashes it.

"Where do we go from here, Violet?"

I take a deep breath and steel my heart. "I've been thinking about you, too, Asa, about how I've been looking forward to this and you inevitably talking me into a walk around town. Maybe watch the sunset from your boat. But I can't. We can't. This has all been a mistake. I should find someone else to take me back."

I start to push back in my chair, but his next words freeze me. "You're married."

"What?" I drop into my seat and lean in, dropping my voice to a hissed whisper. "Why would you think that?"

"You are. You're married and running from your husband."

"How did you know?"

"I didn't, but it seemed like an easy guess. Whatever he's done, he's an absolute fool for not treating you right, Violet."

The silence stretches as I wait for his promises of how he'd do better, as they do in all great works, as the hero woos the heroine, but the words don't come. Maybe, despite his flowery description of how I dance in his dreams, he isn't trying to woo me. Or he's doing it in a very different manner.

"I'll find someone else to take me back. Thank you for everything, Asa." I start to rise again, but he snatches my hand in his.

"No. I'll take you. The fewer who know about you, the safer you'll be."

Mrs. Tilley returns with our drinks, and I take a first bite of the aspic, if only to give myself a moment to consider his words and motives. Asa likewise cuts a mouthful of fish and potatoes to chew while staring at a point in the table's center. The silence stretches into awkwardness, and I'm sure we're thinking the same thing: how different this could be if I were untethered. I thought about him plenty since he caught me at the wheel yesterday, and it's been days more for him. What if we fled to the South Pacific? Maine marriage records would mean nothing there.

No. I was right when I said that I needed to figure this out on my own. If I ran off with Asa, I'd forever be beholden to him. Who would he be in a week? A month? Two years? Edmund was perfectly kind in the beginning, too.

"Do you know what you need from the market?" Asa asks.

It takes me a beat to switch my mindset. "Enough for a few weeks, if I can. There are stores of canned and pickled things at the house, as well as coffee and tea, though none of it's good. Nothing's swollen with botulism, it's just all stale."

His grin returns, casting a twinkle in his eye. "A mix of fresh, canned, and jarred. Weeks will be difficult, but not impossible. We can get some things in bulk and pile the crates on my boat."

We drop my luggage and dresses at his ship bobbing lazily at the harbor and return to a mostly deserted market. It has to be well past noon, so I imagine people are at work. Asa carries the brown sack against his chest, offering an apple for me to sniff and waving for the butcher's attention. By the time the bag is full, as well as the smaller one I'm holding by the handles, my mind has gone through a dozen rapid stages of acceptance, each silently rebutted with a counterargument about why this cannot be. Asa isn't telling me what to buy or making me do all the work. It's a slow progression of us getting more accustomed to each other's proximity while deciding how many cases of coffee are too many.

With only a few of Mr. Sparrow's dollars remaining, Asa sets the last crate on the deck of *By Cod's Grace*. He sweeps a hand through his hair, tugs on his captain's hat, and makes a thoughtful grunt.

"What is it?" I ask.

"Storm's coming." He pulls a tiny brass watch from his breast pocket and frowns. "I feel awful for what I'm about to say, Violet."

The sky's clear except for some puffy clouds on the horizon. There's no sign of a storm, but then, I didn't believe Mr. Farlow when he dropped me at Widdershin, and he turned out to be right.

"It's not safe to leave now," I say.

He nods. "These early summer storms come up fast and hot. The rain'll start before we dock, and on my way back, the sea'll either be a tempest or the fog'll be thick as soup. I'd rather not be known as a cautionary tale about yet another sea captain who overdrew his luck."

My lips part, intending to ask him if he needs to come back right away. I almost invite him to stay the night at Widdershin. We wouldn't even be sleeping in the same wing. We could have tea and read in front of the demon skull hearth. Maybe the cat would come to sit by the fire while the storm rages around us.

His green eyes search mine, waiting for me to decide the next move.

"But my things are already piled up on your boat," I say and cringe at my simpering tone. Asa opened his heart and dedicated the day to me, yet I struggle to be honest with him.

His frown deepens. "Theft isn't much of an issue; your things will be safe. I can walk you back to Miss Morrow's, and we can leave first thing in the morning."

Asa's still on his boat, resting an elbow on his knee with a boot propped on the lip. He'd take me to Widdershin if I insisted and, being a reasonable sailor, weather out the storm there if I invited him to stay. He's been a perfect gentleman, but would that continue once we're alone? What if the Witch's Wail that drove Mr. Sparrow to madness does the same to Asa tonight?

Life is nothing but a series of calculated risks, but this doesn't seem like one I should take. The longer he watches me for an answer, the more I want to step onto the boat. It seems wholly unlikely that he'd suddenly change when we're on the island...

"In the morning, then," I say.

Coward.

Asa blinks and his focus shifts to just past my ear. Is that disappointment? Or is he imagining Chatham behind me?

"Which bags will you need for the night?" he asks, turning to my things.

"Just the leather case on top. I don't want to take up your whole day, Asa. I can manage on my own."

"I know you can. I've left you here before to make that walk into town." With my bag in both hands, he sprightly hops from his boat to the dock.

I grasp the luggage, but he doesn't immediately let go.

He speaks to the leather case. "I'm being stupid, Violet. I've told you how I feel, and you've told me enough to know I don't have a shot. That has to be the end of it."

My heart twists, but I know he's right.

Asa releases the bag, but takes my hand. "Before you say something about finding another captain in the morning, let me stop you. I'll come get you first thing."

My face must be an open book. Everyone can read what I'm not saying out loud. "If you come by Miss Morrow's, I'm signed in as Evelyn Bell."

"Pretty name. I'll see you in the morning."

He raises my hand, but stops short of kissing it. Instead, he squeezes and releases.

The air between us thickens, making it difficult to breathe, until I step back and break the spell. When I reach the beginning of the pier, I glance back long enough to see Asa facing away, both hands on the edge of the roof covering the wheel, head tilted back, gazing up at the sky. His shoulders swell with a sigh.

Miss Morrow is annoyed that I interrupt her card game to fetch my key. But at least, she grumbles, she hadn't cleaned the room yet.

The clock claims it's almost seven, but that can't be right. Where had the day gone? Had we spent that much time in the market? I hadn't rushed my steps while I hopelessly tried to reaffirm my motivations for being in Chatham and Widdershin:

Emancipation. I need Mr. Sparrow's money to start fresh as far from Edmund as possible, and I need to do this without handouts. The second stipulation was never in my original plans, as sketchy as those were, but now it feels essential. I can't live my life beholden to another. Isn't that, though, the very definition of being a woman?

No. That was the life of Sarah Vale, of my mother, of every suffragette who came before me. Last night, I chose between Jane Austen and Clara Ames, opting for the more socially challenging path. Tonight presents the same two options. Stay in, attempt to read, but more likely spend every moment analyzing what I could have done differently with Asa. Or take Sabine up on her invite.

The journey to Widdershin was my first meaningful decision, made entirely for myself. How long will it be until not every subsequent decision feels like I'm making it for generations past and those to come?

Twenty-One

Sabine looks up as soon as I enter her shop. She's with a customer, an older woman who can't decide between two hats, but Sabine shoves the larger one with too many feathers at her to weave through the racks of scarves and accessories, coming at me with arms wide.

"Ah, Violet! I am so pleased to see you again." She squeezes me in an embrace and holds me by the shoulders at arm's length. "You have come for the shoes, yes?"

"Shoes? No, I..." It had only been a few hours, but the visit had been so frantic, I'd forgotten about the concern regarding my despicable footwear. "No, not that. I'm in town another night, it seems, and I wanted to inquire about the... the other thing."

Sabine's eyes narrow, then widen as she snaps a finger. "Yes, yes, Zora's seance."

The older woman's gaze peeks across the store.

"So you can come?" Sabine asks, and I nod. "Lovely. Let me write down the address." She turns toward the counter by the door, but snaps back to me. "This dress, hard to believe my sister held onto it so long. You bring it to life. You are a treasure, Violet."

No matter how I look in it, I *feel* good wearing it. Light, fluid. Everything my conservative frocks are not. The older woman is staring at me over a display of stiff felt hats, so I flash her a grin and rush over to the counter. Sabine is putting the last pen stroke onto the back of a blank invoice and looks up to hand it to me. Her hastily scrawled penmanship is a masterwork of looping calligraphy.

"Be here about ten. Don't worry about bringing a dish."

"I'm glad you said that. I wouldn't have thought about it until I was on my way. Will you be there?"

"But of course. And my sister. If there is nothing else, I'd like to finish up with Mrs. Craig and close up." She nods at the other woman in the shop, who is now pulling heavy scarves out of a bin.

"I'll see you in a few hours."

The door closes behind me just as someone disappears into Madame Solange's shop next door. I recognize the slumped posture from this morning: Hester June. She's probably stepping in to cancel her order. What happens to wedding dresses that are no longer needed? A twinge of guilt twists in me for my half-hearted offer to her. I know I can't help her, but why did I say anything if I hoped she'd refuse?

All I know is I can't be standing here when she leaves. The bookstore has one employee pulling in their signs and another sweeping on the other side of the large glass windows. The coffeeshop's sign says they're open late. My stomach reminds me that I ate hours ago, intending to spend time at sea immediately afterward, and I tuck into the nearest restaurant, simply named Phebe's.

My father often said how food tastes better when someone else makes it. It was his flimsy excuse to never make a meal for the family, but he might have been on to something. The ham on rye sandwich I had yesterday was excellent, even if I ate it in a rush, and the aspic was the best I'd had, though that isn't saying much. Now, my first sip of clam chowder makes my toes curl. Briney, creamy, with the perfect dash of sweetness. The clam is fresh and the potatoes are soft, yet still firm enough. I devour the cup in record time, just as the waiter arrives to take it away and replace it with my entree.

It was a difficult debate on what to order, with the Skipper's Load being a strong contender. Boasting that the sandwich requires a fork and a spoon to eat, it would be everything the delicate aspic was not. Then I considered the Lighthouse Special. Two thick slices of crusty Anadama bread, cold sliced roast beef, sharp white cheddar, crisp iceberg lettuce, sliced tomato, fried bacon, a smear of tangy mustard, pickles, and topped with a fried egg to evoke the image of a lighthouse beacon.

It's utterly ridiculous. A meal for four.

Instead of all that, the waiter places the Widow's Catch before me, a hearty white fish stew served in a bread bowl.

And so what if I'm having both clam chowder and a stew in the same meal? No one's here to stop me. I haven't had clam chowder in weeks, and I couldn't pass up something with a name like the Widow's Catch. It's more than I can eat, but I feel I have a bit of catching up to do, after thinking lunch with Asa would be my last on the mainland for weeks, and settling on an aspic that I barely touched.

Phebe's is clearly meant for the busy Chatham local, with the cash register beside where they prepare the food, and only seating for eight. I slowly enjoy my Widow's Catch near the back, watching the people flow in for their Friday meals. Many arrive with empty, clean glass jars and trade them for another full of chowder. Most leave with one of the mighty sandwiches wrapped in paper. Everyone knows the staff, joking and catching up on their week while their food is made. They all pay on credit, putting it on their tabs. I can't help but fantasize about how nice it would be to be so close to the people of a town.

But also, everyone glances at me in the back corner. Some flash a smile, but most ignore me beyond a casual observance of my existence. They know I don't belong here, and they're right. I should be hidden away, not on display for the whole town to see. Edmund could arrive in a week, describe me to anyone, and they'd say, "Oh yes. You mean that quiet woman wearing the skimpy dress, eating the meal for three?"

That is, if he isn't already in town. Watching me. Waiting for the perfect time to step from the shadows.

The Widow's Catch is suddenly too much. It wars with the clam chowder, and I can't get out of Phebe's quickly enough to the fresh air in the darkened street. I slip into the alley beside the restaurant.

"Deep breath. He's not here. He probably gave up on you. He's prowling for the next girl to torture," I mumble, regaining enough control over my breath to notice the stinking garbage in the alley.

Thunder rumbles in the distance, reminding me of Asa's storm prediction. He could have taken me to Widdershin and returned by now, but he probably needed time away after I yelled at him in the restaurant and rejected him. Just another man who gave up on me, except this one I mourn. I should have asked him to stay the night, to weather the storm at Widdershin. We're two adults, capable of retaining control of ourselves. He could have helped me carry the things to the cellar, and I'd make him breakfast in the morning.

Except... no. What would people say? I worried about Mr. Sparrow staying on the island with me, and it was one of the first questions out of Asa's mouth when he came to pick him up. What will the town think if another bachelor stays out there?

The first raindrops hit the cedar shingles overhead. They accelerate as I run for Miss Morrow's, soaking through my lovely new dress and terrible old shoes.

***

The clock on the mantle reads 9:32. My purple dress and shoes are nearly dry by the fire as I sit on the bed in my underthings. Despite telling myself I intend to stay in and read, and that I cannot risk being seen all over town even more than I already have, my eyes are on the clock more than on Jane Austen. The rain stopped a few moments ago; the clouds swept away, revealing a full moon that lights the street in sharp lines of darkness.

I tell myself I can't go, that I shouldn't go, even as I slip into my dress and pull on my shoes. The risk is too great. I should flee with the two dollars remaining from Mr. Sparrow's funds. Poverty and anonymity are preferable to Edmund finding me. I've gone too far; there's no way I can talk him down or make him understand what I did. I'm not sure I understand it, myself. One thing led to another, and now I'm knocking on the front door of a stranger's seaside bungalow. The issue of getting back to my room after curfew will be an issue for later.

Solange pulls the door open within seconds; the flickering light of a hundred candles behind her gives her an ethereal presence. She snatches my hand and tugs me inside.

The plaster walls are painted a pale blue, where I can see them around the countless framed family photographs and paintings. The sitting room to my right has a bookshelf and overstuffed chairs facing a hearth. The dining table to my right is cleared for the five women sitting around it. Candles, short and fat or tall and thin, cover any horizontal surface, but otherwise, the house is perfectly normal. Whatever fears I had for my immortal soul after attending a seance begin to melt away.

"Ah, good, you made it at last, *mon petit chou*," Solange says.

"Sabine told me to be here at ten." I search for a clock while she drags me to the table. I can't possibly be that late.

"Well, you are here, no matter. Tell me who you know."

I allow myself to acknowledge the others in the room with a wave. A woman in her late forties, who looks to be all sharp angles, sits at the head of the table and considers me through the tiny glasses she holds at the end of her nose. Sabine and Hester June sit to one side, across from another with silvered hair pulled back under a paisley scarf. In contrast to the other unknown woman, her glasses are enormous.

"Hester June, I'm glad to see you again," I say.

"Solange made me come," she says flatly.

"She should be with company." Sabine pats Hester June's hand.

"I haven't had the pleasure with the others. Hello, I'm..." I start toward them with a hand outstretched, but falter. I've introduced myself to these women as different identities.

The door beside me swings inward, and a seventh woman enters, backing through the door with a plate of crackers, sliced cheese, carrots, and celery.

"Clara?" I ask, and hold the door for her.

She passes the tray to Solange so she can hug me. "You made it."

"I thought you were leaving early this morning?"

"I had every intention to, and I'll pay the price by having to rush tomorrow, but I couldn't miss Zora's... *this*." Clara's tone is more excited than skeptical. She winks at me, takes one of my hands in both of hers, and turns to address the others. "Ladies, this is the woman we were telling you about, Violet."

My breath catches in my throat.

Clara notices and continues, "Yes, we found you out. Sabine said she invited a Violet, we asked who that is, and long story short, we concluded that Violet and Evie are the same person. Nothing to worry about, though. We won't tell anyone."

I glance at Hester June, expecting some reaction after our discussion in the conservatory this morning, but she doesn't look up from the slice of yellow cheese she's holding.

"Oh, sweetie. Come sit here," the woman with the thick glasses says as she pulls out the chair beside her. "What you must be going through. I couldn't imagine running from my Nicolas."

Everyone knows my secrets, leaving me both freer and scrutinized.

"I'm Phebe. Phebe Easterday. I never miss a full moon here," says the woman.

"Phebe? Any relation to the restaurant in town?"

"Oh, that?" She snorts and rolls her comically large eyes. "My pa named it that, and my brother kept it when he took over. So, yes and no. It's named after me, but I don't have anything to do with it. Never have, never will. I wouldn't have time, anyway, taking care of Nicolas and our boys. The housework never ends, I'm sure you're aware. Do you have any children?"

Her words come at me like an unstoppable force, syllables rising and falling like the waves, and just as relentless.

"N-no. We don't have children."

"Well, that might be for the best. My boys are my greatest blessing, proof of God Almighty's shining benevolence. I never knew what was missing from my life until I brought each of them into this glorious world. But if this fellow of yours isn't kind to you, children won't make him better. That's not advice you'll get from most mothers, but I believe it's true."

Phebe reaches for the glass of lemonade in front of her.

"And I am Zora," says the thin woman at the head of the table, folding her glasses and tucking them into her sleeve. I imagined her voice would be smoky with a mysterious accent, but she sounds as though she could have been my neighbor in Maine. "I'm pleased to have seven this month. Seven is a powerful number. Miss Peltier, should we begin with you?"

Hester June jerks upon hearing her name, as if being jolted from some inner place.

"Yes, I..." She lifts a small silk purse from her lap and pulls the strings to open it. One piece at a time, she places a scrap of paper from the bag onto the tablecloth. She doesn't have to arrange them for me to recognize the telegram.

Zora picks up a single piece with her long fingers and sucks a breath in between her teeth.

"Powerful," she whispers. Zora places the scrap in front of herself and folds both hands over it. "Speaking with the dead is difficult, but not impossible. Those who have been gone too long have lost their interest in the living. Those who have recently passed away may not yet understand what has happened to them."

Clara grunts to my left, but I'm not looking at her to understand her reaction. Phebe, meanwhile, is nodding along with rapt attention.

"What was your betrothed's name?" Zora asks. This must have all been discussed before I arrived. There's no way Zora could be guessing all these details.

Hester June parts her lips to speak, but the words catch in a restrained sob.

"Louis," Sabine answers for her.

Zora nods. "And what are you hoping to know from him?"

"Is she safe to go back to her father?" Solange answers.

Zora closes her eyes and bites her lower lip with whatever effort she's experiencing. The wind doesn't howl through the drapes, the candles don't flicker and blow out. Other than Zora tilting her head to the left and scrunching up her nose, there are none of the theatrics I expected with a seance.

I glance back at Clara, but she only twitches her eyes toward the head of the table, silently asking me to stay focused.

Zora gasps as if the paper burned her, and her eyes snap open, training on Hester June.

"No." She reaches to take Hester June's hand. "Don't go back."

The younger girl pulls back, raking her hands through her hair. "That's it. My life is over."

"Reply to your father, telling him you're returning, and don't," Clara says. "I leave in the morning, and I want you to come with me."

It's almost the same as my offer, except that they'll be gone in a few days. And Clara's invitation sounds like she actually wants the answer to be yes.

Hester June's breath noticeably slows, and she nods. "Thank you. I can learn to sew or do bookkeeping. I'll be useful."

"It's nothing. I want you safe before you worry about all that, dear," Clara says.

Everyone nods and murmurs their approval. Just like that, it's settled. Hester June Peltier is uprooting her life based on... what? Zora said four words, and it's enough for all of them. But, for the first time, Hester June relaxes, and a smile tugs at her lip.

"Violet, how about you?" Zora asks. "Do you have a question for the spirits?"

"I-I don't know. I suppose so, but I don't have anything physical like the paper, if that's what you need."

"We call them totems," Zora says. "An object with a physical link to the spiritual world. You don't need one. Give me your hand and hold the question in your mind and heart." She stretches her arm across the table, palm up.

"No, thank you. I don't want to... Phebe, Clara, you must have questions."

Phebe shakes her head. "Thank you, dear, but you're new here, and new people go first. Besides, Zora reads for me so often, I frankly don't think I have anything left to ask her."

Solange and Sabine aren't offering any interference, so I reach past Phebe, feeling the chill of Zora's many rings around her bony fingers.

What is my question? Should I flee with Asa? Will I be successful in this whole plan with Mr. Sparrow and selling the collection? Will Edmund find me?

"Interesting," Zora coos with her eyes closed. Her face contorts, as it had while reading the scrap of paper. "A shadow has attached itself to you. Not the shadow we all have, of our regrets and guilts, all the little things we do, yet are ashamed of. This is something old. Not ancient, but old."

I don't believe in any of this mysticism. If she could read my mind and answer my unspoken questions, she would be saying something about a dashing sea captain.

"What could it be?" Phebe asks while ringing a scarf that matches the one on her head.

"At least it's not an *ancient* evil," Clara says.

"When it comes to the works and hearts of men, evil is subjective. Anyone can justify their actions." Zora releases me and leans back in her chair. She traces the gold cross on her necklace with a look somewhere between confusion and horror.

I hadn't noticed the sound of insects chirping and the wind brushing against trees outside until they're gone. My heart pounds in the silence.

Sabine claps once. "I am so happy I asked you here, Violet! What fun we're having."

"Yes. Fun." I stare down at the hand Zora had held, then to each of the other women around the table. Phebe looks as worried as Zora, but the rest are grinning, entertained. Even Hester June.

"We should look deeper," Zora says and pushes back from the table. "Everyone, grab a candle and follow."

She doesn't wait to make sure everyone's in motion, but snatches a tall candle on her way out of the dining room, toward the sitting room on the other side of the front door. Phebe hops to her feet, rushing after with a flame in each hand.

We each follow in line, forming a silent vigil, through the sitting room to a small room at the back of the house. It might have been intended as a bedroom, but dark fabric drapes down the walls, drawing all focus to the round table at its center, shrouded in a deep maroon cloth. Seven chairs tightly surround it in the space reeking of incense and cinnamon.

Zora uses her candle to light a lamp over the table, then licks her thumb and snuffs out the wick. "Blow those out," she says.

"What was the point in bringing them?" Clara asks.

"To transfer the energy to this room. Please, sit. Violet, here, please." Zora pulls out the chair beside her, patting its back, and we all take our places.

Zora slaps her hand on the center of the table, fingers wide, and wads the tablecloth in a fist before whipping it aside. Letters are etched and burned into the pale oak top, the whole alphabet. In addition to the numbers zero through nine, there are question marks, "YES", "NO", "Hello", and "Farewell". It also has "BLACK", "WHITE", and "GREY" across the top.

"Now we're talking," Clara whispers beside me.

Zora opens a drawer on her side of the table and places a thin, circular wooden block with a hole in its center over "Farewell".

"Ladies, I'm sure you've heard of this parlor trick, if you haven't seen it in person. We put our fingers on the planchet, and a trickster amongst us tugs it to spell out sinister things." Zora taps a finger on the table. "But let me put it to you that this spirit board can absolutely work. Either by tapping into the deep recesses of our minds or allowing spirits to act their will through us, this board works beyond known or explainable science. Relax your minds and do not fight it. Now, please." Zora places her index fingers on the block, and the others follow suit.

"This is a lot just for me," I say.

"Maybe a lot, but it is never too much," Zora says, nodding to the paddle. "Please."

There's barely space for me to touch my fingers to the planchet, with twelve others already on it, but I squeeze in. Looking at the other expectant faces in the dim lamp light, I feel silly. This is clearly nothing more than a spectacle put on for their entertainment. Even so, it beats sitting in my room at Miss Morrow's with a book in my hand, pining over Asa.

Zora blows out a long breath and whispers to the room. "To the shadow that clings to our Violet, we open this circle. Come from silence, come from sorrow, come into our keeping. We seek your story, not your harm."

Nothing happens, exactly as I assumed.

Then, the paddle twitches, lurching in bursts toward "Hello".

I glance up, expecting someone to be grinning, but everyone is intensely focused.

"Spirit, do you mean Violet harm?" Zora asks.

The paddle moves to NO.

Despite my skepticism, I let out a little puff of relief. At least it's not Edmund's malevolence that has attached themselves to me.

"When did you find Violet?"

The planchet slides to the question mark.

"I expected that. Spirits don't have a fine grasp on the passage of time," Zora explains. "Where did you find Violet?"

The paddle hesitates, then slides faster and faster, pausing for a fraction of a moment over each letter.

W-I-D-E-R

I pull back, and it freezes over the S.

"Clara! Stop this!" I shriek and jump to my feet, knocking my chair back. My anger is less about her trying to scare me than about her blatantly discarding the trust I placed in her last night.

"It's not me!" she pleads. "Violet, I didn't tell anyone about what... about that."

"You know what it was spelling?" Zora asks.

"Yes. Widdershin. I'm staying there for work. I told that to Clara in confidence."

"You went to Widdershin Isle?" Zora asks.

Phebe gasps and crosses herself.

"Please, Violet. Believe me." Clara squeezes one of my hands in both of hers.

If I don't believe her, it means a betrayal beyond any scope I'd like to consider. Clara was the first woman I opened myself to, though still not fully. I told her all about Edmund, but not my real name. But if I believe her, who or what is controlling the paddle?

With a wary eye on Clara, I right my chair and sit, placing my fingers back with the others.

Zora again blows out a long breath, recentering the room. "Widdershin, an island of ghosts and graves. Some marked, most forgotten. Spirit, what is your name?"

The paddle vibrates under my fingertips, though it may be the adrenaline surging through my veins.

It finally moves, slowly sliding across the letters, over the numbers, and stops at the top of the board.

BLACK

Phebe loudly sighs. "Thank you, Jesus. If it were Erasmus Vale, I'd have called for a priest."

"The spirits sometimes lose themselves over time, forgetting who they were in life," Zora explains. "Maybe this one sees only its shadow."

No, the spirit hadn't forgotten who they were.

"Zora, you said old spirits are hard to contact because they've lost interest in the living," I say. "How long does that take?"

Why do I bother to ask? This is a bunch of hokum, but no one else in the room shows a glimmer of recognition for the name BLACK. Hester June and Clara are just visiting Chatham. Zora has only lived here for three years. Solange and Sabine moved to town six years ago, but have been busy with their businesses. It's perfectly believable that these women wouldn't know the full history and lore of a tiny island off the coast. I don't know Phebe's story, but maybe her history of the island begins and ends with the Vales.

History books forgot the truth of Widdershin, so why should these women know it?

BLACK. Deliverance Black. The Widdershin Witch herself has bonded her soul to mine.

"It depends on the person," Zora says. "How powerful was their soul? How closely were they connected to the world, and did they have any unfinished business? Any deep traumas that would leave an imprint?"

I assume that Deliverance Black would be strong in all those questions, but if none of the other women recognize her name, perhaps my opinion is skewed.

"Spirit," I say, taking command. "Do you have a message for me?"

The paddle drags to YES.

"What is your message?"

R-U-N

Twenty-Two

The rest of the night was a blur. I remember the room closing around me, fleeing out the front door, brushing off Clara's offers to walk me back, tiptoeing past a snoring Miss Morrow, and now I'm staring up at the ceiling in my narrow bed. I yelled at Zora, sure it had to be her, calling her sick and sadistic. But she never asked for money, so what was her grift? To frighten me and delight the others? Except, they hadn't been delighted. Phebe screamed and fell out of her chair. Solange and Sabine looked mortified.

Somewhere in my fevered apprehension, sleep finds me. Nightmarish dreams chase me from it, leaving a residue of primal fear, even if I can't remember any details.

I'm up and use the bathroom before any of the other residents are awake, slipping out as the sun crests the Atlantic. The fisherman cast off an hour ago by the time I reach the dock with *By Cod's Grace*. I've gone back to acting without a plan. All I know is that Asa will eventually come to his boat, and being here will keep me from having to see anyone else.

As I approach, a hatch opens near the back, and a man steps out onto the back deck.

Shirtless, his suspenders hanging around his hips, pants sagging low on his hips, Asa reaches high overhead, stretching his back and shoulders. I try not to stare, and fail miserably. He looks perfect, as if sculpted from clay or chiseled marble.

I clear my throat.

He turns, obviously thinking nothing about who would be approaching his boat at this time. When he sees it's me, he nearly trips down the stairs beyond the hatch.

"Violet!" He snatches a shirt and turns away to hastily button it. "I was going to come get you in a bit."

"Do you sleep in your boat?"

He turns back, raking his fingers through his mess of hair. "Sometimes, yes. I wish you'd let me come get you. I hate the thought of it, every time you make that walk alone." His words come fast, breathless, as he fumbles with the shirt and pulls his suspenders over his shoulders.

"It's an easy road. I didn't realize there was a lower level to this." I stop at the edge of the dock.

"Sure. It's not tall enough for me to stand up in, but there's a bed down there." He offers a hand to help me onto the ship. "And other things, not just a bed," he quickly adds.

Between the smoothing tone of his voice, the glimmer in his green eyes, and the strength in his hand, I can almost forget the horrors of last night. One or more of the women must have conspired to get a rise out of me. Why, I can't guess, but it must be that.

"How was it in the storm last night?"

He frowns. "I expected a lot more from that, sorry. A bit of rain and some waves. They can as easily flip and be the fury of Poseidon this time of year. Do you want to get coffee?" Asa asks.

"If you don't mind, I'd like to get underway as quickly as we can."

"Get underway? You've mastered all the lingo, haven't you? A few moments behind the wheel and you're ready for your own vessel." His grin sours when I don't return it. "What's wrong, Violet? Is it..." He scans the dock past my shoulder and whispers, "Is it *him*?"

"No, it's not. It's... at least not directly. I didn't sleep last night. I think I've had enough of Chatham for a while."

"You worry me, Violet. But if that's what you want, sure. I wish I knew how to help you."

"You've already helped me more than you could guess, Asa."

Asa navigates *By Cod's Grace* from the safety of the harbor, silently maneuvering around the shoals that reach from the Cape's elbow. I feel his gaze on me, but every time I look his way, his focus is straight ahead.

Do I owe him anything? Perhaps a thank you for ferrying me to and from the island. Or for his offers to show me a good time while in town. But more than any of that, for giving proof that a better class of man exists.

So yes, I do owe him something: a truth.

"My mother had just died, and my father wasn't taking it well. He told me how he felt Death's icy fingers in his brain," I say to the hat in my hands, but loud enough to be heard over the engine. "He wanted to see me married, to know I'd be taken care of after he was gone."

Now in the open sea between the Cape and Widdershin, Asa pulls back the throttle to quiet the engine.

"I was seeing Jakob Vogel, but his family's business sank, and they were forcing him to move south with them. Ma died, Pa died, Jakob left, the lawyer took everything from me, but Edmund was there. Out of necessity, I married him. When Mr. Sparrow sent me the letter, offering the work at Widdershin, I couldn't pack quickly enough. I was on the first train as soon as he was out of the house."

Asa runs a thumb under his suspenders' strap and rakes a hand through his hair, but says nothing, granting me space to continue.

"This is my first time alone. My first time from home, if you can call what I have with Edmund that. Maybe it is pride, but if I can't do this on my own, then I'll be forever stuck in a cycle of dependence."

Silence rests between us, interrupted only by the lapping of waves against the hull.

"I understand," he says at last. "It was silly of me to ask you to run away together, with all that you're carrying, and us having just met. It was just a little fantasy that I shouldn't have brought up. I still wish I could help you in some way, Violet, even if that means taking you down to Georgia and us never seeing each other again. You accepted Mr. Sparrow's help when you took the job, but won't accept any more."

His assessment hits deep and true. I set my own rules, yet don't follow them.

"There's you and there was Jakob," I say. "Every other man I've known, even my father, is nasty in their own way."

"And you're expecting my mask to crack."

"No, the opposite. I don't deserve someone like you, Asa. Mr. Sparrow wasn't drunk. I drugged him before you came to pick him up. He was raving and I didn't think he'd let me stay behind, were he of sounder mind."

"He threw up twice on the ride. Luckily, he got it all on himself or over the rail, and not in my boat," Asa chuckles. "Fine then, Violet. I don't agree with it or fully understand it, but I'll leave it be. Thank you for telling me something of yourself."

"Thank you for listening."

"Sure, sure. My Meemaw will be so proud of me."

The engine comes to life with a groan, and Asa pushes the throttle to resume course.

Before long, the ragged dock comes into view, that gnarled gray-white finger in the Atlantic's deep blue. Then the house, cold and silent as the graves behind it. If I finish here and achieve financial independence, could I then take up with Captain Carver? I would have proved what I needed to, though Edmund would forever be a worry. The plan brews like the terrible coffee I have in my near future. Better than the stale cans from the cellar, but far from good.

Asa slows his schooner and glides it to the dock, tossing a rope to hook and pull it secure.

It's about to be over, my little holiday from Widdershin. But more importantly, my time with Asa. My luggage, garment bag, two bags of groceries, and three crates of coffee, oats, and canned things will take several sweaty trips to the house, but I can't ask him for help. Nor can I accept the help will be undoubtedly offer. I could do the world a favor and drop the garment bag over the edge of the dock, giving it to the sea, to lessen my load, but unless I dive into Lavinia's wardrobe, I don't have many other things to wear.

He turns to me with one booted foot propped on the boat's edge. He seems somehow taller, larger than the great trees surrounding the island.

Then I realize I'm still seated. No part of me wants this to end.

"I'll help you carry your things up," Asa says, picking up a bag from the market. He hops onto the dock and offers a hand to me.

His calloused fingers slip through mine, and too quickly, I'm safely on the rotten wood of the dock.

"I can manage," I say. "It'll take a while, but the exercise will be good for me, with all my long hours hunched over books coming up."

His skill at reading me must be rapidly increasing, and he doesn't fight it. He just frowns. "I feel like this is a farewell."

I open my mouth, ready to refute it, saying he could visit any time, but stop myself. There's too much work to be done. Then I open my mouth to promise something for after I'm done here, but stop myself again. At best, I would have to agree with him that this is farewell, but I hope he's wrong.

"Can I ask one thing of you, Violet?" he asks, his emerald gaze enhanced by the afternoon sun reflecting off the water. "May I kiss you?"

I can't stop myself. I shy a step from him. No one has ever asked me that. When Jakob first kissed me, he just did it, and I didn't fight him. Edmund first did it when the priest told him to. My father and uncles all kissed my cheek or forehead without asking.

"You don't have to. You can say no—"

"Yes," I say, cutting him off.

He licks his lips, nervous. With his looks and charm, Asa has to have kissed a hundred girls, yet he doesn't seem to know what to do with his hands. I take back that little step I took from him and place a hand on his chest as our lips meet.

He's gentle. Too gentle. Perhaps this is how kissing is meant to be. Edmund is a slobbering hound who wants to eat my face. My hand on his chest slides to his ribs, and I let my lips part enough to share a breath. The solidness of his frame beneath that loose shirt. The intoxicating scent of his aftershave, splashed on in haste when I caught him off guard. I give in to the one thing I've lusted after and run my hand through his wild mop of hair.

A whispered moan escapes him. His tongue brushes my lower lip. One hand is on my cheek, the other slipping around my neck as he reduces the space between us to nothing.

My hand in his hair moves to his cheek, across light stubble, to the jacket's collar.

It hits me at once, the layers of how wrong this is, and my arm straightens, shoving us apart.

"I can't," I manage through threatening tears.

Again, I expect anger, but Asa looks confused, standing there, touching his fingertips to his lips.

"I know. You're married and... Thank you, Violet." Asa backs up, tripping into his boat. For a few agonizing moments, he unloads the crates, stacking them on the dock. As much as I want to jump in to help, I'd either get in his way or trip into his arms again.

He's about to accelerate away, but remembers to untie from the dock first. Without glancing back, Asa keeps his focus on the mainland as his boat glides from the pier and out from the island.

I catch myself touching my lips, watching him go. His Meemaw taught him well about how to treat a girl, and I start to wonder if I'm the first girl he's kissed. It seems wholly unlikely. With those eyes and smile... Yet, he was mimicking my movements. Not that I'm some great expert in the field of kissing.

Still smiling, I turn from Asa's shrinking form to the awaiting Widdershin House. It feels like we've been apart for weeks, not just two nights. Hopefully, Mr. Sparrow will call soon with good news from the buyer, putting an end to this chapter.

The house greets me with its usual silence when I enter with the first crate from the market. Erasmus Vale glares down at me from the top of the stairs, clutching his poor daughter's shoulder in a way that reminds me of Hester June. She'll be safe with Clara.

Golden eyes shine from the dark between the railing upstairs, considering me briefly before the cat slinks toward Lavinia's room.

By the time I bring the last thing in from the dock, I'm sweating and out of breath. Maybe I shouldn't have declined Asa's help. I could have thanked him with another kiss, maybe a drink from the decanters in the library.

I have been to the attic. It's time to explore the cellar. Not the flooded one in front, that's surely full of rats. No. The back root cellar.

It's time to find out what's breathing behind that door.

Twenty-Three

C hatham was a lifetime ago. The silence of Widdershin wraps around me like a dry, old blanket, equally suffocating and comforting.

The ghost of Asa's lips is still upon mine, his scent deep in my lungs. If I close my eyes, I feel his hand on my cheek, the heat radiating from his body, and the absolute solidity of his frame. If any of a dozen things were different in my life, his proposition... But instead...

I leave my things by the stairs on my way to the kitchen. The cellar door is open wide, exactly as I'd left it. I almost expected the house to reset itself to a state before I arrived, to forget I'd ever come. Before descending, I take the one item I was shocked to see at the market: An Ever-Ready flashlight and batteries. Armed with a personal light source, which hopefully the Widdershin House has no power over, I pull the bulb's chain and start down.

The space at the bottom of the stairs, with the larder to the right and the wine cellar to the left, feels smaller than I remember. It also holds a faint stench, which I attribute to the eggs I dropped in my hasty retreat.

As I cross the threshold into the wine cellar, it strikes me as foolish to have never discovered the cause of the terrible impact that shattered the bulb here.

"A sudden gust caused a swell in the currents, which knotted the underwater power cables to the island. It caused a surge, which almost blew the whole fuse box."

My explanation, said to the dusty wine racks, sounds perfectly reasonable. Knowing essentially nothing about electrical engineering certainly helps.

It all makes perfect sense, making my earlier fears laughable. The house and island are home to birds, insects, one cat, and a number of rats that I don't want to think too hard about, but ghosts or spirits are out of the question.

Shaking my head and scoffing at my earlier silliness, I step around the shattered remnants of the butter crock. There's a smaller jar of another brand on the counter upstairs. It won't be as good as Berrymore Farmhouse Creamery, but it was all the little market had to offer.

There it is, the white-washed door, flaking with neglect, barred tight to keep an unknown something fast behind it. The words scratched into the wood, those of the children's rhyme about the Widdershin Witch and her White Rider, are difficult to make out in the flashlight's glare. They stood out, fresh and raw, before, but now I have to squint and angle the light just right to make them out.

It wasn't all a work of a mind starved for engagement. A breeze presses through the cracks, bringing with it the scent of wildflowers. I smelled that in the garden out back, too. Maybe in Lavinia's room, too?

The chains come away effortlessly, the mortar securing the loop making no attempt to hold back its charge. The wood crossing the door, which I thought would take a crowbar or some other strong lever, crumbles at my touch.

Widdershin House is tired of its secrets, ready to reveal everything to me.

The worn brass handle is the only solid thing, and the door lurches toward me on rusted hinges. Beyond, a black void beckons to me, unnaturally dark, potentially endless, yet with a light, continuous breeze and that delicate, floral scent.

Erasmus Vale was obsessed with the occult, and I grant him full credit for why the secrets lurking in this darkness were boarded over and bound by chains. His superstitions were precisely that, with no basis in reality. They hold no power over me. Yet, despite knowing there is nothing here that can harm me, I catch myself making the sign of the cross.

The flashlight dispels my imagination before it goes too far. The beam of light sets the room's dimensions to an arm's span wide and twice as deep. The ceiling is low, barely taller than me. At the far end, stairs lead upward, but are aborted by another, more substantial wooden barricade with roots and dirt breaking through. Where I stand now is beneath the back patio, in what might have been the house's first root cellar, long ago forgotten and ruined. Other than the stairs, a hip-high metal shelf is the only other feature in the space, held together with more rust than anything else. A small tin box rests on the top, with a fist-sized white stone beside it.

The stone is lighter than I expected, rough in places, but mostly smooth. I turn it in my hand, but see nothing of note, other than the purity of its color, as if it had been bleached.

The box's tin hinges disintegrate on use, and I set the lid aside. A few dozen cardboard sheets wrapped in cellophane are stacked vertically within. I take one out, hold it to the light, and recognize the girl from her portrait at the top of the stairs. Lavinia Vale is at the beach, holding her wide hat in place as a breeze tugs at her white dress. She's younger than the portrait, but what makes her almost unrecognizable is her smile. Wide and carefree. The photograph was taken on a candid whim, capturing a girl's vacation from her island home of misery.

Sarah Vale is in another snapshot at that same beach trip, similarly happy and carefree. It must be Erasmus and Sarah's other children in the other photographs from other trips, posing beside a giant tree trunk or well-dressed at a distant relative's wedding. They quickly paint an image of a happy Vale family, so far distant from the one in the portraits in the attic. It's also not lost on me that Erasmus is not present in any of the snapshots, though I assume he was the one holding the camera. If he wasn't, that alone may explain the genuine smiles. Any chance away from the patriarch is reason to rejoice.

It also explains why this collection of memories is hidden, chained up, in the deepest recesses of the cellar. Erasmus didn't want that joy to be so close, but neither could he toss these photographs into a fire. Nothing, however, explains the white rock.

Laden with my new treasures, I return to the kitchen and spread the snapshots on the tile counter. There is a magnifying glass in the library, but I don't need it to see the unobstructed joy in Sarah, Lavinia, and the rest of the family. Many of the photos have a date and location on the back, with their trips dotting the East Coast and as far inland as Pennsylvania.

Maybe the patriarch wasn't the one holding the camera. Maybe these are photographs taken when Erasmus sent his family away. Either could be true, and either would explain why he would despise seeing such happiness. Destroying the pictures would grant him nothing. He would still know his family is capable of so much without him. No. A man of such severity would clearly wish to control it, and he did that by locking the images away. Holding something prisoner forever shows more dominance over it than its destruction.

Though it begs a question: Why did Sarah never flee while on such a holiday, if Erasmus was not there?

Perhaps for the same reason I didn't flee with Asa to the South Pacific. Heck, Clara Ames might have taken me with her, had I asked her. No, I returned to Widdershin to prove something to myself. Of course, now that I'm back in the dead silence, broken only by the rasp of waves or a distant fog horn, staring at snapshots of a long-dead family delighted to be any-where but here, I regret that choice. It may turn out to be the correct one, the one that will lead to emancipation by my own action, but it definitely isn't the easy one.

The rock, though. That is a mystery. In the kitchen's better light, it reminds me of coral plucked from the sea. It could be a memento from any of the family vacations in the photographs, something nabbed off the beach by a Vale child. Why keep it, but nothing else? If he cared for it, Erasmus would have kept it safe in his library, yet...

There's no point in allowing my mind to spin on something I can never answer. I put most of the groceries into cupboards and take a few of the cans to the larder in the cellar.

Then, back to the library. Mr. Sparrow won't receive my package for days, but he may call at any moment once he reads my telegram, if he hasn't already tried.

I gather up the tin of photographs and the rock and return to my small corner of the world.

Tonight, another storm rolls in from the deep Atlantic, or perhaps the same from the previous two nights returns, seeing now that the island is occupied. Rain falls in a slanted sheet, in time with gusts from the eastern bluff. It lasts less than an hour before the clouds are spent, and the sky opens to the full moon.

Memories of Zora's seance creep forward. I still cannot guess a motive, and may never know one, but one or more of those women had it in for me.

R-U-N

To where? Running without a destination can just as easily lead you back into danger. Why hadn't Deliverance Black been more verbose in her warning?

I venture onto the veranda outside my bedroom and wrap my arms around myself for warmth. A chill on the breeze is like Aeolus clearing the last remnants of winter from his storehouses, yet a low fog creeps in from the dock beyond the rusted iron gates. Unperturbed by the wind tugging at my terrible gray dress, the fog crawls through the overgrown garden, gathering in clumps that hold onto the moonlight a moment too long.

I can hear it in the space between the wind, the steady, low croon echoing through the trees. The Witch's Wail, as I have come to call it. And below, moonlight shifting through the fog. The White Rider's lantern.

The wind and moonlight. One drove Mr. Sparrow, and perhaps Erasmus Vale, to madness. The other has terrified sailors for centuries and woven itself into local legend, enough to be the subject of children's rhymes.

Childish.

I breathe deep of the air carrying that fateful tune, said to be Deliverance Black's wrath, and smile down at the will-o'-the-wisp that is her dear murdered husband. If not for the Sword of Damocles hovering over me, held by a horse hair, primed to be snipped by an unfortunate visitor or disappointing telephone call, Widdershin Isle would make the ideal residence. It may not lend to a lavish lifestyle, but the very features that drive others away create the perfect pocket for one willing to embrace them.

Twenty-Four

The storms return to rattle the windows every few nights, but I barely notice them beyond a casual observation. As another rolls in days after my return to Widdershin, I am relaxed into the leather chair before the demon's skull and empty hearth. The growing summer warmth makes a fire unnecessary, but I consider lighting a small one for the ambience. My slippers are tossed across the room, and my bare feet are tucked under the hems of my dress. I pull the knitted blanket over my legs, just because I can. If only I had a taste for cigars or spirits, to complete the feeling in this little cubby. Better yet, if only the cat were to join me, sprawling on the rug.

The nanny's books—for I've decided she was a nanny, despite lacking evidence of her charges—have me in thrall. Although I attempted to pace myself, with limited books of their kind and more hours than I should have spent enjoying them, I tore through one yesterday afternoon, when I should have been working on my task. The writing is decidedly poor, compared to the classics I am accustomed to. Somehow, that doesn't matter.

Set in late 1800s London, the action is fast, following Deirdre Doyle, a woman detective struggling to balance her career and love life. And what a love life! I set the first book aside more than a few times to let my blushes cool, and the next seems doubly in that vein. Despite all descriptions of the protagonist, in my mind, she's me. The author finds an opportunity in every book for Deirdre to describe herself while looking in a mirror, going into exhaustive detail about her flaming red hair, freckles, and green eyes. I replace all the details with my own. The male leads, who are always tall, dark, and exceptionally handsome, are easily replaceable with Asa. The villains are Edmund.

I know I should be combing the library for the best tomes to show off to the seller, but I feel I've earned a few hours, or even days, of rest. Mr. Sparrow knows only what I've told him about what he's selling or how long it might take me to get through it. My work ethic and honest desire to explore what else the library has to offer will draw me back to it, but for now, I can grant myself a moment.

Had I ever spent so many hours doing nothing? Playing Bridge while gossiping and paying no attention to the cards. Talking to Clara until the early hours. Sharing a moment of vulnerability with Solange. It would be all too easy to acclimate myself to this.

As much as I may want a fire, I wouldn't want the warmth to cut through Widdershin's chilly embrace. The house seems dead and inhospitable at a glance, but that is just part of its charm.

The library and its hidden treasure can wait until tomorrow. Today is for Deirdre Doyle.

***

I wake the next morning, hoping for my first, deep breath to be the comforting dampness pervading Widdershin Isle. It struck me as off-putting and wild those first few days, but now it represents freedom. Something I have never had before. Or, at least not to the extent to which I have it now. I haven't done anything for days, and no one has said a word against me for it.

But my first breath isn't damp and welcoming. It's wet and foul, stinking of filth.

More, my hair is wet. My eyes snap open, and I try to bolt upright, but something heavy weighs on my chest.

The garden cat hops off me and slinks to the pillow to show off the massive, half-chewed rat carcass there. I barely hold back the scream as I scramble away from the cat's offering. The cat observes me from where it sits on the pillow, then loses interest and washes its paw.

"I suppose I should be thankful. I can't imagine you did this for the grumpy old lawyer."

The cat pauses washing to consider me. The pale golden eyes draw me in yet again, analyzing me with beastial intelligence.

"If we're to be friends, we should become acquainted. Even if we weren't friends, it would be rude not to introduce myself." I bite my lip as it dawns on me that I'm having a conversation with a cat. Maybe a few weeks alone on the island are taking a toll on me. I continue. "I'm Violet. Violet Bow. Well, Primrose, as you will hear Mr. Sparrow refer to me. That's my maiden name. He doesn't know I'm married, and I'll thank you not to tell him."

The cat, of course, says nothing.

"Is there really enough to eat on this little island for a colony of cats? Or are you the only one? You probably lived here with Erasmus and Sara. I wish you could tell me what they were like. Not that it should matter. I'm not here for that, but I'm curious."

The cat goes back to washing, now deeply invested in its flank and chest. Mostly dark gray, but with white feet, I only barely manage to resist petting it, deciding I don't want to disturb its rhythm.

Somewhere in the one-sided discussion, I decided the cat is a he. Something about his quiet, giving nature reminds me of a dashing young man I knew before Edmund, Mr. Jakob Vogel. He was tall, strong, charming, but with a quiet intelligence and gentle touch. So much like Asa. I must have a type.

I wanted to love him. I did love him.

I guess I still do, I just hadn't allowed myself to remember that. Proof never surfaced, but I know it was Edmund who spread the rumors that led to Jakob and his family being run out of town. And yet, I still married Edmund.

"*If the world were only ours, Violet... I would ask for your hand this very hour. But it isn't, is it? And I will not see you caged because of me.*"

Those were the last words that Jakob said to me, and I can hear them as clearly as when he whispered them on the dock two years ago. The sun setting behind me burned gold into his amber eyes. His calloused, ink-stained fingers brought mine to his lips for a final kiss. Then he was gone.

"Would it be odd for me to call you Jakob?" I ask the cat. "If I can talk to you, maybe I can pretend I'm talking to him still."

The cat, if possible, loses further interest in me. After a deep stretch, he jumps from the bed and slinks through the open door to the veranda.

"Fine. We'll think of another name."

I watch him go, then turn to the ruined pillow. No amount of soaking and scrubbing, even with a pantry bursting with all the finest French soaps, could I ever use the pillow again. The rat's body weighs down the middle as I lift it by pinching it in the corners at arm's length. The urge to retch is strong, but I get to the door the cat had exited through, pull it open with a toe, step out onto the veranda, and toss the whole thing, pillow and corpse, into the garden below.

With hands on the railing, I lift my nose to the clear blue morning. Had it been so clear since Mr. Farlow first brought me here on his stinking boat? Why hadn't I found Captain Carver to bring me over, and how different would my stay have been with him setting a vastly different precedent?

How many hours had I spent considering that very question, with details fueled by the nanny's books? A blush creeps up my neck just thinking about it.

The veranda is about seven feet deep, perfect for relaxing with a mint julep after a long day of... whatever Erasmus Vale's profession was. The newspaper article had called him a "prominent shipwright and gentleman of leisure", which I understood to mean he came from old money and never knew a hard day's work. I bet the view was spectacular on a clear evening, when the garden was at its best, with the sun setting behind Chatham. There haven't been many clear nights since I set foot on the island. Certainly none since or before the night I returned from town and watched, grinning, as the White Rider wandered aimlessly through the awful garden.

Today, though, is starting out lovely. The air is heavy and still, perfect for savoring a mint julep. If I had a head for gin, I might mix one and sip on it while reading the next book from the attic while I can in the natural light. I never had much tolerance for liquor, though. But reading in the open air will be good for my constitution after being confined to the library's dark corners for so long, eating packaged and canned foods... The fresh things from town are long gone, leaving me with cans and jars, but luckily, Widdershin saps my appetite, making it easy to ration. I prefer not to think about how long the eggs and oats have been in that cellar.

As I walk to the two weathered wooden chairs on the far end of the veranda, a book on the armrest of one of them hurries my pace. Someone already had my idea of reading outdoors, but Widdershin has seen no other visitors since Mr. Sparrow's hasty departure.

A pentagram and eye are embossed into the cover. I trace the grooves to the gold clasp, which appears to have been recently forced open. I immediately recognize the handwriting from the single page I found, and flipping through, I note several others torn from the journal. They weren't neatly removed, but grabbed in a fist and ripped, evidenced by the creases and damage to the remaining pages. How long had this been exposed to the elements? Weeks, since Mr. Sparrow sat out here reading it? Or years before that? As evidenced by Lavinia's room, time only moves where it wants to on Widdershin.

No, Mr. Sparrow must have left this out there. He mentioned a journal.

The first entry, dated April 2, 1840, is penned in a neat, flourishing hand. The handwriting degrades as it goes, as does the care to mark the date of penning. According to the preceding page, the last entry dates back to the late 1850s.

Almost twenty years of Erasmus Vale's life, a priceless relic to someone sharing the man's interests, and Mr. Sparrow left it out in a rainstorm for weeks. I can forget the rest of the library; this is it. If a buyer from overseas is willing to pay such a sum for the collection, this journal will be the crowning jewel. Yet if it had been Mr. Sparrow reading this, why didn't he mention it on the telephone? Had the Witch's Wail scrambled his mind so badly? Or had it been the laudenum?

I relax into the seat, the journal on my knees, flipping the crisp pages and delicately tracing my fingers over the words, feeling where the ink has gathered in places and the quill has dented the parchment. Mr. Vale's words are as tactile as they are rambling. I reach another point where at least a half dozen pages are torn out at once. Had he removed them in a fit of passion, or perhaps Sara? It seems unlikely that Mr. Sparrow absconded with the pages wadded in his pocket. Though... maybe he had. Maybe he read passages over the telephone to convince the buyer. Why, then, would he not take the entire journal as he fled the island? If I can find the missing pages, if they still exist, Mr. Sparrow can ask anything of the German fellow, or so I fancy.

Inhale. Exhale. I pull myself back from the spiral of pointless unknowns.

The morning slips by while I absently run fingers over Erasmus Vale's words, as if I might better understand him by learning the texture of his pen stroke. I have gone through the entire journal, reading very little, more enamoured with the slow evolution of his script. I glean enough in a phrase here and there that Mr. Vale heard what drove Mr. Sparrow from the island. He, too, called it the Witch's Wail. I thought I'd coined that myself, but maybe I saw it somewhere without noticing. But where it drove Mr. Sparrow to near-insanity within a night, Mr. Vale seemed more interested in understanding, and thus capturing, the essence and power of the Witch and Widdershin Isle.

My stomach grumbles. The cat woke me early, but what time was it now without breakfast? Before closing it, I focus on the entry my idle wanderings left me at.

April 9th, 1843 – Widdershin Isle

I stepped onto the island today. Alone.

The trees lean inward, but the center—where the sun lands—is clear and flat, as if made for something. I stood there and felt... known. Not seen, not judged—known.

The air is brined and still. The birds do not sing here. The soil is soft and yet nothing grows without force.

I laid a white stone at the center. Not a marker, but a promise.

I do not intend to tame this place. I only wish to earn its silence.

Had this been his first time on the island, or the first time without company? Did the fisherman at the tavern call him mad for coming to the island alone? Did he consider himself brave? I admit I had similar feelings, asking to be taken to a cursed island and ignoring the locals' warnings, though I didn't allow myself to acknowledge them in the moment. I have never felt as I do here: peaceful and free. I try not to follow that line of thought to the natural conclusion that Erasmus Vale went mad while living on this island, and my early feelings mirror his.

And, curious... I had thought the trees were cleared for the house, but they have never encroached on the place where the manor would stand. Is it from a flaw in the soil? Perhaps providence, knowing the house should one day take this place, though the dust and decay might show Nature's regret in that decision.

Before I close the journal, my eyes return to a scribbled line.

"I laid a white stone..."

I snort and smirk. That's one mystery solved.

My heart jumps to my throat as something shrieks in the garden. The cat is back to work.

So, too, should I.

Twenty-Five

I cannot stay in the room I have been in for the last few weeks. Though I changed the sheets with another musty set from the linen closet, I still smell the cat's gift. My hair feels damp as soon as I rest it on the other pillow. It may all be my imagination, as so much here is, but with a whole house to choose from, there is no reason to stay here.

So, I moved.

I tried one of the two rooms facing the back of the house, but there was something about the view, to the forest with its hidden graves, that I found unnerving. The rooms in the front have larger windows that open onto the veranda, and although the garden is gnarled and overgrown, looking out over it to the dock and water beyond is pleasant. Better than the trees in back, which feel far too close, choking out any view other than them.

I don't dare sleep where Mr. Sparrow had, which, as I would never consider the tiny room in the attic, leaves one final option. Lavinia's bed is too firm, too ungiving, as if it rejects me. I lie atop it, barely denting the duvet, and stare at the lace canopy, finding and losing patterns in the stitching, imagining the long hours spent weaving it, only for it to fall into decay, forgotten. Sleep eludes me, as it has for the last four days since finding Erasmus Vale's journal. I read it as my constitution allows. The man's heavy, poetic tones burrow into my mind, each highlighting something deeper and darker that he left unsaid, unwritten. He names his son Nathaniel and mentions two others indirectly. Fewer than I found obituaries for. The man died only a few years ago, yet piecing together his life comes in fragments like a puzzle. To be fair, I am not actively trying to learn about him.

My morning coffee is long cold, barely touched, but I have started on the shelves along the north wing of the library. With a focus on occult books only, the work progresses at a faster pace. I pull one in ten to record in the ledger, while leaving the others neatly arrayed, though unorganized. Some are obvious from the title, such as predicting or controlling weather, or unusual things to do with plants or trees as they grow. Others are collections of children's nursery rhymes with pages dog-eared at a poem about the Rider in White or a Witch in the Storm. Why can't children chant about pleasant things?

I reach blindly to the back of the bottom shelf, fingers fumbling for any stray pages, perhaps from a certain journal, and instead pull out a small cream-colored box with—

I rush it to the window, to better see the logo stamped into the thin cardboard and ensure my tired eyes aren't playing some cruel trick. Across the lid is the image of an inkwell sprouting a feathered quill with "PRIMROSE STATIONERY COMPANY, Portland, Maine" below it. I stocked hundreds of such boxes in my younger years. I might have handled this exact one. With trembling fingers, I set the box on the desk and pry it open, breathing deeply of the old ink. The smell, that of my childhood, brings me back to long nights in the back of my father's shop. I read by candlelight as he repaired and cleaned typewriters, and my mother balanced the day's books or prepared an order. If I close my eyes and ignore the insects droning beyond the window, I can hear the unsteady clack-clack-clak from my father and my mother's tuneless humming.

I shake my head before falling too deep into the reverie.

Inside the box sit five blackened spools of Evertrue Ink. Looking like withered fruit, their ribbons are tangled and looped over each other. A receipt rests across them, folded once and foxed at the edges, but I recognize the handwriting where the ink bleeds through the thin paper: My father's.

A card flutters loose from the lid, its gold script faded, yet legible, especially since I know it well. I thought of the slogan stamped into it when I was twelve.

"Ink Saved Is Ink Earned — Return Your Used Ribbons and Refill for Less!"

My father ran a special deal where customers could return their used box of six for a discount. My mother rolled her eyes at the idea of such a marketing gimmick at first, saying we had no need for everyone's trash. Her tune changed quickly when she tallied the repeat business.

Mr. Erasmus Vale was one such repeat customer.

That is not enough to say that he knew my parents. My father sold hundreds of these boxes a year. One thing is certain: the box originally contained six, but now holds five. The missing spool could mean it is now on a typewriter somewhere in the house, perhaps with a stack of paper beside it containing the last ramblings of Erasmus Vale.

Where, though? I have been through the bedrooms, the attic, and even found Sara's little sanctuary beyond the hall of portraits up there. The layout of Widdershin House unfolds in my mind as I search for a space I have yet to uncover. The front basement. The bolted room in the kitchen cellar hiding the photographs and the Widdershin Lodestone. The boathouse I never attempted to find.

Then, I blink with the obvious fact that comes to the front of my mind. I stepped into the dining room with Mr. Sparrow, but I have not gone back since. Moreover, there are two other full rooms on the main level that I have never considered entering. What was the label in the fuse box? A drawing room? I pass it every time I go down to the kitchen, yet I never look in. That could be filled to the rafters with more tomes to add to the collection. It might be the perfect location, with windows open to the garden, letting in a fresh breeze of roses and lilacs, for stabbing at the keys of a well-used typewriter.

When I first stepped up to Widdershin, I wondered if I have an adventurous nature. Apparently, I don't.

My mind spins as my hands go through the mechanical process of closing up the box of ink. Though everything since I arrived on the island has happened by coincidence, it's difficult to say Widdershin has not acted as a force, slowly revealing itself to me. Each new mystery is unearthed just as I set aside the last, either answered or abandoned. But to make me ignore a full half of the ground floor? Was it not ready for me to see what those rooms hold, as if this is a bard's tale that must be recited in order? No. There is nothing supernatural at play here. The house, or some essence within it, is not pulling me forward by a string. Yet, thinking back on the last few weeks, I have never felt the slightest interest in exploring the main level. Now I can't get out of the library and down the stairs fast enough.

Downstairs, immediately beside the front door, the space extends to a massive ballroom. The sheer openness and vacancy of the room call to me, begging to answer the question of how I could have left it unnoticed for so many weeks. Cobwebs hang from the corners in sheets, obscuring the cracked wallpaper. Dried leaves congregate along the outer walls. Where the rest of Widdershin House gives a sense of neglect, the ballroom is abandoned, perhaps never once used. Who, after all, would come to a party on a cursed island? Erasmus Vale must have felt it necessary when designing the house. Or, more likely, he plucked the manor's layout from a catalog with intentions that never came to fruition.

I walk around the room's perimeter, noting where the wallpaper is darker, as if paintings have been removed recently, leaving the virgin space behind them fresh and exposed. Maybe the missing art is that which I saw lining the attic. Nothing else in the house felt removed, so why is this room picked bare?

Ghosts and curses may not be real, but the act of tearing portraits from the wall will echo through the decades.

It is not a question I can answer. I see no books, loose journal pages, or typewriters. Nothing to keep me here. Widdershin has fed me another dollop of mystery, but I must be content to move on. If nothing else, I am learning to accept the futility of unanswerable questions. I'll be gone from Widdershin soon and leave behind whatever fragments of mysteries are yet unsolved.

With a last slow circling in the room's center, I envision it packed with partygoers. The men's cigars form a haze that the ladies' fans can't disperse. The string quartet I imagined on the back patio is here, now perfectly tuned, though playing in a minor key. The merriment doesn't last long with Erasmus Vale watching over it with a sour sneer.

I pause, mid-step. I had been dancing a slow waltz without knowing it.

The parlor sits across the hall, pristine and fresh, diametrically opposed to the ballroom. Time moves through Widdershin House at its own pace.

A velvet-trimmed couch and three matching chairs face a low table masterfully crafted of the same dark wood that permeates the house. Roses and fanciful creatures from myth are carved into the wood around the tall windows facing out to the garden, and the gauzy lace curtains are in near-perfect condition. The portrait above the hearth, of a woman in her later forties wearing a stiff collar and billowing black dress, staring down her nose, might be Sara Vale. In every other portrait of her, she sits or stands beside Erasmus, lost and forgotten. The smile in her vacation snapshots makes her almost unrecognizable. This is the image of the mistress of the house, powerful and self-assured.

I can hardly take my eyes from hers, worried as if I might spill something in her watchful presence. Moving across the room, I trace fingers along the buffet with a crystal decanter of wine and a full dozen matching goblets, all without a spec of dust. The candlesticks look recently polished. Even the rug is neat and clean, as if it were taken off the boat from Turkey and rolled out just this morning. Afternoon light refracts through the thousand glass shards of the chandelier hanging in the center of the ceiling, spreading light to every corner.

Why is this room untouched by time? Surely Mr. Sparrow wasn't down here, polishing and sweeping while I worked upstairs. There's no easy explanation for it; nothing short of the supernatural.

A telephone rings from between the glasses on the buffet table, and I fumble to answer it.

"Yes?"

"Miss Primrose, the buyer was quite pleased with the list you forwarded to me. He asked where you were trained, and I told him you were not. Then, he inquired if you would be interested in a position with his patron, but I digress. He wishes to move to the next step, which is a personal tour of the library."

I am trained. My work in the Portal District Library more than prepared me for the task, but it's too much to ask that the lawyer remember any of that.

"Mr. Sparrow, hello. That is amazing! Your ears must have been burning because I've found another item that will be the star of the collection."

"I have never cared for that expression, but go on."

"Erasmus Vale's personal journal, though it is incomplete. He mostly discusses topics beyond my ken, but I imagine anyone so interested in Mr. Vale's work will be delighted to have this."

There is no response for a long span of breaths, just a sound that might be chewing.

"Astounding," he finally says. "We'll be there in a week and a half. I'll need everything sorted and labeled, ready for immediate shipping. I want this transaction done the moment the paperwork is signed."

I press the receiver tighter to my ear, unsure I heard everything correctly. "A week and a half? I can't possibly finish by then. I'm maybe halfway, no, a third, done cataloguing, but how do you want them sorted? Alphabetically? By topic?"

"Do your best, Miss Primrose. With Mr. Vale's reputation and your information, this buyer is extremely interested in the entire collection and has agreed, sight unseen, to a majority sum of the estimated value. Mr. Vale's journal may not be of monetary value, but the sentimentality of it will sweeten the deal."

"A team might be able to get through the library in that time, but I couldn't do it alone," I say.

Again, silence is his response for several rasping breaths.

"Are you not up to the challenge, Miss Primrose? If I hire the team you suggest, that will only significantly reduce your share. My memory was not perfect as Captain Carver took me away, but I clearly recall your insistence on getting paid. Is that no longer the case? What, might I ask, has changed your mind? Guilt, perhaps?"

His choice of words is too intentional. He knows what I did to him, but pride keeps him from making an outright accusation.

"No, Mr. Sparrow. Nothing has changed. You took me by surprise, that's all. I'll..." I have barely touched the books in the hall along the house's North face, which accounts for about half of the collection. But, unless he tries some sneaky lawyer tricks, I'm guaranteed at least half the amount I had been expecting, which is still so much more than I need. "I will devise a scheme for putting the collection's most coveted pieces at the front, don't you worry. This German fellow will double his price and still feel as though he's getting a bargain."

"That's a good girl. I will see you soon."

"What was that about a job offer?"

The line crackles with Mr. Sparrow scraping his end of the connection, and it goes silent.

"Miserable old prig."

The sudden windfall from this work will go a long way, but lasting employment with a foreign office? Sponsorship in another country to continue the work I love? Germany, I hear, is doing well right now, after The War. It's too good to fantasize about in this moment, too great a hope to hang onto with so little known and nothing assured. I came downstairs for a reason, and by the grace of God, I will not allow myself to be distracted by idle fancy.

There, in the corner, is a small table with a single chair. Atop the table, beside a tray of neatly stacked paper, rests an Altamont No.5. The No.5 had issues, but the Altamont No.7, with its low rate of jamming and sleek curves, was an easy sell for years and the basis for my father's small fortune. It was likely a fleet of Altamonts that my father sold to Mr. Sparrow's firm, securing what would enable my family to move to Maine and settle with a shop. My mother often joked about how my father had no choice but to love her forever, because moving the behemoths gave her the arms of a sailor, and no man would want her again.

She also joked about dropping one on his head at night. At least, I assume she was joking. Either way, she never did it.

I settle into the chair and let my fingertips play over the round, silver keys, feeling the embossed raising of each letter. It was at a typewriter just like this one that I told my father I wanted to learn to type so that I could be a great writer, like Jane Austen or Mary Shelley. He would laugh, without cruelty, and tell me that knowing how to type and knowing how to write are unrelated skills. None of my examples had seen a typewriter or half of our modern conveniences. Mary Shelley wrote with a goose feather quill by the light from beeswax tapers. So that was how I began my writing, all while trying to hide how my hand and wrist cramped. My father laughed again and told me that just because greatness was achieved without modern technology, that is no excuse to forgo the advancements available.

The lesson I wish he had instilled in me is that knowing how to write and knowing how to write *well* are also unrelated skills. I'm glad he was only ever supportive.

The ink reel bears the familiar Evertrue Ink stylized name, thus closing the case on what happened to the missing ribbon. Erasmus Vale would have sat exactly where I am now, punching out his addled thoughts until the letters were too faint. He would have packaged up the reel with the others and sent it, for he surely wouldn't go himself, to Primrose Stationery Company for a refill. It seems odd that a man of such apparent prosperity would have cared for my father's minor discount, but Mr. Vale would not have held onto wealth by squandering it. Or maybe he saved every penny after his philanthropic adventures drained him, funding every mad person who saw a link between their tea leaves and the autumn's crops.

I turn over the stack of paper held down by a flat stone beside the typewriter. "Of Shadows and Memory in Maritime Land-forms" is typed across the center. Not just typed, but stabbed. The typist was clearly a novice, using far more force than necessary. I hold the edge of the pages tightly and flip through, noting how the ink fades and surges back to life as the spool was reused more than once, then replaced.

The words mean nothing, as if they discuss an advanced topic I know too little to understand, but this, even beyond his journal, will be the crowning gem of the Widdershin Collection. A piece directly from the mind of Mr. Erasmus Ambrose Vale. This is it, as plainly as a one-way ticket to Paris, France. I hope Mr. Sparrow allows me into the room when the German buyer comes to inspect the library, so that I might be the one to reveal this masterpiece.

On the other side of the typewriter is a glass, wide and squat, exactly like the one I gave to the lawyer. Lipstick is faint, but clear, on the rim, throwing my image of the room upside down. I now see Sara sitting where I am now, typing as Erasmus lounges across the couch, a cigar in one hand and a drink in the other. He sloshes whiskey when the topic agitates him, which it often does. Sara watches the fabric soak up the booze, quietly seething. Her life was just as quickly gone, sponged into her husband's.

With this new treasure, concerns for the missing journal pages drift from my thoughts, gone as easily as booze soaking into velvet. Worries for how I might order the library in preparation for shipping flit away just as easily. I carefully stack the manifesto onto its tray, weighed down by the flat stone. If only Mr. Sparrow had called twenty minutes later. He would have told me to put my feet up and relax after finding this gem.

Twenty-Six

I 'm curled comfortably before the hellmouth hearth, reading the last of the books from the attic. I restarted the series thrice in an effort to prolong reaching its end. Deirdre Doyle is fast approaching the climax of a romantic arc hinted at since the first book. When I started, I thought they were a step above trash. Now I understand the author's delicate genius, which wraps and obscures complex subjects that can only be noticed through careful study.

It's not Shakespeare, but it isn't too far off.

Or I may be allowing myself to invent depth that isn't there as an excuse to read it again.

The first crash of thunder hits, enough to make me jump, but only because I was so engrossed in a particularly steamy scene. The lights dim, but flicker back to full after a beat. To be safe, I note the nearest candle and matches on the mantle. Another crash, sounding as though it might be from a strike immediately on the other side of the wall, but I barely hear it, or the next. The world is nothing but that of Deirdre Doyle.

What I can't ignore is the ringing. Someone is calling, and just as the book is getting to its thrilling climax. I consider ignoring it, but if Mr. Sparrow is calling with bad news about the seller, that would change everything about what I've spent the last week doing. Or rather, not doing. I'll readily admit that my work ethic has slipped since I discovered the manuscript.

Grumbling the whole way, I leave my nest.

"Yes?"

Static is the only reply.

"I can't hear anything. Maybe it's the storm? Speak up."

There is still only static, but I can sense that there is someone on the other end.

"Mr. Sparrow, is this you?"

A rhythmic popping joins the static, but no one speaks.

"Tell your buyer I have found something exciting. Something of exceptional value. I don't want to tell you what it is, not over the telephone, but they should be very excited to see it next week."

There is something more than static. Breathing, perhaps? Slow and menacing.

"Mr. Sparrow?"

For a moment, I hear nothing but the storm, the line shivering with static. Then, not even that, just a hollow emptiness, as if the cut were cut at the root. I hold the receiver for a moment, dreading the thought of who else might know I am here, that there is anyone to call at the Widdershin House. To whom did I just verify my presence, alone, on this island?

Thunder crashes, and this time, I jump from pure nerves. The storm is holding directly over the island, and that was not Mr. Sparrow on the telephone.

I think of retiring early, with the thought that I might sleep through the storm and wake to another foggy morning. This may all appear as a silly worry tomorrow. Leaving everything in the open, I switch off the library lights and stalk down the hall to Lavinia's room. Each flash of lightning across the carpeted path is accompanied by an immediate boom that rattles the artwork and my teeth. I reach the door with my nerves intact, though only barely. When I turn on the lights, the cat looks up at me from the end of the bed, decides I am uninteresting, and settles back in for the night, completely uncaring about the tempest circling the house.

"That was Mr. Sparrow on the telephone. The storm interfered with the connection. That's all."

A deafening crack like the earth splitting in two erupts behind me. Glass explodes against my back, tossing me forward, and the world snaps to black.

***

I have never fainted from fright, and have rolled my eyes at the women in my books who do. Now I understand. When a body is so overcome by shock, fear, or another intense emotion, it simply cannot function. When the mind cannot cope with what it is given, it shuts down and waits for things to change.

My arm and cheek hurt from where they must have hit the floor. Wind rushes in behind me, carrying a kiss of rain.

I force myself to get on all fours and crawl. If I can make it to the bed, I will be safe from whatever hell opened on the other side of the house. Had lightning struck it? If the roof is on fire, I should flee. I should rush back to the library for Mr. Vale's manifesto and flee into the night. How long would I remain stranded on the island before someone notices the house has burned down and comes for me?

I reach the bed, but something tickles my nose as I rise up. I shriek and fall backward. The next distant flash outlines the cat sitting on the edge of the bed, staring down at me as though nothing had happened. He would know. If there is further danger, if the attic were ablaze above us, he would flee.

After a moment to gather my wits, I use the bed's corner post to pull myself to standing. Fumbling across the wallpaper, I find the light switch, but of course, it does nothing. A blown fuse or more, there is nothing I can do in the middle of the night. My hands still tremble as I light a candle, and the cat watches with waning interest.

The storm moved on while I lay sprawled in Lavinia's doorway, but the rain still falls in sheets down the tree thrust through the window in the bedroom across the hall. The ceiling is damaged and bowing downward, though the candle's timid light can barely reach it for me to verify. The room above, the room I still think of as the nursery, must be in ruins. While I hope the power outage is something wider, caused by the storm, and will be repaired within a few days on the mainland, I sense the damage is local.

Nature has come to bring down Widdershin House.

Below, the kitchen will be a wreck by morning due to water damage. My dwindling food stocks in the cellar will be floating by then. What if the tree took out the telephone line, as well? How could I signal a request for rescue? Maybe there is a flare in the boat house, wherever that is. Why didn't I take the one Asa offered when he left with Mr. Sparrow?

Defeated, I pull the door closed. This may be the beginning of my end at Widdershin House, or indeed the end of Widdershin House itself, but if I can shut out this catastrophic damage for now, maybe I can delay it just a little while.

There is nothing I can do tonight. There is probably nothing I can do tomorrow, but that remains to be seen. I pull off my wet dress and get into bed. Within a few moments, the cat stands, circles, and falls heavily against the side of my leg. Somewhere in the rhythmic rocking of his grooming, I find sleep.

Twenty-Seven

Dawn filters through the trees behind the house, outlining the one resting through the window, still dripping water onto the rugs that are already soaked through. Not just through the window, it's through the wall. The bed is a wreck, and I try not to think too long about what my fate would have been had I selected this as my new sleeping quarters. I should try the telephone, try to signal for help, and return to the mainland. A tree smashed through the wall surely has a negative impact on the house's structural soundness. Though there is some solace in thinking this has never happened before in the Widdershin House's long life. The chances of it happening again, of the next storm tossing a tree into Lavinia's room and onto me, are astronomical, though, not zero.

For no reason other than because it's right there, I open the door to the attic. The staircase is smashed in, impassable, halfway up.

I survey the back property from the library window with pity. Mr. Sparrow hired me to assist in selling the literary collection, but if his job included selling the manor and island, last night's storm made his job ten times more difficult. A half dozen trees, each twice as tall as the house, are toppled, either barely leaning against their neighbors or fully knocked to the earth, their roots a gnarled mass of mud. Two, that I can see, are near enough to the house that a slight change in the wind last night might have brought the whole manor down on my head.

The telephone is nothing but a decoration, as dead as the light switch. I will have to find another means of signalling for help.

Widdershin House is quieter than usual as I descend the stairs. It's an oppressive silence, not an absence of sound, as if beams, plaster, and wallpaper are holding their breath in anticipation. The house is licking its wounds, knowing a mortal blow has been struck, and hopes to avoid its hunter just a moment longer.

Under the stairs, three fuses are blown, and the knife switch is blackened. It's a small wonder the whole thing didn't throw a spark last night to bring down the house from within the walls. The dim light shimmers across the water a few steps down. The front basement is now completely flooded. I shudder, thinking about the brackish state of that water, of the drowned rats, and how they would soon make the house unlivable.

The back cellar under the kitchen fared better. The water only reaches the third step from the bottom. There was no sign of previous flooding down there. Last night's storm was unlike anything this island, or at least this house, has survived before.

As I step out the back door, an unseasonable chill greets me, heavy with the sogginess dripping from tree limbs and pooling between the stones under my feet. The view is the same as the last time I saw this space, if not more chaotic from the downed trees. That last time was also the first. Almost six weeks on this island, and have I really only left the back door of the house once? It's the same, yet fundamentally different. Nature makes itself known, remembered, or feared, with every sagging or broken limb.

Giving it a wide berth, I survey the tree that struck the corner of the house. The maple rests on the roof, completely obscuring a third of the back. The weight will shift with every gust until it overtakes the manor's backbone. This tree, which took root a hundred years before the United States won her freedom, is just the opening volley in nature's slow assault. It might take another ten years, but Widdershin House has no chance in this battle.

I look from the house, down the tree's length, to the root ball taller than me. What a shame that such a mighty tree would fall to the soaked earth and a strong wind.

Nothing can last forever.

My eye lingers on the roots and the mud clinging to them. Before my mind can turn too long on the wonders of how such chaos below can organize into the beauty above, I spy something I shouldn't. Or, at least...

I move closer, careful to avoid the wet grass and clumps of muck. I squint, though what I'm seeing is obvious.

The edge of an iron box among the roots.

I have more dresses, and the cisterns are overflowing with fresh, though cold, water to clean up.

I plunge my hands into the cold mud, feeling the edges of the box, assuring myself that this is real. The tree has done its duty holding this unknown treasure, and I easily pull it free. Made of engraved wrought iron, the box is eight inches on a side and half as deep. The weight, although manageable, is uncomfortable, and I rush it back to the table by the back door.

There is no lock, only a turning clasp to keep it shut. That snaps as I turn it, and the hinges crumble and crack as I lift the lid. The box has fulfilled its purpose for existence and is dying before my eyes. Within, oiled leather covers something that fits perfectly into the space. I pull away the damp hide to reveal a cedar box with "DB" carved into it. A box in a box. Someone really wanted the contents protected.

DB... No... I shake away any mounting conclusions. This will reveal itself within a few breaths.

There is just enough space for me to slide my fingers inside the iron box and pull out the cedar one. There are no latches or hinges; the lid fits snugly into the body. My time at the Portland District Library taught me something of the care and handling of ancient or delicate artifacts and manuscripts. All of that is tossed aside as I wipe my hands on the leather and force the swollen wood box open with a grunt.

Within it, sitting atop another layer of things wrapped in oiled leather, a note awaits me. The linen should not have survived its time in the ground, a testament to the layers of wax expertly applied to it. Other than a bit of wear at the edges, as nature attempted to destroy it, the note could have been written a week ago.

The house is still. I have barred the door. I do not think it matters.

He came in the night as I knew he would. The rider, at last. His voice was no longer my husband's. It was hunger and hatred given breath.

I thought perhaps I would see a sign—a shadow behind his eyes, the Devil's hand upon his shoulder. Surely such evil must bear a mark.

But there was nothing. No dark spirit. No foul enchantment. Only a man who believed himself righteous in his violence. And that was worse.

He raised his hand to strike me. I asked aloud for the Lord's mercy, for some grace to descend between us. None came. Not even the Devil bothered with him.

We struggled. He dragged me toward the cliffs. I remember the sky: clean and wide, without witness.

I gave him fight, thought Samsom could not match his strength. But, as David brought down mighty Goliath, a stray pebble underfoot was all I required. When his balance broke, I knew I was free.

The blood, the endless blood, where his head struck

the stone. I knew it should have ended him, yet I would not trust such a thing to the mercy—or neglect—of any wandering Providence. His chest shook with gasps as a dying fish. His eyes, wide and unseeing, searched for help that would never come. His lips moved with a verse no one would hear. I fetched this knife—the same I once took from Master Josiah Pike—and drew it across his throat, sure and slow.

Then I gave him to the sea.

I stood there after. Waiting to feel sorrow. Waiting to feel anything but relief.

I have sinned, or so they will say. But I will live. I will live until this island no longer wants me or an uncaring power comes to fetch me.

Deliverance Black
June 1693

Widdershin House, Widdershin Isle, is tired of holding its secret, is ready to confess its past, and so it throws everything upon me. It has served me morsels as it thinks I am ready, and now it's time for the main course.

Deliverance Black stood where I do now, two hundred and thirty years ago. Having killed her husband, she was free at last.

I trace fingers across her cold words. She drew the knife across his throat. She gave him to the sea. Had she been so clear in the moment, or had her passions cooled before penning this passage? Even as Absalom dragged her to the cliffs, probably to toss her off the bluff, she still held some thread of hope for Almighty intervention.

She received none, so she did what she must.

Within the second layer of oiled leather, I find a bundle that feels like a book wrapped in waxed vellum, a few bundles of herbs that still smell of sage and thyme, and a delicate dagger with a jeweled handle. It is not a murder weapon, not exactly. His fall to the rocks sealed Absalom's fate, but Deliverance used this to ensure her husband's demise. Or grant him a swift, merciful death. The point is still sharp enough to prick my thumb, and I suck at the ruby drop.

I unwrap the book next. Time has been less kind to it, leaving the hard leather binding cracked and flaking. The pages resist me, threatening to cling to each other and rip, rather than allowing me in. Persistence wins, and I pull apart two pages enough to see who has signed the entry.

Absalom.

The writing is little more than chicken scratch, barely legible when fresh.

I shift the journal in my grip, searching for a better light to read the entry.

December 1692

She does not speak. I do not need her words.

The devil's mark is not always seen. It is quiet, like her. It simmers beneath the skin—how she stares when I pray, how she writes her dreams, how she withholds herself. She has always withheld herself.

She offered me cider the night I fell ill. Sweet as sin. She touched the cup.

I awoke and could not move my legs. She said it was the Lord's will.

Her fingers bruise fruit just by picking it.

I know what must be done. I brought the papers. The Lord sees my cause.

If I die, let this record testify: She was not my wife. She was the devil's bride.

My blood chills with every line. I never asked for this knowledge, but Widdershin Isle forces it upon me. Absalom accused Deliverance of witchcraft in December. She fled in January and thought she was free, here, until he arrived for her in June.

Time has slipped away for me, such that I am unsure of the exact date, but I know it is currently June.

A deep crash rattles the door's glass beside me. Is the house falling apart?

I wrap the knife in a scrap of the leather, the book in its vellum, and tuck both into my satchel. I rush into the house, intent on saving Erasmus Vale's manuscript, if nothing else, but know right away that the crash wasn't a collapsing beam or falling art. It's something much worse.

The front door.

A man stands in the tiled entryway, wearing the white suit and hat that he always prefers while traveling. "White means wealth," he would say to me. He considers me with eyes narrowed by barely contained rage, his lip curls upward with a mirthless smirk.

"Violet. I've found you."

I bump into the glass doors behind me. There is nowhere to go. The knife weighs heavily at my hip, but do I possess the constitution to use it?

"Edmund."

Twenty-Eight

"You worried me, Violet. You didn't even leave a note. You were just... gone."

He's within arm's reach before I notice him move. He shoots out a hand to rest a palm on the glass beside my head, pinning me in place.

"How should I understand what you did to me, Violet? Help me to understand."

His aftershave overwhelms all my plans. Escape, freedom, Paris, the South Pacific with a rugged captain... gone in a cloud of citrus and clove. He's only taller than me by a few inches, but his presence fills my periphery. My world is nothing but Edmund.

"I... got a job."

"A job?" he snorts. "I take care of you, Violet. Don't I take care of you? Don't I buy you anything you want? What have you done to this dress that I bought for you?"

He picks at the sleeve. He's too close for me to look down at myself, but I know I'm covered in mud from pulling out the iron lockbox. Thank all the gods of fortune that I slipped on my old, dull gray thing today, rather than the new purple frock.

"I... I..." No words will come. Each uttered syllable is weaker than the last.

"You what? You worried me, Violet," he repeats and finally pushes from the glass. He turns his back on me to survey the kitchen and dining room on either side of the hall. "You took a job here? In this condemned pit on an island that God turned His back on? So far from any semblance of civilization? So far from me?"

He wheels back on me and must confuse my fear and disgust with guilt. He could never identify my emotions.

"The man who brought me over told me all about you, Violet. You were alone with him? A stinking fishmonger? Tell me he tried to touch you. Tell me, so I have a reason to..." He punches himself in the chest, breathing hard.

Asa wouldn't have betrayed me, which leaves... "Mr. Farlow? No. He wouldn't dare. I—"

He snorts. "All men would dare, Violet. It's our God-given right to dare. Only a stupid, silly girl would believe otherwise, and I wouldn't marry a stupid, silly girl."

The repetition of my name grates on my wrecked nerves, but also gives me something to grasp onto.

"I mean, he wouldn't dare cross you. I told him how powerful you are. Not directly, but I talked about you in a way such that he wouldn't do something to upset you."

He grunts, dismissing the topic, pleased for the moment that I might use the threat of him to fend off another man's advances.

Edmund is on me again, snatching up my left hand, twisting it painfully, and bringing it close to my nose. "Where, then, is your wedding ring?"

"Upstairs. I wouldn't risk getting it dirty or damaged with what I was doing outside." The first part comes easily, as it contains enough truth. My ring *is* upstairs, buried at the bottom of my suitcase. "Is Mr. Farlow still at the dock?" What is my plan? To pit Edmund against the fisherman?

"No. I knew you were here, so I dismissed him the moment I stepped off. He doesn't need to be any more involved in our relationship than he already is. When you came rushing in from the back, did you think I was your Mr. Sparrow? You thought I was him calling last night."

My heart sinks, surprising me that it could go any lower. Of course, it was him. I could sense the malevolence through the line, even if I hadn't recognized it at the time.

I force a smile, hoping Edmund can't tell it from a real one.

"I am so sorry, dear. I wrote you a letter before I left, but I was so excited by the opportunity. I probably packed it with my things, rather than leaving it on the table. You know how absent-minded I can be. How about I make you tea? I'm sure you're tired after such a long trip."

His scowl softens upon hearing "opportunity."

He waves for me to proceed, takes off his jacket and hat, tosses them over the back of a dining room chair, and falls into another. I move to the kitchen and light the stove. The ceiling is darkened, but the water hasn't yet soaked through from upstairs. The tea, coffee, and a few other things I brought up from the cellar are, by some grace, untouched by the tree thrust through half the house. While the water rises to a boil, I search the cabinets again for a box of arsenic, but find none. It isn't until I'm considering searching the other bathroom for more laudanum that it strikes me what I actively want to do.

I drugged Mr. Sparrow to get him out of my way. I want Edmund gone forever.

My mother would be turning in her grave if she knew her daughter had such un-Christian thoughts. There must be a compromise. Edmund Bow is a businessman, but more so, he's a schemer. Nothing is too underhanded for him if he ends up with what he wants. Perhaps I can dangle the thought of some great opportunity in front of him like a carrot before a horse. Or cheese in a mousetrap.

When I enter the dining room with two steaming cups on a silver tray, he's leaning back in the chair, blowing a cigar smoke ring to the ceiling with his leather boots propped on the table. He watches me drop a sugar cube into his, then take a seat on the other side of the table.

Edmund looks up slowly. "Have we been apart too long? I take mine with cream."

"The cream is in the larder, but that was flooded with last night's storm."

He grunts and pushes the cup away from him. "Who is Sparrow?"

Good. He wants to start with his insecurities.

"Mr. Sparrow is the lawyer representing the Widdershin Estate: this house and its contents." I gesture to the room around us, much like the lawyer did when he arrived. "He was a friend of my parents and contacted me to organize the literary collection here."

"I see. And it never occurred to you that I might have something to say about that? That he should have come to me first? I am your husband, the master of my house. Is that why you waited until I was gone? So you could sneak away in the night? Like some..." He doesn't know how to finish the sentence, so he puffs on his cigar.

He may be the master of our house in Portland, but Widdershin has chosen me as its mistress. The cat certainly agrees, and I don't need more opinion than that.

"The timing is purely coincidental, dear. He could have sent me the letter a month earlier or two later, when you were at home. And I did write you, but you know how I am."

"Yes." He sucks on his lower lip for a long moment. "I know you would never betray me. That is why it came as such a shock when I returned to an empty house. How much money is in this? It better be worth my time."

My feelings surge forward. My mother's spinning corpse be damned. The knife at my hip still has a keen edge, waiting to spill blood. But I focus on keeping my feet planted on the floor and my palms flat on the table top.

"Many thousands of dollars. I was..." I choke back a sob, using what he would expect from an obedient, regretful wife to grant me a few breaths and come up with a story. "I was hoping to surprise you with a present."

His anger evaporates. "Thousands for some dusty books? When do we get paid?"

There should never have been this "we". There should have been me, Jakob Vogel, and an apartment in Paris. Captain Asa Carver and watching the sunset over the Philippines.

"Mr. Sparrow has a buyer coming... I fear I've lost track of time, but soon."

"You are forgetful, Violet," Edmund chuckles and takes out his pocket watch. The barest mention of time was enough for him to flash the gold and inlaid silver. "Soon, you say? A few nights for a tidy sum sounds reasonable. Think of it as an unplanned holiday."

"I should get back to work, though. Mr. Sparrow needs the library organized." I reach across the table for his teacup.

Quick as a snake, Edmund snatches my wrist. His brow creases. "Find a better way to say that, Violet. Do not let me think about how you are seeing to another man's needs."

I swallow the dryness in my throat and stare down at his fist. "I have work to do. You can watch me, but I worry you'll find it dull."

"So now you worry about me?" he scoffs, but releases me. I step back. "Show me your letter," he says.

"Letter?"

He sucks his teeth. "You're forgetful, but not stupid, Violet. The letter you meant for me to explain all this. You said you must have packed it by accident, in your overwhelming excitement. Bring it to me. I want to read how you justified letting me return to an empty house."

"Yes. Yes, of course. It must be in my things."

"Then fetch it so I can put off this nagging suspicion that you didn't want me to find you."

I have no plan, but the dark glint in his eye tells me that I'd better come up with one quickly.

"Right away, dear. I'm glad you did, honest. How... May I ask how you found me, so far from home?"

"I hired a detective, at no small expense, who specializes in this kind of thing. He hardly seemed worth the price. Just discovered that you were traveling without my name, Miss Primrose." He says it through clenched teeth.

I nod along with a false grin. "Very smart of you, dear. They wouldn't let me buy a steamer ticket if they knew I was married."

He accepts my lie with a dismissive wave and takes a long drag from his cigar.

I flee to the library and gasp for breath with the familiar tomes surrounding me. The shelves, which felt cozy and inviting only this morning, are now distant and cold. Dead trees bound with dead horses, filled with the words of dead people. There is no path forward that does not include Edmund. He will stay until Mr. Sparrow arrives. Mr. Sparrow will express confusion over the state of my marriage, further infuriating Edmund. The lawyer might cancel all contracts with me, or my husband might simply take the money for himself. Either way, we will return to Maine, and his leash around my neck would be that much tighter.

I snatch a loose piece of paper from the desk and scrawl out a quick note.

Dearest Edmund,

I do hope this letter finds you well. I've taken on a temporary engagement in Massachusetts, assisting with the cataloging of a private library. It was rather sudden, but I couldn't pass up the opportunity.

If you should need to reach me, Mr. Clarence Sparrow, Esq., of Boston, will gladly see your correspondence forwarded.

I shan't be away long, and will make it up to you in full upon my return.

Yours devotedly,

Vi

I read it back once, hating myself as I do, then fold it neatly before wadding it into a ball. Fleeing to Lavinia's room, I hope Edmund can't hear my movement on the first floor.

I only brought enough to fill one bag, but had since mingled my dresses with far nicer ones still hanging in the armoire. After tucking the note into my coat pocket, I make a show of tossing everything across the room. Across the bed, the chair before the vanity, over the fainting couch. A weight at my waist calls for attention, and I pull out the jeweled dagger and Absalom's journal from the satchel. I hide those in the nightstand drawer and slam it shut.

Tossing everything else out, I dig through my bag and slam my wedding band onto my finger.

"You've lived like this for weeks?"

I jump at Edmund's booming words from the doorway. He strolls in, nose curling as he looks over mine and Lavinia's discarded things. "They'd kick me out of the Club if they knew I allowed my wife to live in such squalor." He picks up my coat and pulls the note from the pocket between his index and middle fingers.

"You found it!" I jump a step toward him, but shy back. He went straight for the coat. I'd placed it too intentionally.

His face softens to neutral as he reads. "You certainly were in a hurry. You didn't let the ink dry before shoving it in your pocket. A strange thing to do when you meant to leave it for me in the open." He tosses the note onto the bed, his eyes dart around the room, taking in the soft, feminine details. "Of course, this is your room. I want to lie down before dinner."

I busy myself hanging everything back in the armoire while he sits on the fainting couch to pull off his boots.

Edmund says nothing, rolls himself onto the duvet, and tosses an arm over his eyes.

The nightstand is within arm's reach. I could wait until he's snoring, then use Deliverance's stolen knife as she had. History loves little more than repeating itself.

What would be more difficult to explain to Mr. Sparrow? Who is this man claiming to be my husband? Or who is this dead man?

She drew the knife across his throat.

My fingers creep to the drawer's edge and pull it open. It's silent, not a whisper or groan, as though the nightstand, or the house itself, is conspiring with me. I take Absalom's journal, then the knife, feeling its weight and sensing its purpose. The dagger knows what it did so long ago, and is eager to do it again. It would be so simple with how his neck is exposed. Even though I have no reason to know where to cut, that wouldn't matter with enough enthusiasm.

Edmund chokes back a snore and turns his face to the side, away from me.

This isn't me.

I rush back to the library, to the overstuffed chair in front of the demon's skull, and bury my face in my hands.

I sob until I am hoarse.

Twenty-Nine

December 1692

They looked at her, not me. Brother Pike said the sickness could be bad air. Bad air! As though the Lord's punishment floats like smoke. No. It is her.

She walks the woods before dawn. No woman does that unless called by devils. She hums to the trees. She kissed one once. I saw her.

My hair falls in clumps. My nails yellow. The Book trembles in my hands when I pray aloud.

She watches me like I am small.

The Elders did nothing. They fear what she is. I do not.

December 4th, 1692

She does not sleep as I do. She walks at night, bare-footed, in her shift. I asked her what drew her from bed and she said, "The moonlight." That is not an answer. That is a poem, and poems are dangerous.

Her hands are always warm. Even when mine are not. When I lie beside her, I forget my prayers. When I close my eyes, I dream of fire and roots.

She looks at the snow as though it might part for her. I saw her whisper to the hearth before she lit it.

Perhaps beauty itself is a kind of trial. Perhaps the Lord sends it to test the faithful. She is not a woman like the others.

I love her still, but I do not understand her. And what I do not understand, I must watch closely.

June 1693

They say the sea is calmer after noon. The fisherman takes no women, but I am no woman. He will take me.

They speak of an isle with no name, or many names. Widdershin, they whisper, like it is a curse. It waits in fog. A crown of pines. Guarded by a Hellcat, no doubt the same she took from home. Nothing could end the beast.

She built it, I think. Or the Devil built it for her. A temple to her pride.

I will knock. She will open. I will see her eyes and know. And then the Lord will have His due.

She will not laugh again.

I read Absalom's journal as I am able. Time in the earth was not friendly to the paper, but the man's frantic ramblings would have been difficult to decipher before the ink dried.

My heart breaks for Deliverance, a woman two centuries gone. Her mad husband accused her, placing a death sentence upon her head, then hunted her down when she fled.

The parallels to my plight cannot be ignored, as if Widdershin draws the same story to itself over and over.

History does love to repeat itself.

Edmund and I have shared Lavinia's bed for the last two nights, as I could think of no excuse not to. Both nights, without preamble, he performed his husbandly duty while I regretted the house's lack of ingredients to brew Deliverance's tincture. Had foresight been kinder, I would have bought something from the market in Chatham. He complains endlessly about the power and telephone being out, but offers no solutions. He spent the first half of yesterday sighing and huffing behind the library desk, asking me endless details about every book I recorded. I managed to get him to leave by asking if he could find a way to bypass the damage caused by the tree and regain access to the attic.

He gave up in less than an hour.

I asked him to draw a floor plan of the house. He returned shortly with a sketch that an eight-year-old could improve upon. I praised him and traded it for a book.

On the Moral Nature of the Mind by Dr. L.C. Bellweather is a dense text in the field of moral psychology. When I found it weeks ago, I thought to toss it in the trash after catching a few of the lines while flipping through its pages.

"Where woman weeps, man must reason. Nature did not craft both to govern, lest the house collapse in sentiment."

"A gentleman's moral compass is set not by circumstance, but by the iron lodestone of his breeding."

"The mind of the male is an engine; the female mind, a mirror—apt to reflect, but rarely to originate."

I pointed out such lines to Edmund. "The buyer would love it if you could circle the best passages," I said, handing him a fountain pen.

That was almost a day ago. A day of relative peace while he sits below me in the dining room, a glass of whiskey and an ashtray for his cigars in front of him.

The glass doors to the back patio slam, and his voice comes to me from the bottom of the stairs a moment later, cooing my name in a gentle sing-song. "Violet. Oh, Violet. Come to me, my dear."

It chills me to the bone, but I know better than to ignore it or feign deafness.

He's standing in front of the doors, hands behind his back, and offers a hand and a smile when I peek around the corner at him.

"I've found something I'd like to show you," he coos.

"Were you out back?" I ask from the first step.

"Yes. If I'm to be trapped on this awful island, I should know it. I need you to see what I've found." His fingers curling, beckoning. He's discarded his suit coat, and his dark suspenders stand out against the light pinstripe of his shirt. I thought he was so handsome when we first met. He is just as attractive now, but I know the bitter ugliness of his soul.

He'll drag me out if I don't come willingly. Taking the stairs slowly, keeping a hand tight on the banister, my mind goes to the overgrown graves. Except, now I imagine one recently opened beside a pile of fresh dirt and mud. The shovel is stuck at the top, ready to help fill the hole again.

His fingers dig through mine, his wedding band cutting against my knuckles, and he pulls me not towards the back door, but to the side parlor.

"This typewriter is just like yours at home," he says, pushing me toward it.

Mine is far nicer, supporting a quicker typing speed and takes half the time to switch a reel of ink, but I say nothing out loud.

"Take down a letter for me, dear," he says, still in that devious, gentle tone. There's nothing I can do but sit where Sarah Vale had and load a piece of paper.

"To Mr. Sparrow. No. What is his Christian name?"

"Clarence."

Edmund draws in a deep breath, clearly upset by how quickly I answered.

"To Mr. Clarence Sparrow. I must object in the strongest terms to your recent correspondence, addressed not to me, but to my wife, Mrs. Violet Bow." He pauses, giving me time to catch up. The Altamont No.5 had its place in history, but it's a marvel anyone got through anything of length with the force I must stab the keys with. Poor Sarah Vale's hands must have been a wreck after typing her husband's thick manuscript.

"All matters pertaining to Widdershin House, its contents, or any business thereof or therein must be directed through me, as her husband and head of household. I am assuming ownership of any and all contracts and promises made without my knowledge with my wife. All future communications must be directed through me directly."

He again waits for me to finish typing.

"It is unseemly, and indeed inappropriate, for a lady to be burdened with such affairs, which lie far beyond her province. I trust you will, in the future, respect the proper order of things and spare her any further distraction from her domestic duties. Without further patience, Edmund Bow, Portland, Maine."

I pull the page free and stare at the words, focusing more on the tiny imperfections and differences in ink saturation and key alignment, rather than the content.

"Read it back to me."

I do, keeping my voice even and lifeless, and he nods along, tapping a finger to his lips. Mr. Sparrow will never see this letter. These words are meant for me.

"Quite good for a first pass. There may be room for improvement. Now, for what I really wanted to show you." He extends his hand again, and I stand to take it, noting how cold and clammy he's become.

His grip is a vice. His ring cuts into my hand, but I dare not cry out, as he pulls me out the back doors, past the fallen tree, and down the narrow path. My mouth opens to ask where we're going, but I don't trust my voice not to betray my fear. Edmund wants to hear me afraid, wants to hear what power he holds over me.

We pass the graveyard, looking undisturbed, but he yanks me off the path a few steps later.

A well with crumbling masonry rests beside a few light-starved saplings. A pile of planks sits beside it, having been recently ripped from the top.

"What's this?" I ask, circling away from Edmund when he releases my hand.

"A well," he announces, still smiling. "I thought it strange that there would be a well on a tiny island, surrounded by salt water. Isn't that strange, Violet? It's all salt water down there."

"A shallow well would capture the rainwater floating over the denser salt…" I start, but quickly catch myself. "No, you're right. That is strange. Why do you suppose it's here?"

He strolls to the well, places both palms on the ancient masonry, and raises one to beckon me over. "Maybe they were hopeful. Maybe they were stupider back then and didn't know that you can't drink saltwater."

I join him at the lip of the well. Motes of light twinkle back from the water's surface a dozen feet down. One of the Vale children, I don't remember their name, drowned in a well on the island. Probably this very one.

"Or perhaps," Edmund says, shifting closer to me. "They tossed their unwanted children down there. Maybe not to drown them, but to teach them a lesson in the cold dark." His hand slides across my lower back. "To leave them treading water, not knowing if what sins brought them down there would be their last."

His palm presses against my spine, enough that I snap out my hands to brace against the doubtful well wall.

He's close, his breath on my ear. "I won't be made a fool of, Violet. Whatever game you're playing, flitting about in the library while feeding me inane tasks, I see it. I see you. I'm going to find a way off this God-forsaken island, and you're coming with me. Things won't be so easy for you, as leisurely for you, when we return home. You must, apparently, be kept on a shorter leash."

He's still pressing on my back. Mortar crumbles under my fingers, dropping into the water with a dull plop.

"Edmund…" If I try to twist away, I'll tip into the water. The mortar and stones under my hands won't take another ounce of pressure.

"Yes, Violet?" He's still so close. "Tell me what you need from me."

"You're hurting me."

"Am I? I'm barely touching you."

"You're scaring me."

"Am I?" Though I can't see him, I can hear his grin in his mocking tone. "What about how you scared me, Violet? When I came home to an empty house, with no idea where you had gone or what had happened. Are you still thinking only of yourself, Violet?" He presses his shoulder against mine, pulling a gasp from me when my hand slips. "Were you thinking of me when you took off your ring for the sailors and fishmongers?"

He shrieks, and the weight at my back is gone long enough that I dare slip away.

"Wretched beast!"

I follow Edmund's gaze and fist shaking at the streak of gray disappearing between the trees. He clutches at his calf, where blood is freely soaking through the white.

Saved by the cat.

"I'm sorry, Edmund. I'm so sorry. I know I've wronged you. I understand that now. Please grant me the mercy I know you have within you." The traitorous words flow from my lips a little too easily, but they work.

Edmund glances back at me, the well, the cat, then back to me.

"I will get us off this island. More than flowery words, I will ensure that you understand what you have done until I am fully satisfied. Maybe I'm partially to blame, allowing you to be the spoiled brat who believes she can do as she pleases. I won't make this easy for you, Violet, but it is necessary."

He rolls back his shoulders and, leaving a trail of blood, stomps into the trees.

Thirty

It's only mid-afternoon, but the library darkens with the approach of yet another storm. Maybe this one will be stronger than the last, knocking down the whole house and freeing me from this misery. I've used most of the house's meager supply of candles, which means tonight will be early to bed. Edmund will be asleep a few sweaty minutes later while I cry into the pillow.

There are more candles on the shelves in the back cellar, but it's still flooded. The water, waist-high after the last storm, would still reach my thigh. It's a shame that Edmund drained the flashlight's batteries almost immediately. Though a beam of light is better suited for searching than for working.

Of course, none of this matters. I will work until we find a means to leave the island, or he kills me.

Edmund returned from the boathouse an hour ago, grumbling about the lack of flares. He barked at me to make him tea and settled himself in the dining room. The last thing I heard him mumble was about a plan to burn the house down to catch someone's attention. I couldn't tell how serious he was being, but neither did I want to engage him in conversation.

The medicine cabinets have nothing left to offer. If I want to be free of him, it'll take blunt force trauma or a mortal wound with a knife, and I lack the skill with either to overcome his strength and conviction. Widdershin House has thus far revealed itself to me as it sees fit. Maybe there is one last trick it can offer me.

The sky had gone nearly black in my few moments of thought. Wind rattles the panes and shutters. I should hurry for candles before this gets worse. Maybe my dear husband will brave the dank water for me. Maybe...

There it is, the low whine of wind through the bluffs and trees. I never noticed it before a few weeks ago, since returning from Chatham. Now it's as clear as anything.

I can walk Widdershin House with my eyes closed, and I descend in the dark to the dining room. Edmund has a candle lit with a long, dancing flame at its end. He leans forward, over the terrible book of bitter misogyny, grasping fists through his graying hair.

I stand across the table from him, and he looks up, his face sweaty and drawn.

"What is wailing?" he asks, breathless.

"The Witch's Wail," I say, folding my hands before me and looking down on him.

"It's burrowing into my brain like some parasite. Why doesn't it affect you?"

"I need your help in the root cellar, my dear."

"Help? No. No. We have to get off this cursed island. It's like knives stabbing through my ears."

"Only men can hear it, so only a man can break its curse, Edmund. You could do it." The words spill from me faster than I can think them. They don't even make sense, yet Edmund doesn't seem to notice.

His face is drawn, stretched. His single word comes out as a plea. "How?"

"There is a door in the cellar, past the racks of wine. The answer is behind it."

"The answer? What is the question?"

I shrug and extend a hand. Dazed, he accepts it and stands. I take his candle and lead us into the kitchen, to the awaiting maw of the root cellar. The windows shudder with another powerful gust, and I try not to dwell on the massive tree hovering over us as I point down the steps.

"It's in the back of the wine cellar, to the left. You go first." I pass him the candle. "I'll be right behind you, though there is nothing I can do."

Emotions war across his face in a clear progression: fear, anger, confusion, pride. Yet, he accepts the candle and descends the first step.

I have no plan, at least none that I am aware of. I simply give in to the force driving my false words.

Edmund looks back from the last dry step, and I encourage him by starting down as I promised. He steps into the murky water, to his calf, past his knee, and sloshes forward once toward the wine cellar door.

He glances back once more, and his expression shifts from wide-eyed fear to outrage within a breath. I rush up the few steps, slam down the door, and drag a heavy chest over the iron ring. The latch is missing a lock, but I flip it over the eyelet anyway, for one last line of defense. He's pounding at it and screaming, cursing my name a breath later, but I can barely hear it over the tempest outside and my heart thundering in my ears.

How long will it hold him? Edmund might summon the Devil's strength at any moment to fling the chest aside and come for me. He might escape through the door past the wine cellar, through some hidden passages, to exit safely elsewhere on the island. I performed only a cursory examination of the root cellar when I was in there with the flashlight. I may have inadvertently told him how to escape.

I can't wait to find out, but I have nowhere to go.

The rain soaks through my hair and dress as soon as it hits me, as I flee out the back door. Maybe it will flood the kitchen cellar to the top and solve my problems. My feet trip over themselves, but they know enough that I must get away from the house, toward the source of the Witch's Wail. Toward the bluffs.

An explosion blasts behind me, like dynamite in a quarry.

The lightning bolt holds in the air for a long moment, tearing into the north end of the house in brilliant, divine fire. By the time I can blink away its afterimage, the fire has engulfed half of the upstairs.

The library. It's all gone, as simple as that. Destroyed in a single shot by Almighty Zeus.

The flames lick high, eager to consume the entire manor, reducing it to ash before the beating rain can quench them.

I fall to my knees, my shoulders and jaw slack. My mind spins too fast to focus on anything. However, I know I should put as much distance as possible between myself and the house. If the fire should leap to the fallen tree, then to the forest... The heat is already becoming unbearable from my distance.

Up the slope, toward the eastern bluffs. The rain has given up by the time I reach the brief clearing before the slick rocks tumble to the sea. The wind has lessened, allowing me to hear the snapping conflagration of Widdershin House behind me. Despite all my feelings for him, I hope Edmund didn't suffer long.

I sink against a tree to catch my breath.

The mainland will see the blaze, and Asa or Mr. Farlow will come with others. Everything that happened here was an act of God. Everything that I would repeat, that is. I will fare far better with Edmund's estate than I did with my father's. I just hope he doesn't secretly have a mountain of debt. He seems the kind that would live beyond his means to project the desired air.

The thought of reading Edmund's will before he is confirmed dead tickles a chuckle from my chest. Even if his debt and obligations leave me destitute, that is a price I would pay to have him gone.

I accepted Widdershin House, and it became my husband's coffin.

A twig snaps, and I turn in time to dodge a monster flinging itself at me.

Not a monster, a man. Filthy with mud.

Edmund.

His eyes glow with hellfire.

"I should have known you'd do it," he slurs. A great gash across his forehead weeps blood into his eyes and down his cheek.

His fist is around my throat, pressing me against the tree. He leans close, his nose an inch from mine.

"You're the curse, Violet. You wretched witch. I should snap your skinny neck. That'll end it."

Darkness creeps into the edge of my vision. I claw at his arm, pointlessly.

"I gave you everything, and this is how you show me love. You want to know a secret before I kill you?"

His grip is iron. I won't live to the end of his next sentence. He leans close to my ear.

"I killed Jakob Vogel." He backs away to see my shock as I stop struggling. "I shot the Kraut in a back alley and left his body for the street cleaners. No one cared."

Rage grants me a final surge of strength, and I raise my knee up, squarely between his legs. He releases enough that I can pull away, scrabbling across the stone and gasping for air.

He looms over me, grunting and panting. "No more playing around. I'm done with you, Violet." He bends to pick up a rock with both hands, raising it over his head to throw down on me.

A weight bounces off my shoulder and throws itself at Edmund. A mass of matted gray fur and claws. Edmund drops the rock behind his head to swat the cat away, but the act pulls his balance backward, and he staggers.

The cat lands at my side, hackles raised and fangs bared.

Edmund's heel hits the rock he meant for me and trips. His hands clutch at the air, and he's gone

It happens in an instant. He's there, then he isn't.

I don't know how long I wait, absently stroking the cat, who had taken to his grooming routine. When it no longer feels like a dream, I stride to the edge with confidence the rocks do not deserve.

There he is, a tangle of awkward limbs on the rocks. The sea has washed away the mud, leaving him clean in his cream suit. Each wave tugs at him, beckoning him to join the depths. I watch until he does, slipping off the rocks to be lost beneath.

It doesn't feel real. It was too easy.

I can't stay here. I can't be a grieving widow to this man.

There is only one chance left.

Edmund found the boathouse, so too must I. With a mild idea of the island's topography, I know it is likely on the south end, not far from the docks. The trees snag at my terrible dress, but more to tease than ensnare. The clouds part, and the moon outlines a ramshackle wooden structure at the shore. It's led me directly here. Behind me, flames lick high above the trees, curling black smoke into the night.

The bottom of the rowboat is dry, and the oars seem to be in one piece. Chatham isn't far, just a few miles. A few hours from now, and I'll be back at Miss Morrow's. Even if all my Bridge friends have moved on, Miss Morrow will remember me and take some pity. Maybe in the morning, Asa's offer will still be open.

I pause a hundred yards from Widdershin Isle, reflecting on what I hoped, gained, and lost there. The cat should be fine, continuing his life of solitude.

Maybe such a dark collection of occult work should be forever lost to the world.

Clouds swirl to cover the moon, reminding me that the night is far from over and I am sitting in an old rowboat in the Atlantic Ocean. My back and arms burn from rowing, though the island looks no farther away. A gust pushes against my tiny boat, rocking it. Over my shoulder, the Chatham lighthouse sweeps across the dark water, impossibly far away.

"What am I doing? This is madness!" I can wait at the dock. Edmund is dead. Someone will come when they see the fire. I have nothing but time that I can spend crafting the perfect tale.

I dig the oars deep into the water to turn my craft, pulling with my left and pushing with my right. It's working! I'm turning! Another few moments and I'll be safe on dry land.

A wave slams the side of my rowboat, flipping it without effort, tossing me into the icy, inky void. Saltwater rushes down my throat as I kick and grasp for the edge of my capsized vessel.

Widdershin burns, and the sea takes me.

Thirty-One

"You lied to me, Miss Primrose."

I know the voice, but everything hurts. My arms are heavy. I can barely flutter my eyelids open.

The room is too bright. Sterile white curtains and glass bottles hanging beside where I lie.

"Or should I say, Mrs. Bow."

It's Mr. Sparrow. He's sitting in a chair beside me, twisting a dagger between his hands. A nurse helps me to sit up and pushes a cup to my lips. I sputter and cough, as though my raw throat has never known water.

"What happened, Mrs. Bow?" Mr. Sparrow asks.

We aren't alone. Other than the nurse, a uniformed police officer stands by the door.

"Where am I?" I ask. The answer is obvious, but I need a moment for the fog to clear.

"Boston. The local hospitals weren't equipped to handle a coma victim."

"Coma? For how long?"

"Barely a week. I suspect they wanted to be rid of you. What happened that last night on Widdershin?"

It rushes back to me. The fight at the well, the despair, the storm, trapping Edmund in the cellar, the fire, his return, the cat... Edmund's broken body on the rocks.

Mr. Sparrow sighs and turns to the police officer. "Give me a moment with my client."

I don't watch the officer leave, but hear the door click.

"I've had some time to make inquiries. You're married, Mrs. Bow. Or were. Your husband's body was found the morning after the fire with some suspicious wounds. The local police are inquiring about what happened leading to his death. I'd love to help them and help you, but imagine my shock to learn he exists."

"I..." A fiction is easier with a grain of truth. "I'm sorry I never told you about him. You assumed I was unmarried, and Edmund was not good to me. I thought your job offer was a chance for a new life, but he caught up with me."

"And you were together on the boat?"

"Yes. That's right. We reconciled just in time for the fire, a lightning strike, and escaped together on the boat. I lost him when we went over. The currents must have dragged him away. You said he had suspicious wounds?"

"The coroner says he died of blunt force trauma, not drowning. Bashed with a rock, he suggested." Mr. Sparrow clears his throat and shakes his head. "Not that I think it will come to it, but try adding some emotion into your story if this goes to court. The jury will be hard-pressed to deny a grieving widow."

"Widow... So he is dead?" I let out a gasp, though I'm not sure why. Mr. Sparrow sees through my act.

"They don't get much deader."

"May I see him?"

"The coroner may appreciate an identification, but the gold watch in his pocket was enough to fill out the death certificate. I recommend against an open casket, if you don't mind me being forward. The currents must have bashed him against the rocks before he could drown. Simple as that."

"I see..."

"The destruction of the Widdershin Collection has freed up my schedule, and I took the liberty of looking into the estate of your late husband while I waited for you to wake, something I should have done months ago. He was far from a Vanderbilt, but farther from poor."

That perks me up. "How much?"

"Settle down now. Getting excited about a late husband's finances never looks good. But unless you're quite careless, you won't need to worry about money. You are the only claimant, and I am willing to offer my services as an estate lawyer. I'll draw up the paperwork to have everything put into your name, though, do not expect a discount on my fee."

"Yes, thank you. Will the police be a problem? They can't think I had something to do with his..."

"No. The wounds can be explained away with rocks and sharks. They didn't take blood samples to test for laudanum, if that's what you're concerned about." He doesn't look at me, just keeps focusing on the dagger in his hands. Deliverance

Black's jeweled dagger. Did I have that on me that night? I must have.

"The last thing I remember was falling into the water," I say, hoping to pull the conversation away from when Mr. Sparrow and I were last together. "How did I get here?"

"A sailor was out in the storm and saw you draped over the rowboat. He brought you back to Chatham, and you ended up here."

My heart jumps. "A sailor? Who? What's his name?"

He shrugs. "I wrote it down so I don't have to remember it, and that notebook is elsewhere. Tall, black hair. That probably describes half the men in town. Younger. That would narrow it."

It might, but it describes one in particular. "Captain Carver? Captain Asa Carver?"

Mr. Sparrow squints, then shrugs again. "Perhaps."

"What was he doing out in the storm?"

"How should I know? Maybe to come rescue you when he saw the house ablaze."

Maybe. Or maybe Asa overheard Mr. Farlow say he had taken a man to Widdershin the other day, and he was coming to inquire about it—to rescue me, not from the fire, but from Edmund.

"There is also the matter of this dagger. It was found on you when they pulled you from the water. Local historians and jewelers have assured me it would fetch a tidy sum to the right collector. Am I right in assuming you didn't bring this with you from Maine, and that you found it on the island and intended to flee with it? That this is a piece of the Widdershine Estate and not your personal goods?"

If he knows the dagger is worth anything, he knows, or at least suspects, its connection to Deliverance. There is no point in lying. I nod.

"But I wasn't trying to steal anything. I, we, were getting away from the fire, for worry it would spread to the forest."

He sighs and pushes on the chair's armrests to stand. "We are not in the clear yet, Mrs. Bow. There will be a mountain of paperwork for you to sign and people to talk to when you are a bit more recovered."

"What will happen with Widdershin?"

He pauses at the foot of my bed and turns. In the hospital's harsh lights, he looks a decade older than when I last saw him. "There is no Widdershin. The manor is a pile of ash and charred studs and bricks."

"I mean the island. You were going to sell it after the collection was appraised, yes?"

He straightens, and his brow crinkles. "Even with the state the house was in, it was viable and repairable. Now there is nothing. The island will sit in ruins until some eccentric person comes along, willing to purchase something all the locals say is cursed."

"What if I wanted it?"

Mr. Sparrow's brow crinkles even further. "And why would you want that?"

He wouldn't understand it. I don't understand it, but I feel it. An ineffable draw to the island. It changed and saved my life.

"That doesn't matter. Could I afford it? I could sell the house and everything in Maine."

"As I said, other than having electricity from the mainland, the island has little value. If you are serious, I can make some calls. I assume you will want to build a new residence, which is never inexpensive. Assuming you avoid murder charges, we can make this happen."

"Thank you. And, Mr. Sparrow, call me Violet."

He snorts and rolls his eyes. "Very well, Violet. Get some rest."

I wanted to escape to Paris or the South Pacific. I never wanted to stay on Widdershin. But now there is no one behind me. I am free. I'll use Edmund's money to create a shrine to all the wronged women. Lavinia and Clarinda. To all the widows of Widdershin: Deliverance, Sarah... Me.

The chuckle starts low and slow, then breaks into a rolling laugh. All my bodily aches melt away with the simple realization that I am free. I arrived a wide-eyed girl so coddle that I was using a key for the first time. Now, my sides are hurting from laughing about my husband being nibbled on by fish for a night. The island changed me, molded me into something I didn't know I wanted to be.

The Widdershin Widow.

Final Entry

From "Purity and Panic: Forgotten Witch Trials of the Colonial North" by Dr. Eliza Godfrey (published 1907)

Chapter Seven: Deliverance Black – The Witch of Widdershin Isle

It is worth noting that Mistress Deliverance Black was never formally tried, nor executed, and yet her name appears in no less than eleven prayer records concerning wayward women.

Surviving documents suggest she fled from Beechfield in early 1693, following escalating accusations of hexery, bodily harm, and the death of a neighbor's dog—matters which, while mundane

by modern standards, were cause for frenzy in those days.

Of particular interest is the theory that she escaped to a small isle east of Chatham, where her husband, Absalom, reportedly joined her months later.

He returned never, and local legends persist of a white rider seen pacing the coast each June, the month of his supposed demise.

Some speculate Deliverance killed him; others suggest the island itself consumed them both.

No body was ever found. No children. No grave. Only the story.

The Cape Cod Times

October 16, 1982

Chatham — Mrs. Violet Primrose-Carver, longtime resident of Widdershin Isle, died peacefully at her home on Sunday. She was 82.

Born Violet Primrose in Boston in 1900, Mrs. Primrose-Carver moved with her family to Port-

land, Maine, in her youth. In 1925, she came to Chatham, where she later married Asa Carver, a fisherman and boatman of the town. Together, they rebuilt the historic Widdershin House and raised their family there.

In addition to her life as a mother and home-maker, Mrs. Primrose-Carver was active in civic and social causes. She was an early supporter of women's suffrage and continued throughout her life to advocate for equality. In 1948, she helped establish the Primrose Center for Women, a safe haven for women fleeing abusive households, which remains in operation today.

She was also a devoted member of the Chatham Bridge Club, where she rarely missed a Friday game for more than fifty years. She served on the library committee, was a tireless cataloguer of rare books, and inspired generations of young women through her mentorship and example. In 1971, Mrs. Primrose-Carver founded the Widdershin Foundation, a non-profit society dedicated to the collection and preservation of rare literary works.

She is survived by three children, seven grand-children, and a wide circle of friends and neigh-bors who remember her warmth, wit, and quiet strength. Few will remember seeing her at home without a cat in arm's reach.

Funeral services will be held Thursday at First Congregational Church, Chatham, with interment on Widdershin Isle.

Historical Fiction

While this is a work of fiction, many of the details are based in reality.

At the harbor, the waves chop and buck with the slightest breeze.

Walking up Stage Harbor Road, the high steeple of the First Congregational Church marks a welcome to town.

The Nickersons were a prominent family in Chatham, with William Nickerson considered to be "the Father of Chatham".

The Rider in White is pulled from local folklore, though little is written about it.

While walking Main Street, beside the lighthouse, during a nor'easter, I heard the low drone of the Witch's Wail, a detail I created before visiting the town.

The clam chowder is delicious.

About the Author

Award-winning author J. M. Samland is a mathematician by training, a web developer by profession, and a martial artist and writer by passion. Math nerd, cat dad, gamer. He's always loved to write, but what started in force during the 2020 lockdown has become a driving passion.

Inspired by the comedy of Terry Pratchett, epicness of Brandon Sanderson, and the genre spread of Martha Wells, he's gone from epic sword and sorcery to modern romance to Gothic historical fiction. He doesn't care about standard genre expectations and focuses instead on telling the story he needs to tell.

He lives in Michigan with his husband and their furbabies.

As an indie author, he relies on reviews and word of mouth, so please consider leaving a review on GoodReads and at your

point of purchase. Find him on the socials or at jmsamland.co
m.

Also By

Books by J. M. Samland:
Realms of Terswood (2020)
Trials of Throk'tar (2021)
Necromancer of Urbus (2022)
Seeds of Farsil (2022)
Ooo Shiny! Volume 1 (2022)
Arcanym (2023)
The Invisible Castle (2023)
Ooo Shiny! Volume 2, Holiday Edition 1 (2023)
Cracking the World (2023)
Grave Mistakes: A Necromantic Adventure (2023)
Ooo Shiny! Volume 3: Vampires! (2024)
The Widdershin Widow (2025)
Ooo Shiny! Volume 5: The Search for Shiny 4 (2026)